MW01120652

Operation Majestic

Operation Majestic

by Scott M. Baker

Also by Scott M. Baker

Novels

The Chronicles of Paul: A Nurse Alissa Spin-Off
Nurse Alissa vs. the Zombies
Nurse Alissa vs. the Zombies: Escape
Nurse Alissa vs. the Zombies III: Firestorm
Nurse Alissa vs. the Zombies IV: Hunters
Nurse Alissa vs. the Zombies V: Desperate Mission
Nurse Alissa vs. the Zombies VI: Rescue
Nurse Alissa vs. the Zombies VII: On the Road
The Ghosts of Eden Hollow
The Ghosts of Salem Village
Frozen World
Shattered World I: Paris
Shattered World II: Russia
Shattered World III: China
Shattered World IV: Japan
Shattered World V: Hell
The Vampire Hunters
Vampyrnomicon
Dominion
Rotter World
Rotter Nation
Rotter Apocalypse
Yeitso

Novellas
Nazi Ghouls From Space
Twilight of the Living Dead
This Is Why We Can't Have Nice Things During the Zombie Apocalypse
Dead Water

Anthologies
Cruise of the Living Dead and other Stories
Incident on Ironstone Lane and Other Horror Stories
Crossroads in the Dark V: Beyond the Borders
Rejected for Content
Roots of a Beating Heart
The Zombie Road Fan Fiction Collection
The Collector

A Schattenseite Book

Operation Majestic
by Scott M. Baker.
Copyright © 2021. All Rights Reserved.
Hardcover Edition

To Scott Ferguson

My high school Astronomy teacher who instilled in me my love for science and, even more important, trained me to think critically in all situations.

A Note on Historical Inaccuracies

As I'll discuss in the acknowledgments later, I did intense research to make this novel as accurate as possible. However, I included two historical inaccuracies for the sake of the plot and want to bring them to your attention before you begin reading.

By all historical accounts, in September 1917, Maria Orsic was contacted by the Anunnaki. Since this is a science fiction novel, I opted to change the Anunnaki from their typical anthropomorphic style to the mantis-like Mantid aliens that appear in several UFO sightings. The reasoning for that is purely literary. I thought the Mantids portrayed a more menacing species than those originally described. I hope followers of ancient alien theories will excuse my change.

Second, I want to apologize to Gudrun Reinhardt. Little is known about the *Vril Gesellschaft*, or the *Vril Damen* as I refer to them in this novel, and even less is known about the women other than Maria. By all accounts, each of the five members of the *Vril Damen* were lovely individuals who saw only positive prospects for the future by maintaining relations with the Anunnaki and abhorred the evils perpetrated by the Third *Reich*. However, I needed a female antagonist for the plot, and Gudrun got that role. I hope I'm forgiven for that indulgence.

BOOK ONE

Chapter One

Giza, Egypt
Present day

A N INTENSE MID-DAY sun blared down on the desert, reflecting off the sand so brightly that not even the Rayban sunglasses Pierre wore could fully lessen the glare. The shimmering heat distorted the Pyramids of Giza two miles to the north, rendering their image on the horizon like that of a mirage. Even within the shade provided by the tent, the temperature topped one hundred degrees. As soon as Pierre swiped a cloth across his forehead, more beads of sweat formed and ran into his eyes, stinging them. He did not let the heat and discomfort bother him. A few minor hardships were a small price to pay. He was on the brink of hopefully making one of the most significant discoveries in Egyptian archaeology since the unearthing of King Tut's tomb nearly a century ago.

Pierre stood at the entrance to his tent, watching his crew. Several dozen local excavators supervised by two of his graduate students from Cambridge University dug up the surrounding fifty acres. A year and a half ago, ground-penetrating radar mapping the desert around the pyramids detected an anomaly of three buildings two miles to the southeast. The structures were far enough removed from Giza not to be associated with the construction site yet large enough to have some significance. Finding the location was the easy part. It required nearly a year of negotiating with the new director of the Ministry of State for Antiquities, a man who did little to conceal his anti-Western bias, before the Egyptian government finally granted permission for Pierre to excavate the site although under two stipulations. First, a ministry official would share the lead on the excavation with a team comprised primarily of ministry members. Second, any artifacts found belonged to the Cairo Museum. Pierre agreed.

So far, the pieces uncovered had been neither numerous nor extraordinary: a discarded sack of pottery, probably that fell off a trading caravan; an abandoned campsite; and sundry other objects. However, what fascinated Pierre was that the depth of each discovery correlated to an era coinciding with the construction of the Pyramid of Khufu, indicating they were excavating a pristine location not seen by human eyes in millennia. His expectations were born out nine weeks ago when his team uncovered the wall of an intact building composed of the same material used to construct the worker compound near the pyramids. The shards of pottery found inside confirmed the structure was four thousand five hundred years old. Since then, another structure had been discovered and the roof of a third unearthed a week ago. With luck, his team would learn something new about this era that would earn them accolades from the Egyptology community.

"A watched pot never boils." The voice came from Hans Erntsmann, who sat at Pierre's desk. A contributor to *Mitteilungen der Deutschen Instituts Abteilung Kairo*, known within English-language circles as the *Communications from the German Institute Department, Cairo*, one of the leading German journals on archaeology. Erntsmann had been following Pierre's dig since the expedition began four months ago. A positive article by Ernstmann would not give Pierre the same popularity as would a mention in *National Geographics*, but it would provide him considerable cachet in the academic community.

"I can't help it." Pierre stepped back inside the tent.

"Don't you trust Janet?"

"It's Janice." Pierre opened the cooler and removed a plastic bottle from the ice. "And yes, I have full confidence in her.

She's the best grad student I've ever worked with."

"Then what's the problem?"

Pierre sat down behind his desk and opened the bottle. "The problem is I'm stuck in here when I want to be out there involved in the dig."

"We have to pass the torch to the next generation at some time."

"I don't see you stepping aside," chuckled Pierre as he swigged a mouthful of cold water.

"Don't let my charming presence fool you," teased Hans. "I originally intended to write about the presence and influence of Asiatic races in the Middle Kingdom, but apparently someone has already drafted something along those lines."

Pierre smiled. "And you're here because you got sloppy seconds, right?"

"That, and because I like you."

Pierre laughed. "I'm touched."

"You should be." Hans raised his bottle of water in a mock toast.

"I'm afraid this will be my last dig."

"Is the university pressuring you to spend more time lecturing?"

"Yeah." Pierre frowned. "Don't get me wrong. I love teaching. But fieldwork is my passion."

"At least you'll end your time in the field on a high note."

"What do you mean?"

"With luck, you're about to make a major archaeological find."

"Do you think so?"

"Of course. Your team has uncovered a village buried for almost five millennia. Who knows what you'll unearth? Most importantly, if it's something extraordinary, your name will be associated with it."

Pierre smiled. "I hope you're right."

"Of course, I am. I've been in this business—"

A commotion broke out at the excavation site, with the workers yelling in Arabic. A moment later, someone ran toward the tent.

Hans pointed toward the approaching footsteps. "See, you're about to go down in history."

One of the Egyptian workers burst into the tent. His panting to catch his breath mixed with excitement made it more difficult than usual to understand him. "Come quickly. You're needed at the site."

"Is everything all right?"

"Janice sent me to get you."

"What's all the excitement about?"

The worker ignored the question and moved toward the exit, waving for Pierre to join him. "You're needed at the dig. Please, hurry."

Pierre jumped up and raced after the worker, followed by Hans. The three wound their way through the dig to where a group of workers stood around the rim of a twenty-meter-square excavation unit overlooking the partially covered third structure. He knew by the fear and anxiety on their faces that whatever caused the uproar was not good. As Pierre and Hans reached the workers, they moved aside, allowing the two men access. Janice stood on the slope, taking photos with her cell phone. Her usually calm manner seemed rattled.

"What's going on?" asked Pierre.

Ini-herit, the foreman, turned to Pierre. "I wouldn't have believed it if I hadn't witnessed it first-hand."

"Witnessed what?"

Ini-herit pointed to the base of the building they had unearthed. Only a few days ago, they had discovered shards of pottery dating back to the 4th Dynasty at this location. Now they had unearthed the lintel from above the entranceway, which lay on the ground, the edges still covered by sand. Pierre's attention focused on the symbol etched into it. He was speechless.

Hans mumbled, *"Mein verdammter Gott."*

Descending the slope of the dig, Pierre crossed over to the symbol and ran his fingertips across its surface. "This can't be real?"

"It is," Ini-herit replied. "It has the same weathering pattern as the rest of the wall. As best as I can tell from a visual examination, it's at least four thousand years old."

Pierre stared at the symbol, shocked by the implications. His name would be associated with this discovery, but not in the way he had hoped. Removing his cell phone from his back pocket, Pierre took several photographs of the symbol, wondering how he would explain this to the university.

Chapter Two

Manchester-Boston Regional Airport, Manchester, New Hampshire
One Week Later

A COOL SPRING wind blew across the tarmac, kicking up dirt and sand. Agent Patrick Brady lowered his head and closed his eyes. When it died down, he blinked several times and brushed off his suit jacket. On the last swipe, he glanced at his watch. 10:23. Shit.

Brady folded his arms across his chest. He had picked up several agents at the airport in the past and was used to them being late, but those involved commercial flights. The agent from Washington was arriving on a privately chartered flight, which seemed unusual. The urgency of the situation also seemed strange. Brady had received a phone call from the special agent in charge of the Boston Field Office just before seven that morning ordering him to pick up a Suburban and meet a special agent at the airport at ten. Normally he would not mind, except he was on vacation this week. If Brady thought he had a tough time unsuccessfully attempting to talk the SAC out of making him come to work, informing his wife Stephanie they had to cancel their plans for the day proved more difficult. To help soften the blow, he promised Stephanie he would take her to dinner at Hanover Street Chophouse when he got back. At this rate, he would be reneging on that promise as well.

The noise of a jet approaching from the southeast caught Brady's attention. Using his hand to block the sun, he scanned the skies. A Gulfstream approached from five thousand feet and descended rapidly. He watched it draw closer, relieved to spot the FBI logo on the engine nacelles mounted below the horizontal stabilizer. The jet touched down with a screech of rubber and slowed. A few minutes later, the Gulfstream pulled up parallel with the Suburban and stopped. Once the twin jets shut down, the entry door lowered.

A man centered himself in the open hatch. The black suit and tie, and the mannerisms, gave him away as a special agent. Brady had seen it dozens of times since joining the Bureau, the demeanor of someone with years of experience who had witnessed things most civilians would never see and been hardened by it. Brady took him for a career agent, with at least fifteen years under his belt, judging by the graying hair and lines around his eyes and lips. The pissed-off expression on his face told Brady this guy wanted to be here even less than he did.

Spotting Brady, he rushed down the steps and approached the Suburban. "Are you the guy who's supposed to be meeting me?"

"I am." Brady stepped away from the vehicle and offered his hand. "I'm Agent Patrick Brady."

"I'm Special Agent Gary Carbone." He gave Brady's hand a firm pump. "Are you ready?"

"Don't you have any luggage?"

"I don't plan on being here long. I want to interview this guy and get back to Washington as soon as possible." Carbone paused halfway into the Suburban. "How far away does he live?"

"An hour, maybe a little more."

"Then let's haul ass." When Brady did not move, Carbone tapped his hand on the roof. "Come on."

Brady slipped into the driver's seat, started the engine, and pulled away. He waited until they reached Interstate 293N and had merged into the flow of traffic before speaking.

"So, do you intend to fill me in on what's going on?"

"You've been dragged into some major bullshit, kid."

"What kind of bullshit?"

Carbone flashed him an aggravated glare. "Haven't you been watching the news the past week?"

"You mean the discovery of the Nazi emblem on that four-thousand-year-old Egyptian structure?"

"That's the one. Seems the guy I'm here to interview talked about it several decades ago, only then nobody listened to him."

"Why?"

"Because he's a fuckin' nutjob," Carbone sneered. "He makes some stupid ass claim that, by a freak chance, happens to pan out, and now the Director thinks this guy's a fucking psychic. And for some reason, I'm the SA that has to interrogate him."

"I think you mean interview."

"Whatever. They should just let this guy talk to the media. Sending me down here is a waste of time and resources."

Brady gunned the engine and passed a slow-moving tractor-trailer plodding along in the left lane. "Why am I here?"

"To take notes and write the report."

"You're kidding?" Brady kept his eyes on the highway. "I got called in from my vacation to be your chauffeur and secretary?"

"Sorry, kid. Shit flows downhill and, on this one, you're at the bottom of the slope."

Brady said nothing for the rest of the trip, internally fuming that a fellow special agent would treat him this way. Rather than wallow in his anger, he concentrated on driving. The highway took them only as far as Lake Sunapee, the remainder of the trip via back roads and a dozen small towns. They finally reached the lake in the town of Newbury. When the GPS led them off the road onto an unpaved driveway that went on for half a mile, Brady thought the system had erred. He was about to back down to the street when the dirt and gravel merged into asphalt and opened onto the main property after another one hundred feet. A colonial-style eight-room house stood directly in front of them. To the left was a two-car garage connected to the main residence. Lake Sunapee sat two hundred feet behind the property. The lawn out front was carefully maintained, the grass a lush green. Blooming flower beds lined the walkway from the driveway to the front door.

Carbone huffed. "The nutjob has done pretty well for himself."

Brady parked the car in front of the garage. Both men climbed out and proceeded along the walkway. As they neared the front porch, the door opened. A British bulldog waddled out and stopped by the double steps, its tail wagging furiously. An older gentleman emerged dressed in jeans, a white cotton shirt, and loafers. He stood at six feet, erect and without a slouch, with a full head of hair whitened by age. The man's eyes were azure, yet their attractiveness belied the knowledge that lay underneath. Brady could tell that this man was highly intelligent and had witnessed things most men could not even imagine. The agent figured him to be in his late seventies, but with the mental and physical acuity of a man two decades younger.

As the two approached, the bulldog barked in excitement.

"Winnie, be good." The man crouched and scratched the bulldog behind the ears. "You know you don't bark at guests."

Carbone ignored the dog. "Are you Matthew Evans?"

"I am."

Carbone reached into his inner jacket pocket, withdrew a wallet, and flipped it open with his right hand. Brady removed his and opened it with both hands. "I'm Special Agent Gary Carbone with the FBI. This is Agent Patrick Brady. Do you have a few minutes to talk?"

"Of course. Come in." Evans waved for them to follow as he stepped through the front door. "I've been expecting you."

Carbone seemed confused. "You knew we were coming?"

"Not you in particular. But I figured someone would show up."

"Why did you assume that?"

"I've been watching the news all week." Evans smiled at Carbone, not so much out of pleasantry but as one who knows he has the upper hand. "When I heard they found the *Reichsadler* in Egypt, I knew it'd only be a matter of time before the Bureau sent someone to talk to me. I'm surprised it took so long."

"You have a unique perspective on this situation."

"More so than you realize." When both agents and Winnie had entered the house, Evans closed the door. He led the way to the living room.

"So, you know why we're here?" Carbone asked.

"Of course. You have a lot of questions you want to ask me. And I'm happy to answer them." Evans gestured to the couch. "Please, have a seat."

"Thanks." Carbone sat on the sofa in front of a coffee table.

Evans headed for the kitchen, with Winnie rushing along behind him. "I'll get us some iced tea and snacks."

"No need for that." Carbone did not attempt to conceal his irritation. "This won't take long."

Evans chuckled. "Trust me, it will. I'll be back in a few."

After Evans disappeared into the kitchen, Carbone leaned back against the cushions. "Shit. We'll be here for hours."

Brady ignored the special agent. He placed his notebook down on the coffee table and strolled around the room, taking in the details. Evan's living room also served as his study. Built-in mahogany bookshelves lined the interior wall. Brady scanned the titles. Most of the books pertained to Egyptian history, World War II, American politics from the 1940s to the present, the Cold War, astronomy, physics, UFOs, and the science of time travel. An old Army Air Force officer's cap rested in a display case on one shelf, flanked to the left by another display case with a pair of 1940s-era gold leaves and a military intelligence badge, and to the right by a black-and-white 8x10 photograph. Brady studied the image. Evans crouched in the center of the photograph with a lieutenant and a U.S. Army staff sergeant to his right and left; a line of seven soldiers stood behind the others, one of them an African-American corporal.

Crossing the room to the fireplace, he checked out the photos on the mantelpiece. All of them were of Evans and a beautiful woman with shoulder-length red hair, presumably his wife, in front of various landmarks. Brady recognized the Pyramids and the Brandenburg Gate amongst the backgrounds and could tell by the varying textures and clarity of the photos they scanned from the mid-twentieth century to the present. Another thing he noticed was that the couple aged gracefully from photograph to photograph, appearing only slightly older from one image to the next.

"What are you doing?" asked Carbone.

"Getting a feel for what the subject is like."

"Check his desk drawer. If you find a tinfoil hat, you'll know everything you need to."

Brady strolled over to the sofa and sat down as Evans entered holding a tray with a pitcher of iced tea, three glasses, and a plate with sliced cheese and cold cuts. He placed the tray onto the coffee table and sat down. Winnie jumped onto the sofa beside him.

"So, how can I help the FBI?"

Brady picked up the notebook and opened it to the first page as Carbone leaned forward and rested his forearms on his knees. "We want to know how you predicted an archaeological dig would unearth a Nazi symbol on a structure forty-five hundred years old?"

"Do you want the long or short version?"

"The short version should be sufficient."

"That's easy." Winnie barked, so Evans removed a slice of

pepperoni from the plate and fed it to his dog. "The Nazis changed the original timeline so they could win World War II, and I went back in time to correct it."

Chapter Three

THE TWO FBI agents stared at Evans, incredulous. Carbone spoke first. "Are you fucking kidding me?"

"Didn't you read my file?"

Brady attempted to be more conciliatory. "What file are you talking about?"

"The report I wrote for the CIA when I returned to the present.'

Carbone shook his head. "No one ever showed me such a report."

"Oh, my God." Evans laughed out loud. "No wonder you looked at me like I was crazy."

"Excuse me." Carbone stood and headed for the front door. "Given the circumstances, I have to check in and see how the Director wants me to proceed with this."

Once Carbone had left, Evans poured himself a glass of iced tea. "Your partner dislikes me."

"He's not my partner," protested Brady. "And I don't think he dislikes you."

"He thinks I'm crazy." Evans leaned back into the sofa with his glass of tea. "So do you, but you're more diplomatic about it."

"It's not an easy story to believe."

"I know that better than anyone. I wouldn't believe it myself if I hadn't lived through it."

"How come you never told anyone about this before?"

"And let the whole world think I'm insane?" Evans smiled. "I wouldn't be talking to you and your colleague if that

Reichsadler hadn't been—"

The front door opened and closed. A few seconds later, Carbone stepped into the living room. Brady could tell by the pissed-off look on his face that the conversation did not go well.

"What did your boss say?" asked Evans.

Carbone took his seat on the sofa. "He never heard of your report either."

"That doesn't surprise me. It was either thrown away or locked up where no one would ever see it. I'm amazed Washington didn't do the same with me."

"You'll get a chance to tell the story again." Carbone sighed. "The Director wants a full report on what you know."

Brady grabbed his notebook and placed it in his lap.

Evans swirled the iced tea around his glass. "I guess the best place to begin is where it all started for me."

Brady pressed the push button on his pen. "Where's that?"

"Roswell, New Mexico."

Chapter Four

Roswell Air Force Base, New Mexico
2 July 1947

E VANS SAT AT the counter of a dive bar a few blocks from the air base's main gate. He nursed a warm Schlitz from a tall glass dripping with condensation, occasionally puffing on the Camel that dangled on the edge of the ashtray by his right hand. Three ceiling fans rotated on the slowest setting possible, barely churning the stagnant air and creating lazy swirls from the stale cigarette smoke that hung like a mist above him. The only relief from the heat came from a six-bladed Emerson fan set up by the cash register, the bent blades slapping against the metal casing and creating as much noise as it did wind. Evans did not mind. The breeze it made dissipated some of the heat, and the clanging distracted him from news reports coming from Berlin that played on the 10-inch RCA television that sat on the other side of the cash register.

He did not drink often, and never before noon, and usually would not be caught dead in a place this seedy. Today was different. Today Evans drank not for pleasure or to relax but to escape from this shithole mess he had gotten himself into. Or, more appropriately, the mess he had been placed in.

As an intelligence officer, Evans held elected officials in low regard. They ignored the facts for political expediency, fucked things up nine out of ten times, and then either blamed the intelligence community whose advice they refused to listen to or ordered them to covertly correct their mistakes. Not all of them, though. While Evans disapproved of FDR's progressive domestic policies, he appreciated that the president realized the danger presented by the rise of fascism in Europe and had done everything he could, within the confines of the law, to assist Britain in its struggle against Germany. The Neutrality Act and "cash and carry." Lend-Lease. The Destroyer for Bases deal. All these measures were intended to keep America's ally from collapsing until the president could figure out how to overcome the nation's isolationism and join the conflict.

It probably would have been successful if Nazi Germany had not secretly developed nuclear weapons and ballistic missiles. Hitler used them on the first day of Operation Barbarossa to decapitate the Soviet political and military leadership, allowing the blitzkrieg to defeat the Soviet Union in less than two weeks. Less than two months later, a coalition of Liberal Party parliamentarians and Conservative Party members dissatisfied with Churchill's handling of the war removed him as prime minister and placed Neville Chamberlain back in 10 Downing Street. King George VI abdicated the throne for Edward VIII, who was much more amenable to Nazism. Chamberlain signed a peace protocol with Berlin that ended the conflict between the two governments while allowing the United Kingdom to keep its sovereignty and a large modicum of independence, much like Vichy France. The most devastating war in history ended, and most of the world enjoyed the peace that followed.

That peace doomed FDR. In frail health, he refused to seek his party's nomination in 1944. After a contentious campaign and an even more brutal national convention, Henry Wallace finally won the nomination. More like a sacrificial lamb to the slaughter. The country was tired of twelve years of Democratic leadership and returned both houses of Congress and the White House to Republicans. Thomas Dewey became president and adopted a policy that was isolationist internationally and pro-business domestically.

A high-pitched tone interrupted the newscast. Evans

glanced over to the television as a test pattern appeared on the screen. A few seconds later, the image returned, only this time showing a medium shot of a correspondent holding a microphone and standing in front of the camera. The Brandenburg Gate appeared over his left shoulder, each of its columns bedecked in long red banners with the swastika emblazoned in the center of a white circle. A military parade passed through the arches. Four lines of troops, each three soldiers wide, marched across *Pariser Platz*. The black uniforms with twin runes on the helmets identified them as the SS, the *Schutzstaffel*, Hitler's elite troops. They marched with the rigid precision one expects of Germans. Behind them, four columns of *panzers* rumbled through the arches, two columns of King Tigers on the inside and one column of Tigers on the flanks, each painted with a fresh coating of *feldgrau*.

"This is Edward R. Murrow reporting to you live from Berlin where Germany is celebrating the anniversary of their victory over the Soviet Union. Six years ago today, in Warsaw, Nikita Khrushchev, the head of the Communist Party in Ukraine and the highest-ranking official to survive the war, surrendered to Germany and formalized the dissolution of the Communist Party and the Soviet Union, bringing peace to a continent ravaged by the second great war in as many decades."

Evans snorted derisively and swigged a mouthful of beer. He despised the hypocrisy of the media. Seven years ago, Murrow reported nightly from London on the Blitz as the *Luftwaffe* tore the city apart, making the world aware of the atrocities the Nazis were capable of committing. Now he sang their praises. Not that Evans could blame him. The Soviets were as great a threat to world peace as Nazis. No one, except for socialists around the world, missed their demise.

Only those in the U.S. intelligence community realized the ensuing peace had a thin façade. Werner von Braun, the scientist who had developed the ballistic missiles that destroyed

Moscow and a dozen Soviet cities, had covertly begun work on *Projekt Amerika,* the development of long-range ballistic missiles that could reach anywhere in the United States. Most sources reported that Hitler did not intend to use these weapon systems in a preventive strike. He wanted them to ensure Washington would not try to assert its influence in the future, a Germanic version of "peace in our times," so long as Hitler dictated the terms of that peace.

The discovery of *Projekt Amerika* raised alarm among Dewey and certain members of his administration who did not want America to be taken by surprise the way the Soviet Union had, so they decided to explore the problem behind the scenes. Which meant the administration needed someone who did not stand out to travel the United States and get a boots-on-the-ground assessment on the nation's preparedness, especially its ability to develop ballistic missiles and nuclear weapons to counter the Nazi threat. That someone was him. It turned out to be a more thankless and disheartening job than he ever could have imagined.

The military had no ballistic missile program, not even a proposal on paper in someone's office. Other than a few pilot programs to develop short-range rockets for anti-ship and anti-aircraft defense, no one had even considered the concept. Only slightly better progress had been made on the atomic weapons front. After the start of the war in September 1939, FDR had established the National Defense Research Committee on Uranium to study the prospects of nuclear weapons. However, with the end of the war two years later, the committee was disbanded and no further research conducted. When it came to its conventional military, the United States was just as badly off. The 180,000-man army ranked 19th in the world. Although the navy possessed seventeen battleships, more than Germany did, most were Great War-era vessels and could not compete with their Germanic counterparts. America did have an advantage in the 20th Army Air Force based out of Roswell

Army Air Field, nearly fifty of the latest B-29 bombers that could drop one hundred thousand pounds of bombs on Berlin in a single raid. When England capitulated to the Axis, their surrender deprived the B-29s of the staging area needed to reach Berlin.

The United States remained decades behind Germany in missile and nuclear technology and had no means to use their single asset to their advantage, leaving the country at the mercy of Adolf Hitler. All because elected officials who could close the gap when they had the opportunity squandered it for political purposes. And next week, Evans got to tell President Dewey and his cabinet the disquieting truth and why America was in that position.

The scene on the television switched to in front of the *Reich* Chancellery. Hitler and half a dozen political and military dignitaries stood on the same balcony from which the *Führer* greeted his supporters following his ascension to power in January 1933. A string of eighteen-ton FAMO half-tracks drove past the balcony, each pulling a seventy-foot-long trailer carrying a Super V2, the three-stage missiles used against the Soviet Union. A Daimler-Benz G4 staff car passed by with *Feldmarschall* Sepp Dietrich, the head of Germany's missile command, standing in the rear. As he passed the balcony, Dietrich snapped to attention and saluted Hitler with his *feldmarschall*'s baton. The *Führer* and those around him extended their right arms at a forty-five-degree angle and bellowed "*Sieg Heil.*" The crowds along the *Wilhelm Strasse* cheered.

Evans had enough. "Will you turn that TV off? I'm sick of watching all this Nazi shit."

"Sure thing, mac." The bartender paused from cleaning the glasses long enough to shut off the television. "Sorry. I wasn't even listening to it."

"No problem."

"I don't blame you. Somebody should have stopped them damn Nazis back in the mid-30s. Now they're too powerful.

Ain't nothin' we can do about them."

That's for damn sure, thought Evans. Pulling a dollar from his pocket, he placed it on the counter.

"You need change?" asked the bartender.

"Keep it."

"Thanks, mac."

As the bartender scooped the bill off the table and stuffed it into his pocket, Evans put on his service cap and exited. The late morning sun blinded him. He adjusted the cap so the visor blocked most of the glare. The heat was already becoming oppressive. Evans climbed into his jeep and started the engine. He would go back to the airbase, interview some more of the pilots and crews, and then knock off early. A swim in the pool, a few drinks at the officer's club, and a good night's sleep, and maybe things would not seem quite so bad in the morning.

Chapter Five

Berlin
2 July 1947

AS THE LAST military vehicles in the parade passed by the Chancellery, the Nazi dignitaries on the balcony basked in the accolades of the cheering Berliners. All except Hans Kammler, who surreptitiously slipped away from the others and entered the building, stepping to one side until he was no longer visible to the crowds. As an officer, he detested these public displays. Newspaper headlines and mass events were for politicians who craved popularity. Soldiers like himself preferred the anonymity of behind-the-scenes operations over the spotlight, for that is where wars are fought, victories are achieved, and peace maintained. Kammler would gladly have passed on attending except that Hitler had asked him to be there, and no one dared turn down a request from the *Führer*. Besides, he had no legitimate reason to decline. He had not been asked to participate as an *SS Obergruppenführer und General der Waffen SS*. Or as the Head of Office C and Office D within the SS Main Economic and Administrative Office, the branches of government that designed and constructed the *Reich*'s concentration camps and oversaw their administration, respectively. Or as the man responsible for building the underground facilities to house Germany's various secret weapons projects. Or even as the director of the nation's ballistic missile program.

Hitler had asked Kammler to stand with him on the balcony as the man who single-handedly orchestrated the defeat of

23

the Soviet Union.

An outburst of cheering from the crowds filtered in through the double doors. The others entered. *Reichsmarschall* Hermann Goring, the head of the *Luftwaffe* and first in line to lead Nazi Germany should something happen to Hitler, lumbered through the doors. Once the leader of the infamous *Jagdgeschwader* 1, Richtofen's Flying Circus, and a key figure in the rise of the party, Goring's dual addiction to morphine and opulence had turned him into a visage of his former self. He had forsaken the duties entrusted to him by the *Führer* to plunder Europe's art treasures for his personal gain. Obese and flamboyant to the brink of perversion, Goring was a disgrace and an embarrassment to Hitler and the party. Bedecked in his white cap and tunic, including gold *Reichsmarschall* shoulder and collar tabs as well as ribbons and numerous medals, he reminded Kammler of the doorman at the Adlon Hotel. At least Goring did not attend this function in a toga and make-up.

Reichsführer Heinrich Himmler followed. He looked diminutive, average in height and slim in build, with a thin indistinct face high-lighted by small, circular, wire-rimmed glasses and a Hitler-style mustache. His appearance was deceiving. As head of the SS, which included all aspects of the police, investigative, and security services as well as the entire system of concentration camps, the *Reichsführer* was the most feared and evil man in the *Reich*, more so than Hitler himself. One word from Himmler and someone would be confined to a *lager* for decades or simply disappear. To get on his bad side could end one's career, at best, or one's life. Those who curried favor with Himmler had a protected status few in the *Reich* could hope to obtain. Kammler had achieved that status when he saved Germany from defeat two years ago. By making certain the accolades were directed to the *Reichsführer*, Kammler solidified his relationship with Himmler, becoming his most loyal and trusted confidant next to Reinhard Heydrich.

Martin Bormann, chief of the Nazi Party Chancellery, exited the balcony and moved to one side. Kammler appreciated the man. Bormann, much like himself, also thrived in the shadows. Shunning flamboyance and ostentation, he preferred to blend into the background, a cunning man who watched out for his *Führer* and mentally filed away everything he heard or saw. His power came from controlling access to Hitler of both people and information. While no one would ever say Kammler and Bormann were friends, they got along well together and saw things eye-to-eye. Kammler had unfettered access to the *Führer* and would ensure the door was always open by occasionally passing damaging gossip about high-level party officials and military officers to Bormann.

Propaganda Minister Joseph Goebbels hobbled behind Bormann, unable to completely conceal the limp caused by his clubbed foot. Obsequious and pandering, most party leaders viewed him as a necessary evil, a master of public opinion and propaganda who knew how to get the most out of any photo opportunity. Goebbels prided himself on being a member of Hitler's inner circle, but everyone knew that the connection belonged to his wife, Magda. Magda and the *Führer* possessed an emotional and philosophical bond, some would even say a possible physical bond, though they would never admit to that in public. Magda had the true access to the inner circle. Goebbels merely rode on her coattails. No one knew whether Goebbels was truly aware of the reality or simply made the best of a bad situation. In either case, the minister beamed with pride and happiness.

Hitler entered the room last. Only this man was not the same amphetamine-addicted, anxiety-ridden, delusional shell of his former self that brought Germany to total defeat while he lived out his final days in the *Führer* bunker as if life was normal. That medical nightmare resulted from the incompetence of Hitler's personal physician, the obese and foul-smelling quack Dr. Morell. In this new timeline, with the war concluded and

Germany victorious by late 1941, Himmler pried the *Führer* away from the doctor's clutches by trumping up charges of sexual perversion. Morell later had an "accident" in Dachau. When the SS went through the doctor's files, they discovered that Morell had been injecting the Führer with seventy-four different chemicals from vitamins, opioids, and morphine to toxins and commercial poisons. Once off the deadly concoction, the *Führer*'s health and mental acuity improved within days. Five years later, Hitler had returned to his normal self, though greying along the temples and with a distinct shaking in his right hand from Parkinson's.

Goebbels limped over to Hitler, overflowing with enthusiasm. "*Mein Führer*, Germany will remember today with great pride."

"As they should," Goring blustered. "We promised the German people that if they had faith in the party and the leadership, we would bring them justice, peace, and prosperity. That's what we have done."

Hitler gestured toward Kammler with his left hand. "Thanks to the *obergruppenführer*." Goring made little attempt to hide his sneer.

"I only fulfilled my duties as a member of the SS," Kammler replied with as much modesty as he could muster.

The thinnest hint of a smile pierced the *Reichsführer*'s lips.

Hitler chuckled. "We all know what you, Maria, and the others did for the *Reich*. Though I must admit, sometimes I find it incredible to believe."

"It's all true, *mein Führer*."

"I've never doubted you. The story fascinates me. It's all so Wagnerian."

"Thankfully, that's not our timeline anymore," Bormann reassured the *Führer*.

"Even so, the story is inspiring," added Goebbels. "It's a shame we can't tell the people what happened."

Hitler shook his head. "I agree, Joseph. But they're not

ready for it. It'll upset them more than comfort them. But I enjoy hearing the story. Walk with me and tell me again how history played out in that alternate timeline."

Kammler fell in beside Hitler and retold for the umpteenth time the original history, beginning with Operation Barbarossa and its failure to defeat the Soviet Union, progressing through the catastrophe at Stalingrad and the eventual Red Army onslaught that overwhelmed East Europe and Germany. He spared no details about the destruction of Germany, the raping and pillaging carried out by the Russians, and the final days in the bunker. Kammler did make a few changes to the storyline. He never told the *Führer* that, in the last days, both Goring and Himmler made powerplays to take over the leadership of what little remained of the *Reich* and attempted to negotiate peace treaties with the West. It served no useful purpose and would alienate both men, which Kammler could not afford. Knowing where their true loyalties lay gave him the upper hand. In Kammler's version, Goring and Himmler stayed in the bunker with Hitler until the end and, rather than committing suicide as actually happened, the leadership died heroically defending the bunker from Russian soldiers. It never hurt to stroke the ego of your patrons.

Kammler timed the pace of his story so it concluded as they reached the reception hall. The two SS guards on either side of the double doors opened one, allowing Hitler and his entourage to enter. A small reception of thirty or so high party and military leaders was in progress. Upon seeing the *Führer*, everyone in attendance snapped to attention, extended their right arms, and shouted, "*Heil* Hitler."

"Please, please." Hitler gestured with his left arm for the others to be at ease. "No formalities today, my friends. It's a celebration for the contribution to victory made by Task Force Kammler and the *Vril Damen*."

The party-goers resumed their festivities as Hitler and the others mingled. Kammler broke away and strolled over to one corner where he could remain out of the limelight and did what he was best at, watching and observing. The twenty members of Task Force Kammler mingled around the hall, each dressed in their SS dress uniforms, some talking amongst themselves, a few flirting with the young ladies from the Chancellery secretarial pool invited for just that purpose. Admirals Erich Raeder and Karl Donitz and Generals Wilhelm Keitel and Alfred Jodl stood in the opposite corner, laughing and joking, blissfully unaware of the extent of the defeat the *Kriegsmarine* and *Wehrmacht* suffered in the alternate timeline. The political leadership—including Minister of Armaments Albert Speer, Minister of the Eastern Occupied Territories Alfred Rosenberg, Minister of Economics Walter Funk—patted themselves on the back as if they had any contribution to the final victory. Wives and mistresses joined in, laughing and flirting with the leadership, basking in their husbands' and lovers' popularity. SS *Obergruppenführer* Reinhard Heydrich, Himmler's right-hand man, stood by the window overlooking the garden chatting up Traute, Sigrun, and Heike, three of the famous *Vril Damen* for whom this reception was dedicated.

"Looks like one of my colleagues will be getting laid tonight," a sultry voice said from behind him.

"I wouldn't be surprised if it's more than one." Kammler glanced to his right. Gudrun Reinhardt, one of the *Vril Damen*, moved up beside him. She presented a striking figure in her red dress and matching heels, five-foot-six inches in height, slim and well-endowed in the right places. She focused on him with brown eyes that mirrored her sensuality. Unlike the rest of her colleagues, Gudrun kept her brunette hair cut short in an asymmetrical bob. She smiled at him, the tip of her tongue sliding across her upper lip. "How come you're not with them?"

"You know I'm a one-man woman." Gudrun slipped her hand over his and squeezed before breaking her grip. "Besides, he couldn't handle me."

"I see Maria decided to skip the reception."

Gudrun's smile faded. "Officially, she's suffering from a migraine caused by the stress of her telepathic abilities."

"Unofficially?"

"The bitch is having pangs of morality over what she did for the *Reich*. I think the *Führer* should place her in front of a firing squad rather than on a pedestal."

"At the moment, she's a hero of the *Reich*, and we have to deal with that."

"Hero of the *Reich*." Gudrun nearly spat the words. "I could have done what Maria did."

"But you didn't. And that's why Maria is the woman of the hour."

Gudrun glared at Kammler and started to storm off. She took only one step before he grabbed her right arm and squeezed tight.

"You're hurting me."

"You do not walk away from me like that. Ever." Kammler spoke the words in a cold tone far more threatening than if he said the words in anger.

Gudrun averted her gaze. "I'm sorry."

Kammler released his grip. "For some reason, they decided to contact Maria rather than you or the others. That was a matter of chance. Don't forget, you were an integral part of *Projekt Vril* and as important to its success as anyone on the task force. And don't forget that I'm the one who makes sure the *Führer* is aware of that."

"I appreciate it." Gudrun's seductiveness had returned, although this time partially forced. "And I'll show you how much later."

"You will. But for now, it's time to suck up to the leadership and let them think our success was because of them."

"I understand." Gudrun swiped her hand across his as she stepped into the crowd, making her way toward Goebbels.

Kammler stayed in the corner. He would let his men and

the *Vril Damen* bask in the limelight and pound the flesh with the leadership. They deserved the attention he shunned. Besides, they were much better at it. Kammler had more important matters to attend to, especially how to deal with Maria if she became a problem.

Chapter Six

Berlin
2 July 1947

M ARIA ORSIC STOOD on the balcony of her apartment reserved for privileged members of the party. A warm summer breeze blew through her auburn hair, barely moving the strands due to their length and weight, and ruffled the black satin nightgown she wore. She rarely used the balcony because of all the construction around her. Today was a holiday in honor of the ceremonies, so she decided to take advantage of the quiet. The apartment was located a kilometer from where workers were constructing the *Volkshalle*, the steel girders of its dome structure towering three hundred meters over Berlin. Right now, the neighborhood was noisy and a bit disheveled. In ten years, once completed, this spot would be the prime location in Berlin. The center of the *Reich*. The heart of *Germania*.

A *Germania* she had helped create.

Which she would regret for the rest of her life.

Maria stepped back inside her apartment, slid shut the door, and crossed over to the bar. She usually did not drink and, when she did, it was red wine. Today she needed something stronger. Considerably stronger. Maria opened the door to the mini-freezer and removed a brand-new bottle of vodka. She took a shot glass from the mirrored shelf, stared at it a moment, and replaced it with a tumbler. Pulling the stopper from the bottle, she filled the tumbler halfway, swirled the alcohol around, and took a long swig. It felt good. Being cold, it slid down her throat. Only when the vodka hit her stomach did she begin to feel the burn, a comforting sensation that would slowly spread. Soon Maria would be drunk and, at least for a few minutes, be able to forget the last six years. Or was it two years? She could not even be sure of that anymore.

Ironically, this all began to benefit humankind before the Nazis became a viable political party.

Maria had possessed psychic abilities since she was a teenager. Yet hers were not parlor game skills that allowed its bearer to read the playing card in someone's hand or guess their middle name. Maria's talent was far more advanced. Hers began when she collapsed at the age of nineteen. While in a trance, she had visions of extraterrestrial beings made of light. At first, she dismissed it as a hallucination until she fainted again several weeks later and had a similar vision. Maria's ability probably would have gone to waste had she not befriended the like-minded Traute Blohm from Munich, a woman with similar abilities.

In retrospect, maybe those talents should have gone to waste. Back then, as a young woman still in her teens, she was intrigued by the possibilities that lay before her.

Traute introduced Maria to the *Alldeutsche Gesellschaft für Metaphysik*, more commonly known as *Vril Gesellschaft* or the Society of *Vrilerinnen* Women. Those within the physic community commonly referred to the women as the *Vril Damen*. Maria was flattered to be in the company of such noted psychics as Traute, Sigrid Kuenhiem, Gudrun Jentzsch, and Heike Erhardt. These ladies did not engage in the pomp and circumstance of other secret societies and did not adorn themselves in robes or perform elaborate rituals. The *Vril Damen* dressed moderately, the only accouterment they allowed themselves being necklaces displaying the *Vril* symbol, a lightning bolt. Maria allowed the experience to consume her.

The peak of excitement occurred when Maria, while in a trance, began receiving mediumistic transmissions containing technical data to construct what the extraterrestrials called *jenseitsflugmaschine*, or other world flight machines. Maria thought these visions were delusions, a symptom of an overactive imagination, or perhaps the beginning of a mental collapse. As she received further transmissions during future trances, she began what would be the venture of a lifetime. The technical data became more voluminous. It soon became apparent to Maria that the extraterrestrials instructed her on how to build a saucer-shaped craft that used an anti-gravity engine that not only powered the craft but allowed it to engage in interdimensional time travel. The *Vril Damen* referred to it as *flugscheiben*, or flight disc. Over the course of months, Maria transcribed hundreds of pages of documents from these transmissions, which were in an ancient eastern language later identified as Sumerian. Sigrun and Panbabylonists from the Thule Society translated the data and deciphered the mental images.

As Maria wrote down the documents, she also learned a lot about her communicators. The telepathic messages came from the Anunnaki, a race of aliens from Sumer-e in the Aldebaran system within Alpha Centauri, sixty-eight light-years away. The aliens had visited Earth thousands of years ago and assisted the local inhabitants in building the ruins of Larsa, Shurrupak, and Nippur in modern Iraq. Maria also learned that the Anunnaki were one of two clans, the clan of the Black Sun that inhabited the Aldebaran system. The other was the clan of the Golden Sun.

Maria still remembered fondly the thrill of communicating with an extraterrestrial species, making first contact with a life form not of this world, and being an integral part of a scientific discovery that would change the world.

She downed the rest of the vodka and refilled the tumbler. For a woman who prided herself on being intelligent, and who possessed an extraordinary psychic ability, she never foresaw the nightmare she helped to create.

When the Nazis lost the election of January 1933, no one had anticipated that President Hindenburg would offer the Chancellorship to Hitler to form a coalition government. Most Germans seemed happy with the decision, especially as the economy boomed and the nation's prestige rose. Even though Maria herself never supported the party and was appalled by their anti-Semitism, she fell under their thrall during those first few years, especially since Himmler, a believer of the supernatural, gave his support for the development of the designs transmitted by the Anunnaki. The *Reichsführer* supported the Aldebaran Project, the initiative to develop a craft that could travel through a dimensional tunnel independent of the speed of light to explore human habitable planets in the Aldebaran system. He created SS-E-IV, the SS *Entwicklungstelle* IV, to build these machines. Some of the most brilliant minds in Germany worked on this project, and it became one of the nation's priorities. The program followed two tracks: the original design concept, which the SS referred to as the *Haunebu II* project, a larger saucer-shaped craft, and the smaller bell-shaped *Die Glocke* program. Even as the *Reich* collapsed and Germany's enemies approached the borders, work on the *Haunebu II* continued, with the first test flight taking place in late 1944. It was far from a success. The craft's outer skin aged considerably and suffered damages in several places during the procedure. Even so, they proved it could be done.

What Maria did not know at the time was that SS also adapted the Anunnaki's technology for weapons of mass destruction to turn the tide of World War II, thankfully without success. When she discovered the truth, she was furious to the point that she wanted to storm into Himmler's office and demand to know why he had diverted the Anunnaki's peaceful technology for military purposes. Thankfully, Sigrun talked her out of it, convincing Maria that she would be throwing away her life. She convinced Maria that the war would be over soon, the Nazis would be deposed, and their terror weapons would not have a chance to be used in combat. Maria felt more at ease with the situation.

Until that fateful day in January 1945 when the Anunnaki contacted Maria again, the first time in fifteen years. They provided Maria with technical data that corrected SS-E-IV's errors, though it confused her as to how the extraterrestrials knew about their failures. The Anunnaki also advised Germany how to win the war even with its enemies crossing the nation's border on two fronts. What they offered seemed bizarre. No, that was too weak a word. Horrifying more appropriately defined it. The Anunnaki showed a path to victory more destructive than the current conflict. Maria did not need to be a psychic to predict how this alternate path to victory would end for Germany. For all of Europe. For the Jews. Yet she could not ignore the advice, could not choose to conceal it from the party and military leaders because, by this time, Gudrun had started helping her with the translations.

Gudrun had begun an affair with Kammler, hoping that he would save her along with himself when the final collapse came. Maria could not trust Gudrun to keep her secret, and so Maria revealed to Kammler everything the Anunnaki had told her.

That's a lie, and you know it, Maria chastised herself. She swigged a mouthful of vodka, anticipating the well-deserved burn. By now, she had drunk so much she did not even feel the alcohol as it slid down her throat. Maria could have kept the secret from Gudrun and made sure Gudrun did not assist in that part of the translations. Even if Maria could not have kept it secret, she could have… should have at least tried. She had not feared for her life. That, at least, would have had some rationality to it. Despite her reservations about sharing her knowledge, despite knowing the horrors that would result from it, Maria went ahead and passed along the information for the most selfish of reasons–she wanted to. Her desire to experience space and time travel, to be one of a handful of people engaging in the adventure of a lifetime, overrode her trepidation for the horrors the future would bring.

Now the Third *Reich* and its sphere of influence ran from the United Kingdom to a line in the east running from Arkhangelsk in the north to Astrakhan in the southeast. Most of the Baltic States and a quarter of the Ukrainian and Belorussian population, people whose blood was not contaminated by mixing with the Slavs, were Germanized and allowed to remain on their land, sharing it with three and a half million Germans who migrated east for new lives as farmers. Everyone not deemed suitable was either deported across the Urals into western Siberia to fend for themselves or isolated inside the *Reich* and deprived of food. One Foreign Ministry diplomat she knew once told her in confidence that the SS banished twenty million men, women, and children to Siberia and another thirty million starved to death in east Europe.

The apartment provided by the party for her heroic efforts to ensure victory remained a constant reminder of her weakness. Maria found her view of the *Volkshalle* apropos. For Hitler, it represented a monument to the *Germania* he had established. For Maria, it was a constant reminder of her complicity.

Maria finished the last of the vodka in her tumbler. She reached for more. Her hand slapped into the bottle, knocking it on its side. It rolled toward the edge of the table, pouring a swirl of vodka along the surface in its wake. Maria fumbled for it, grabbing the bottle a second before it plunged off the table. Moving slowly, she turned the bottle upright and placed it back on the tabletop. The sleeves of her satin nightgown dragged through the spilled alcohol, soaking them. She had too much to drink, and not for the first time. She headed for the bedroom, taking only one step before her legs grew weak and the room spun before her eyes. Maria stumbled over to the sofa, attempting to gracefully lie down but crashing into the cushions instead. She curled up into a fetal position, ignoring the damp of her vodka-soaked sleeves. Grabbing the crumbled blanket from the back of the sofa where she had left it after her last drinking spree, Maria pulled it over her. It only covered half her body, leaving her legs and feet exposed. *Screw it*, she thought. *I'll be asleep in a few minutes.* And that bothered her.

When Maria dreamt, she relived the day that changed the world.

Chapter Seven

East of Hamburg, Germany
1 May 1945

THE THUNDER OF artillery echoed in the distance. Occasionally, a round would overshoot the intended target and land closer than anticipated, the blast more intense than the others, the shock wave causing the ground to tremble. With the complete collapse of the *Reich*, the British rapidly closed in on the city and would overrun this area within hours. Despite the approaching bombardment and the threat of imminent death, no one seemed concerned. Excitement buzzed through the group. Years of research and testing were about to come to fruition. They were about to make history.

They were about to change history.

Kammler stood by the rear of the *Opel Blitz* utility truck. Behind him, Dr. Hans Albrecht and his team of sixty-seven scientists and engineers worked feverishly at the pair of make-shift control panels to prepare for travel. Coils of wire stretched across the grass from each panel to one of two craft that sat a quarter of a mile distant. The first was officially referred to as the *Do-Stra*, short for *Dornier Stratosphären Flugzeug*. Due to its original research taking place on deserted farmland in the Hauneburg region of eastern Germany, those involved in the project called it the *Hauneburg Gerät* or, more commonly, the *Haunebu II*. *Haunebu II* was eighty-five feet in diameter. The bottom portion had a saucer-like shape, allowing it to accommodate twenty individuals as well as cargo. The upper appeared like an inverted bowl and contained a cockpit that sat six. Three cupolas on the undercarriage and one directly on top each held three 20mm cannons for defense. Two smaller cupolas on the dome bore 7.97mm MG42 machine guns. The *Haunebu II* rested ten feet off the ground on a triple strut landing system. A hatch with stairs descended from the craft's entry port to the ground. The crew members of Task Force Kammler had painted a *Balkankreuz* the size of a bedsheet on the hull.

The smaller of the two, called *Die Glocke* because of its bell-like shape, stood fifteen feet in height with a width close to nine feet and was made of a harder and heavier metal than the *Haunebu II*. The craft could carry only two people. Kammler understood little of the scientific jargon of the scientists and engineers regarding the propulsion process. They bragged about two counter-rotating cylinders filled with a violet-colored, mercury-like substance they referred to as Xerum 525 stored in a tall, thin, thermos-like flask three feet high and encased in lead. None of it mattered to Kammler so long as it worked.

Turning around, Kammler studied the others gathered for this momentous occasion. The *Vril Damen* stood one hundred meters away. Each wore a sand-colored uniform like those used by the *Afrika Korps* and adorned with their custom-made shoulder patches designed for this mission—the three-pointed lightning bolt of the *Vril* on top and the outline of the *Haunebu II* on the bottom encased within two golden oak leaves on either side. None of them would be here today if not for these women. As much as he despised taking them into potential combat, their presence would be an integral part of the mission's success and one he would have to tolerate.

Between the *Vril Damen* and the Opel, twenty *Waffen* SS soldiers led by *SS-Standartenführer* Kurt Fuchs milled around, laughing and smoking cigarettes. Fuchs was the quintessential Aryan: six-foot-one, short-cropped blonde hair, cold blue eyes, stern visage, a chiseled physique, and a reputation for an unemotional devotion to the *Reich*. Like the women, each wore old *Afrika Korps* uniforms, though truth be told, the women did better justice to them. These were the toughest, bravest, and brightest soldiers the *Waffen* SS had to offer from the survivors of the battlefields of western Europe and the slaughterhouse of the Eastern Front. Each had lost good friends. Each knew the goal of this mission. Each had volunteered for the chance to wreak some payback on the Soviets for what they put Germany through. They wore the same patch as the *Vril Damen*, except theirs was encircled in a red-rimmed white banner with the embroidered words in red *Für den Dienst. Für Deutschland. Für die Rache.*

For Duty. For Germany. For Revenge.

A hundred meters to the side stood a dozen SS soldiers in *feldgrau* uniforms waiting to fulfill their role.

Kammler had hoped to use a larger force of *Haunebu II*s for this mission. Two additional craft had initially been assigned to Task Force Kammler, which would have boosted his command to seventy-eight. One had been near completion at the underground *Die Reise* facility near Sokolec inside the Gontowa Mountain. The Soviet advance on the facility forced its evacuation in February. Kammler destroyed the craft and caved in that section of the tunnel complex to prevent the technology from falling into Moscow's hands. The remaining two *Haunebu II*s and *Die Glocke* were transported by rail to a site east of Hamburg. One of them ran into an air raid on a rail junction, obliterating all evidence of its existence. Although the loss of the two saucers was disappointing, it did not mean the end of his mission. Kammler could make do with what he had.

If the engineers could get them to work.

The *obergruppenführer* moved over to the consoles and hovered behind the scientists and engineers.

"Are we almost ready, doctor?" Kammler spoke the words more as a threat than a question.

"Yes, *Herr Obergruppenführer*." Albrecht was so excited he

failed to detect the nuance. "Everything checks out. We can proceed."

"Excellent." Kammler moved away from the monitors and approached his unit. Fuchs came over to meet him, followed a few seconds later by an *untersturmführer* from the SS.

"Is it time, *Herr Obergruppenführer*?" Fuchs asked.

"It is. Board your team."

The *SS-standartenführer* snapped to attention, gave Kammler the Nazi salute, and returned to his men.

Kammler faced the *untersturmführer*. "You know what you have to do?"

"Of course, *Herr Obergruppenführer*. I won't let you down."

"Thank you."

The *untersturmführer* also snapped to attention, saluted, and rejoined his team. Kammler strolled back and stood behind the monitors.

✦   ✦   ✦

"This is it." Haute gestured toward the group of *Waffen* SS soldiers dressed in *Afrika Korps* uniforms.

Maria followed her gaze. The members of Task Force Kammler formed two lines.

"We better get going," added Gudrun.

Each of the *Vril Damen* hugged Maria before falling in with the soldiers. Haute kissed Maria on the cheek and whispered, "See you on the other side."

Maria watched as her sisters and the *Waffen* SS marched toward the *Haunebu II*. As they boarded, five engineers disconnected the wires from the craft and dragged them one hundred feet away. Once everyone had entered, Maria crossed over to the control panels and stood beside Kammler. Both watched as Albrecht began the final countdown.

"*Standartenführer* Fuchs." Albrecht said into the microphone on his headset. "Are you ready?"

"We are."

"Then initiate launch procedures."

A moment of silence passed before an electronic hum emanated from inside the *Haunebu II*. A shimmering field of electromagnetic energy formed around the craft and expanded outward over five hundred feet. The green grass within the zone turned yellow and decomposed into a grease-like substance. When the expansion zone passed over the five engineers who had disconnected the wires, they screamed in agony. Four collapsed onto the sludge that had been grass only moments before. The fifth dropped to his knees. Crystals formed in their tissues, transforming their skin, muscles, and insides from organic to mineral. Their blood gelled and separated, clogging their veins and depriving them of oxygen. In torment, the engineers thrashed about as life was torn from them. After nearly a minute, their bodies went limp, their skin pale and glistening in the sunlight.

The *Haunebu II* elevated, one strutted landing gear lifting off the ground seconds before the other two. The craft hovered for a moment before elevating, rising a few yards every second until it floated at one thousand feet. The humming increased again, the intensity becoming so great Maria placed her hands over her ears to blot out the noise, but to no effect. Just as Maria thought she could not take anymore, the *Haunebu II* excelled upward and disappeared. A few minutes later, an explosion like a sonic boom rattled across the field, shattering the Opel's windshield and blowing back Maria's hair. A moment later, everything went quiet.

Kammler spun around to face Fuchs, his expression confused. "What just happened?"

"The *Haunebu II* has entered interdimensional flight."

The uncertainty drained from his face. "Do you mean…?"

"Yes, *Herr Obergruppenführer*. *Projekt Reisen* was a success. The craft is on its way to the prescribed time and coordinates. We've entered the same calculations into *Die Glocke*. You should arrive at the same time as the others."

"You've done a superior job, Dr. Albrecht. The *Reich* owes you a debt of gratitude."

"It was our duty, *Herr Obergruppenführer*. And our pleasure."

Kammler turned to Maria. "Are you ready, *Fraulein* Orsic?"

A panoply of emotions swirled inside Maria—uncertainty, trepidation, fear, anticipation. Excitement won out. She headed for the craft. "I've been ready for this for twenty years."

As Maria passed by Kammler, she did not notice the *obergruppenführer* look over at the *untersturmführer* and nod.

Die Glocke rested on the ground, allowing Maria to enter without assistance. Only two seats and a control panel filled the compartment. Maria took the seat by the six-inch-round portal and strapped herself in. Kammler entered, closed and secured the hatch, and took the remaining seat. She watched as he manipulated the controls. Beneath their compartment, an electronic whir vibrated through the craft as the gyroscopic rotors switched on. As with the *Haunebu II*, the noise increased, only this time muffled by the sound-proof lining surrounding the exterior of the compartment. A pale blue light radiated from *Die Glocke*'s exterior.

Maria glanced out the portal.

Her blood went cold.

The SS soldiers under the *untersturmführer* surged forward and fired their MP40 submachine guns at the sixty-two remaining scientists and engineers. Albrecht stepped in front of a colleague and begged them to stop, his plea cut short by a burst of fire that tore through his chest. The bullets propelled Albrecht back, knocking over his assistant and crashing into the control panel. One engineer ducked in front of the *Opel* and attempted to use it as cover to escape. An SS soldier spotted him and moved toward the front of the truck, gunning down the man as he raced for the distant woods. As the soldiers loaded the instruments onto the *Opel*, the *untersturmführer* withdrew his *Luger*, walked up to each engineer and scientist, and administered a single shot to the back of the head.

A jolt distracted Maria from the slaughter taking place outside. The view changed as *Die Glocke* rose. After several seconds, she could no longer see the *Opel* or the SS soldiers. She estimated they were between eight and nine hundred feet off the ground. The humming became louder, this time accompanied by a rocking motion as *Die Glocke* vibrated. Maria glanced over at Kammler to ask if everything was okay. Before she could speak, he pressed a red button on the control panel. The craft accelerated at a speed she had never experienced before. Through the portal, the image went from a daytime view over a grassy field to one of darkness. Not darkness, though. Light passed by, but so rapidly it could not form into images, almost like a kaleidoscope rotating at incredible speed. Maria leaned forward against the glass to get a better look. The effort made her dizzy. Her vision blacked out and her head slammed against the headrest of her seat. She tried to call to Kammler but passed out before the words left her lips.

Chapter Eight

Roswell Army Air Field
3 July 1947

E VANS WOKE WITH a start to a bright flash of light and a distant rumble. He thought the Nazis had launched an atomic attack on the States and braced himself for the shock wave that would end his life. A few seconds passed and another flash burst through the window, followed by thunder.

Asshole, he thought. *It's only a summer storm.*

Once the realization sunk in that he was not about to die, Evans settled down. Only then did he realize his heart pounded and his pulse raced. Lying prone, Evans took a deep breath, held it for ten seconds, and slowly exhaled through his nose. He felt his body relax and his nerves settle. Evans repeated the process until the tension dissipated and drowsiness washed back over him. He checked his watch. A few minutes after midnight. Closing his eyes and rolling onto his side, Evans flipped over his pillow and placed his head on the cool side. With luck, he could get another five or six hours of sleep before morning.

✦   ✦   ✦

LIGHTNING LIT UP the sky across the desert, and thunder rattled the windows while a heavy rain beat against the roof. William Brazel sat in a rocking chair by the living room window, watching the splatter against his pick-up truck. He had experienced many thunderstorms during his years as a foreman on the Foster Ranch outside of Capitan. He enjoyed extreme weather, especially out here where mother nature could run its course with nothing to get in its way. It was the primary reason he worked in the middle of nowhere. Sure, there were better paying and easier jobs in Roswell and Albuquerque, but that also meant living in a city with its large populations and all the commotion. That was not for him. Brazel preferred rural life.

However, for a reason Brazel could not put his finger on, he felt uneasy, enough so that he took the shotgun off the mantle, loaded it with buckshot, and placed it across his lap as he enjoyed the show.

Brazel started to doze off when the cattle bellowed in their pen, snapping him awake. The cattle being disturbed was not unusual. Coyotes roamed the desert and frequently neared the pens, searching for an easy meal. They were not fussing about a predator but expressing fear.

Brazel went over to the door, slid on his work boots and jacket, and grabbed a flashlight from the shelf by the jamb. He stepped out onto the porch and listened. Other than the snorting and disturbed movements from the livestock, he heard nothing unusual. Turning on the flashlight, he held it in his left hand, rested the barrel of the shotgun on his left wrist, and slowly panned the area, expecting to see some animal stalking the cattle. Nothing was visible. Moving off the porch and into the rain, he made his way toward the rear of the pen, swinging the flashlight from left to right so nothing could sneak up on him.

A metallic hum came from the northwest, like the spinning of a turbine, only much more intense and loud enough to be heard over the torrential downpour. It was probably one of those bombers from Roswell. Damn Army Air Corps pilots were always barnstorming across the desert, scaring the shit out of his herd. He had complained several times to the base commander and always received the same line about someone looking into it, which they never did because the pilots would be back barnstorming a few weeks later. Doing it in daylight was one thing; taking such risks on a stormy night put everyone in danger. Next time he was in town, he would swing by the sheriff's office and—

The humming increased rapidly. A bright light appeared on the opposite slope of the dune to the northwest and grew in intensity. The cattle panicked, several of them head butting the wooden fence attempting to break free. Brazel felt the same way. He had seen dozens of military aircraft flying over the desert at night, but nothing like this. Moving back toward the house, he hoped to reach it in time to provide some sort of cover.

The aircraft crested the top of the dune and flew directly over the ranch, passing between his house and the pen. For a moment, its brightness blinded him. Brazel closed and averted his eyes. Even then, he could still see the glow from the craft. The humming decreased in pitch as it headed southeast. He opened his eyes and searched for it. It was already over a mile away and heading for Roswell. Between its speed, the rain, and the distance, he could not identify the make. The craft looked like a giant wing without engines. He had never seen a design like it before.

Once it passed, the cattle settled down. Brazel headed back to his house. Still, he could not get the unusual shape out of his mind. Whatever it was, hopefully, it was one of the Army's aircraft.

✦　✦　✦

CORPORAL JAMESON SAT in front of the radar screen inside the air traffic control tower at Roswell Army Air Field, fighting to stay awake. Every night shift played out the same: sit in front of this screen for eight hours, watch the green line make a 360-degree circle, and wait for nothing to happen. At least tonight, he could follow the path of the thunderstorm moving through the area north of the base. It provided the only break in the monotony.

On the opposite side of the tower, Staff Sergeant Bowen poured a cup of freshly brewed coffee. "Corporal, do you want a cup?"

"Is it strong?"

"I added two extra scoops. Is that strong enough?"

"I hope so." Jameson closed his eyes and ran his thumb and forefinger across them until he reached his nose. "If I keep this up much longer, I'm going to nod off."

Bowen laughed as he poured a second cup. "I wouldn't do that. That's considered a dereliction of duty. Could land you thirty days in the brig."

"I could use the rest." Jameson opened his eyes and resumed studying the screen. "This is the most boring job I've—"

A green blip appeared on the radar.

"The most boring job what?"

"Sarge, check this out."

Bowen finished pouring the coffee and carried the two cups to the console. "What's up?"

"That." Jameson pointed to the green blip when it appeared again.

"Holy shit." Bowen placed down the cups quickly, coffee spilling over the brims and running down the sides. The blip appeared again, only this time much closer. "What's the speed on that son a bitch?"

"I can't determine, but it's faster than any aircraft we have." Jameson looked at the sergeant. "You don't think it's one of them Nazi rockets, do you?"

"I doubt it." Bowen pointed to the screen. "It's slowing down and changing course. Looks like it's going to circle the airfield."

The sergeant picked up the phone directly linked to the base CO. "I'm going to get the commander on the line. You alert everyone else that we have a bogey approaching rapidly."

✦ ✦ ✦

EVANS WAS STARTLED awake again, this time not by the thunder but by the air raid klaxon. He jumped out of bed and quickly dressed, all the time expecting to hear explosions from incoming missiles. None ever came. Grabbing the keys off his night dresser, he raced for the jeep parked in his driveway, started it, and backed out at close to forty miles an hour. As he rushed through the housing area, the base bordered on panic. Military personnel reacted normally, but this was the first time their families had ever encountered anything like this. He passed by several homes where soldiers tried to get to their assigned duty stations while calming down frightened wives and crying children. It took over a minute for Evans to clear the housing area and turn right onto the main road where he could floor it. Less than five minutes after leaving his quarters, he screeched to a stop by the tower. Racing up the exterior stairs, Evans burst into the air traffic control room.

"Jesus." Jameson jumped when the door flew open. "You scared the shit out of me."

"We're all scared at the moment." Evans crossed the room and stared at the radar screen. "What type of an attack are we looking at?"

"I'm not sure it's an attack," answered Bowen.

"Then why did you sound the air raid alarm?"

"Because I have no idea what we're facing." The sergeant pointed to the radar. "This bogey isn't behaving like anything I've ever seen before. It's traveling at over five hundred miles an hour."

"So, it's a ballistic missile."

Bowen shook his head. "Look at its trajectory. It's not flying in a straight line as a missile would. It's been circling the base for several minutes, and a few times has backtracked along its path."

"It moves more like an aircraft," added Jameson. "But as

far as I know, no one has the technology to allow aircraft to fly that fast, not even the Germans."

Evans knew otherwise but said nothing. Intelligence had determined that the Luftwaffe had developed jet technology, building the ME-262 fighter and the Arado Ar-34 bomber, which could achieve speeds of five hundred and forty and four hundred and sixty miles per hour, respectively. Even if these aircraft were operational, neither had the range to reach the East Coast, let alone New Mexico. Which brought him back to square....

"The bogey has changed course." Jameson tried to keep his excitement under control. "It's heading right for us."

"Where?" asked Evans.

"Here." Jameson spun his chair to face Evans. "It's heading for the flight tower."

Evans headed for the door. "From which direction?"

"It's coming in from the northeast."

Evans went outside and circled the metal balcony around the tower to get a better view. He spotted the bogey a mile out and approaching fast, heading for the revetment area where the B-29s were parked. He braced for a bombing run, but nothing happened. Even more unusual, for some reason the pilot kept his running lights on, making him an easy target. Once clear of the revetments, the bogey veered southwest and flew the length of the runway at an altitude of two hundred feet, its speed decreasing. Only then did Evans get a better look at it. The illumination did not come from running lights but from the bogey itself as if it glowed. He had never seen a configuration like this before, a swept-wing aircraft with no visible fuselage or engines, the tips of the wings turned up at a ninety-degree angle. For a second, he thought it would land but then realized it had no landing gear. When the bogey reached the end of the runway, it reversed direction. As it approached, the craft veered toward the tower, lessening its altitude and speed. Evans did not hear the roar of traditional engines, only a low-pitched hum. It stopped three hundred feet from the tower, hovering over the tarmac as three landing struts extended from the lower fuselage. Once the struts were in place, the craft lowered itself onto the tarmac. The hum from its interior and the glow of its exterior stopped.

A pair of two-and-a-half-ton trucks pulled up alongside Evan's jeep. Two dozen soldiers poured out of the back, each armed with M1 Garands or Thompson sub-machine guns, forming a semi-circle around the craft. The officer commanding them was a green lieutenant fresh out of officer training school who had been on base less than a month. Evans feared the situation could quickly go FUBAR under the lieutenant, so he rushed down the stairs and joined the soldiers on the flight line.

"I'll take it from here, lieutenant."

"Thank God." The young officer sighed with relief.

Evans spoke loud enough so the others could hear. "The rest of you, hold your fire. But if any Nazis come out of that ship, blast them."

A minute passed. Evans took that as a good sign, not wanting to be responsible for starting a war. However, he faced the problem of how he would contact the occupants when they exited. He was still trying to figure this out when a mechanical hum came from within the craft. A rectangular section broke away from the nose, lowering to form a ramp leading inside the ship. Around him, the soldiers cocked their weapons.

"No one fires unless I give the order." Evans hoped they were listening and not overcome by emotions.

When the ramp extended, a lone figure descended onto the tarmac. He was male, approximately six feet in height and weighing in at one hundred seventy pounds, with wavy dark hair and brown eyes, which ruled out his being Aryan. The only thing unusual about his appearance was his uniform. Evans had never seen anything like it—a one-piece tunic, soft silver in color, like aluminum foil, with no pockets, cuffs, buttons, or zippers. The boots were made of the same material. The figure made his way toward the line of soldiers, his hands palm up by his side in a gesture of good faith. Evans moved forward to greet him. When they were ten feet apart, Evans paused and raised his hand.

"That's close enough."

The man stopped and nodded his understanding. "Are you in charge here?"

At least he didn't say, "Take me to your leader."

"I'm one of those in charge."

The figure stepped toward Evans and extended his hand. When the major did not respond in kind, the figure became embarrassed. Evans approached and grasped the figure's hand. His skin was as soft as a baby's, yet he had a firm grip.

"By now, I'm sure you have surmised I'm not from this planet."

"Yeah, I'm still trying to wrap my head around that."

The figure bowed his head in greeting. "My name is Valthor."

"I'm Major Matthews Evans. United States Army Air Corps. How can I help you?"

"You have it all wrong," answered Valthor. "I'm here to help Earth."

"Help Earth how?"

"To restore your timeline."

Chapter Nine

Roswell Army Air Field
3 July 1947

E VANS WAS IN way over his head. As an intelligence officer, he had experienced some bizarre shit, including a covert trip to Africa to debrief a *Luftwaffe* Me-262 pilot in Spanish Morocco who had faked his disappearance in the Mediterranean. That paled in comparison to hosting an alien from another planet.

Lieutenant General Jimmy Doolittle, the commander of the 768th Bomb Squadron, and Colonel William "Butch" Blanchard, the base commander, had flown to Washington the day before for a meeting with Hap Arnold, which placed the responsibility for this incident squarely in his lap. First, Evans restricted access to the base, allowing only military personnel to enter and banning anyone, especially civilians, from leaving. Next, he cut off all phone calls to and from the base and made sure the only ones allowed in were from Doolittle or Blanchard, and those would be routed directly to him. The gate guards and operators told anyone who asked that the base was engaged in a routine but surprise lockdown exercise. As for Valthor's craft, Evans placed an around-the-clock guard on it and swore to secrecy under penalty of court-martial those who had observed it land. Evans knew every effort to keep this under wraps would fail. He only wanted to delay the leak long enough for the generals to return and let it be their concern.

How to deal with Valthor presented an entirely different dilemma. Under normal circumstances, Valthor would be moved to a secure location and extensively debriefed until Evans felt confident he had gotten as much information as possible from him. However, Valthor did not fall into the category of defector or enemy combatant. Evans considered him a guest, so he took the calculated risk of bringing Valthor to the base guest house, a two-room residence near the main gate. He posted guards around the guest house, not to keep Valthor contained—Evans doubted Valthor could be restricted to quarters if he wanted to leave—but to keep others from barging in.

As Evans brewed a pot of coffee and bided his time while he figured out what to do next, Valthor walked around the living room, examining each item in the room, almost like a child seeing these things for the first time. He paused in front of the television and turned it on, stepping back to watch the grainy image on the screen.

When coffee half-filled the pot, Evans removed it and filled a mug. "Would you like a cup?"

Valthor ignored him for a second, his attention focused on the TV variety show. "I am sorry. Did you say something?"

"I asked if you wanted some coffee?"

"No, thank you." Valthor shut off the television.

"Do you want me to order you anything from the mass hall?"

"I do not obtain nourishment the way humans do, through the chemical breakdown of organic matter. My kind achieves sustenance by absorbing energy from the stars through our skin, much like a process humans call photosynthesis."

Evans added cream and sugar to his coffee. He headed back to the dining room table when a knock sounded on the door.

"Who is it?"

A man six-foot-two-inches in height stepped inside the hall and closed the door behind him. He wore fatigues with the three chevrons and three rockers of a staff sergeant on each arm. A well-toned physique from ninety minutes a day at the gym was evident in how his biceps and chest filled out his uniform. Staff Sergeant Allen Kerdoshian always made a striking first impression, not only for his size but because he was black. It was highly unusual for coloreds to work outside the support ranks in a military still segregated, particularly military intelligence. Evans saw beyond the difference in skin color. One look into Kerdoshian's piercing brown eyes showed his confidence, as it should. Kerdoshian was brilliant, a self-taught man who read every book he could get his hands on and became well versed in science, history, and politics. Evans had first met him a year ago while investigating a suspected thief in the motor pool stealing military gasoline and selling it off base for a profit. Talking to Kerdoshian for an hour convinced Evans of the sergeant's intelligence and intuitiveness. Despite minor opposition from the base command, Evans brought Kerdoshian over to military intelligence to serve as his deputy.

The sergeant snapped to attention and saluted. "You wanted to see me, sir?"

Evans half-heartedly returned the salute. "Cut the formalities when we're alone. Did you bring a notebook like I asked?"

"Yes, sir." Kerdoshian held up a notebook the size and thickness of a hardcover novel. The cover was made of reddish-tan leather. A clothed-covered elastic cord attached to the outer rim of the back cover wrapped around the width of the book, preventing it from falling open.

"That doesn't look like a notebook."

"It's a blank diary, but it's all I could find on short notice."

"It'll be fine." Evans waved for the sergeant to enter and ushered him toward their visitor. "I'd like you to meet Valthor. He's the pilot of the craft that landed here a few hours ago."

"Staff Sergeant Kerdoshian, sir." He extended his hand. "It's a pleasure to meet you."

Valthor reached out and clasped the sergeant's hand.

"I asked Sergeant Kerdoshian to join us so he could take

notes. I hope that's not going to be a problem."

"Not at all."

Evans sat in one of the chairs at the dining room table. Kerdoshian sat on the nearby sofa, crossed one leg over the other to use as a table, and opened the notebook.

Valthor slid into the chair across from the major and smiled. "Sorry, I don't mean to be rude. I find it... I think the word you use is quaint... that you still use pen and paper."

"We must seem so primitive to you."

"My planet prefers the term developing."

"That doesn't sound much better."

"On the contrary. Your society is much like ours was ten thousand years ago, torn between incredible scientific discoveries and interminable war. We have been observing your society for centuries and are impressed with your progress."

Evans attempted to hide his surprise. "How often have you visited us?"

"Hundreds, maybe thousands of times. Each trip has been to study what goes on here. My planet has a strict policy of not interacting with other societies until they have developed the ability to travel through time as we have."

"Which brings me to my first question. Where are you from?"

Valthor leaned back in his chair. "In the vast realm of the cosmos, we are next-door neighbors. My people inhabit the fourth planet from the star you call Proxima Centauri, just over four light-years away."

"Next door neighbors?" Evans sipped at his coffee. "You make it sound like there are others out there."

"Why would there not be? Your planet possesses a wide array of species. Even amongst humans, there are many races, religions, and philosophies. The universe is no different."

"How many...?" Evans stumbled to think of the correct word.

"Aliens?" Valthor offered.

"…inhabited planets are out there?"

"Hundreds that we are aware of. Probably hundreds of thousands throughout the universe. A few are at our level of development. Some are so far beyond our technology we cannot grasp their advances. We have found a dozen or more that are extinct, having been killed off by time, cosmic disasters, or self-destruction. Most are still advancing along their path of scientific development. A handful are not interested in improving themselves, preferring to wallow in their primitive-ness and barbarity. Sadly, even among the advanced societies, some prefer to pursue more nefarious purposes."

"How so?"

Valthor's demeanor became somber as if remembering an unpleasant episode from his past. "Not too far from my home planet is a civilization that refers to itself as the Anunnaki. The Anunnaki inhabit a planet they call Sumer-e in the Aldebaran system, approximately sixty-eight light-years from Earth. They are a warrior society dedicated to dominance and conquest. They refer to themselves as the Black Sun and call us the Golden Sun, which is meant to be derogatory. The Anunnaki visited Earth thousands of years ago and assisted some of your earliest societies as part of their attempt to colonize as many planets as possible and expand their empire. Nearly two thousand years ago, my planet and several other peaceful clans battled the Anunnaki in a bloody and costly war to prevent them from taking over this portion of the solar system. We eventually reached a truce. All parties, including the Anunnaki, agreed not to interfere in the events of developing societies. Once a society advanced to the point where they could time travel, representatives from each planet could make first contact and petition that planet to join their cause. The truce maintained the peace and balance of power in our sector of the universe for two millennia. Until two years ago."

Evans glanced over at Kerdoshian, who kept scribbling in his notebook. He turned his attention back to Valthor. "What happened?"

"It started approximately twenty years ago when a group of females in Germany called the *Vril* telepathically reached out into the cosmos hoping to communicate with the extraterrestrial world that had visited your planet thousands of years ago. Unfortunately for everyone, the Anunnaki initiated contact with them through the lead psychic, Maria Orsic. The Anunnaki took advantage of this opportunity to pass Miss Orsic the schematics and designs for anti-gravity and time travel vehicles. Originally, the *Vril* and other mystical societies in Germany wanted to use the time machine to travel to your ancient past and search for Aryan gods. Then the Nazis took control of Germany and began weaponizing the schematics the Anunnaki had passed to Miss Orsic."

"That's when they traveled back in time?"

Valthor shook his head. "Despite their levels of technology, the Germans were not advanced enough to develop the designs the Anunnaki had provided. Before the collapse of Nazi Germany, the Anunnaki re-established contact with Miss Orsic and provided her with the information the German scientists needed to complete the weapons."

"Hold on," Evans interrupted. "What do you mean 'before the collapse of Nazi Germany'? They won the war. Hitler used atomic weapons against the Soviet Union to knock them out of the conflict within a few weeks of the beginning of Operation Barbarossa and then accepted terms of surrender from England."

"I refer to the original timeline, the one Nazi Germany altered." Valthor leaned forward and rested his forearms on the table. "In that timeline, Hitler did not defeat the Soviet Union. They suffered horrendous casualties but eventually slowed and turned the tide of war against Hitler. Great Britain never surrendered, and the United States entered the war after the Japanese attacked Pearl Harbor in 1941. The Allies eventually invaded and defeated Germany. However, German scientists had perfected the Anunnaki craft and possessed the ability to travel through time. The day after Hitler committed suicide and Berlin fell to the Soviets, a German military unit traveled back to the era of the Pharaohs where the Anunnaki had established a camp. They obtained nuclear weapons from the Anunnaki and returned to early 1941 where those weapons were used against the Soviet Union, altering your timeline."

Kerdoshian cleared his throat.

"Do you have something you want to ask, sergeant?"

"Just that Washington is going to want verification of what Valthor is telling us."

Evans chastised himself for not considering that. He turned back to Valthor. "I assume you can provide proof of everything you've told me."

Valthor smiled. "I would not expect you to believe me without being able to prove it."

"And the proof will be enough to satisfy our superiors?" asked Kerdoshian.

"It will be."

"I don't see how it matters now." Evans leaned back in his chair. "Hitler has already changed things."

"That's why I am here." Valthor straightened in his chair. "My people have agreed to take you back in time and stop the Nazis from altering the original timeline."

Chapter Ten

Roswell Army Air Field
3 July 1947

E VANS STOOD NEAR the nose of Valthor's aircraft, his gaze fixed on the vehicle, not so much studying it as giving him something to focus on. At the suggestion of Colonel Blanchard, Valthor had agreed to have his ship moved beside Building 84 where it would be less conspicuous.

Not that it helped. The rumor mill had already gone into overdrive. Blanchard realized the longer the lockdown occurred, the more suspicious those in town would become, so he decided to lift the telephone restrictions while keeping the base off-limits. Before he did, the colonel assembled all the base commanders via telephone, advised them of the situation, and had them order their men to say nothing about what was going on. A few lower-grade officers were assigned to travel into Roswell and discreetly spread a rumor that the lockdown resulted from an experimental aircraft having to make a forced landing. One of the more reliable operators would pass the same rumor to select individuals who called in.

Yet Blanchard was not a fool. He covertly had all incoming and outgoing calls monitored for breaches of security. It took only ninety minutes for one lieutenant, an NCO, and two privates to violate the restrictions. Those four were currently sitting in the brig and the people they talked to were detained and isolated by the Roswell Police. Everyone knew they could not keep the lid on this much longer.

The presence of an extraterrestrial visitor was only the tip of the iceberg. The public would panic if they knew Valthor's reason for being here and his solution to the problem. When Valthor met with Blanchard upon the colonel's return from Washington, Valthor advised the best way to prove what he had told Evans was to show them the original timeline. He explained the concept of a multiverse, although Evans did not fully understand.

When the Nazis altered the past, they created a parallel universe. However, the original timeline still existed. Valthor proposed visiting the original timeline, which would verify everything he had told them. Valthor had explained the process for multi-universe travel, but neither himself nor Blanchard fully comprehended it. All he knew was that Blanchard assigned him to this adventure.

"Major, it's time."

Evans walked back to the table behind him. Valthor and Kerdoshian stood on either side of Blanchard. Only thirty-one years old, an age belied by his white hair, the colonel rose quickly through the ranks because of his proficiency as a flight instructor. When America started the B-29 Superfortress program as a deterrence to the *Luftwaffe*, Blanchard was assigned to train the first bombing wing forming in Salina, Kansas. Then the war in Europe ended. The government created enough Superfortresses to equip one squadron, based it out of Roswell Army Air Field, and placed the colonel in command.

"All set?" asked the colonel.

"No." Evans' attempt at levity sounded more ominous than humorous.

"I still think I should be the one to go," said Kerdoshian. "I'm expendable."

"You're far from expendable." Evans placed a reassuring hand on his friend's shoulder.

"You're as qualified as the major," offered Blanchard. "We have a meeting in Washington at 1200 tomorrow to brief the

President's advisors, and the findings carry more weight coming from an officer than a sergeant."

"I understand, sir."

"Don't worry," said Blanchard. "You're going to be involved in this operation. More so than you may want."

"Should I change my uniform for civilian clothes?" asked Evans.

Valthor shook his head. "Where we're going, you'll blend right in."

"Can we bring something with us into the other timeline and return with it?" asked the colonel.

"Yes," Valthor replied cautiously. "I must warn against bringing anything with you that, if left behind, could in any way alter that timeline, otherwise you run the risk of creating a third multiverse."

"I want the major to bring a camera to record what he observes."

"That should not be a problem."

"Thanks." Blanchard stepped back and motioned for a captain holding a Keystone K-774 8mm movie camera with a two-bulb lighting system.

"Are you ready, colonel?"

"In a minute." Blanchard glanced around the area until he spotted an MP standing guard by the entrance. "Corporal, come here."

The corporal rushed over and saluted. "What do you need, sir?"

"I want you to observe what's about to happen. You are not to reveal this to anyone without my permission. Is that understood?"

"Yes, sir."

Blanchard nodded to the captain. "Proceed."

The captain raised the movie camera, switched on the twin bulbs, and began filming.

Blanchard opened a suitcase. Inside sat a U.S.-made Kodak

35 camera. The colonel removed the camera and spun it face down so the serial number showed. "Captain, zoom in on the serial number and record it."

"Yes, sir."

After several seconds, Blanchard opened the back of the camera and laid it down inside the briefcase. The colonel stepped back, called the MP over, and handed him a black marker.

"Corporal, in the pocket is a roll of 35mm film. I want you to write a five-letter code on the box and the same code on the film, then put the roll of film in the camera. The major and I are going to step away so we don't see the code. Captain, make sure you get the code on film."

Evans, Blanchard, and Kerdoshian stepped away. A moment later, the corporal announced, "Done, sir."

"Good. Take the box and keep it with you. Can we turn around?"

"Yes, sir."

The others moved back to the table. "Do you still need me?"

"For a minute." Blanchard took a roll of masking tape, tore off four pieces three inches in length, placed two of them horizontally on the side of the camera so they covered the opening to the back panel and the other two perpendicular across the first pieces of tape. He handed a fine-tip marker to the MP. "I want you to write your initials along each of the overlaps on the tape."

The corporal followed orders. Evans and Kerdoshian did the same, followed by Blanchard. When finished, the general said, "You're excused now, corporal. And remember, only discuss this under my express orders."

The MP snapped to attention and saluted. "Understood, sir."

When the MP returned to his post, Blanchard handed the camera to Evans. "Take this with you and get proof that no one can question. And good luck."

Blanchard held out his hand. Evans shook it. "Thanks. Hopefully, I won't need it."

"You won't," reassured Valthor. "This part is easy. Follow me."

As Evans followed Valthor, Blanchard ordered the captain to keep the camera running.

"Please explain to me what's going to happen," asked Evans.

"There's no need to be nervous, Major Evans."

"That's easy for you to say. This is my first experience with time travel."

"Technically, we're not time traveling right now. That's a much more complicated process." Valthor stopped one hundred feet in front of the nose of his aircraft. "We're going to be visiting the alternate universe, the original universe as it existed before the Germans changed history and created this one. We'll do that via a wormhole."

"A what?"

"A wormhole." Valthor raised his right wrist. He wore what at first appeared to be a watch. Its surface was two inches square, containing numbers and mathematical signs, and a display screen like a calculator. He entered equations into the device as he continued.

"Throughout the universe, at the submicroscopic level, exists what your civilization would call quantum foam. In this foam, space does not have a definitive structure. Adjacent regions in space exchange this foam back and forth, sharing it. My civilization has developed the technology to manipulate this foam. We can create two ring-shaped singularities, one in this multiverse at this exact moment and the second at the time and location of the multiverse we want to visit. These singularities are spherical. Once they move closer to each other, they begin sharing the foam, generating a tunnel between the two spheres that allows us to travel from one multiverse to the other. Another name for it is…."

A bright, glowing spot appeared ten feet in front of them. It pulsated for several seconds then slowly expanded. As it grew larger, an outer rim formed, a vortex of whirling matter similar to storm clouds within a tornado. When it reached seven feet in diameter, it stopped growing. The outer rim continued to pulsate. The center shimmered, distorting the image behind it. Valthor turned to Evans and smiled.

"… a wormhole."

Evans stepped closer. The image on the other side looked familiar, like a street at night, or at least something from this world. He stretched out his hand and approached. The palm passed through an invisible barrier. On the other side, it became as distorted as the image beyond. He felt a slight stinging sensation in his fingers and quickly withdrew it, half expecting his hand to be missing. Thankfully, it was still intact. Evans massaged it with his other hand.

Valthor joined him. "That tingling you feel is high-energy particles passing through the wormhole."

"Aren't those things deadly?"

"Normally, they would be. My civilization created a new element that absorbs the particles and channels them back into the tunnel, ensuring it remains stable so long as we stay within a mile of the wormhole." Valthor patted his watch. "It has allowed us to develop multiverse travel."

"What's it called?"

"Your civilization is centuries away from that level of technology. For now, let us call it exotic matter. Are you ready?"

Evans glanced over his shoulder at Blanchard, who stood dumbfounded. When the colonel saw his hesitation, he motioned for Evans to proceed.

"I guess I'm as ready as I'll ever be."

Valthor extended his hand, motioning toward the wormhole. "After you."

Evans stepped forward, pausing for a moment at the singularity's sphere. He took a deep breath and stepped through. Valthor followed.

Both men proceeded through the wormhole and left this multiverse.

✦　✦　✦

EVANS AND VALTHOR emerged into a filthy alley. A few dozen rats rummaging through a dumpster overflowing with garbage scurried in all directions upon their arrival. Evans barely noticed, attracted instead by a loud commotion in the street beyond. A moment later, he recognized the sounds of yelling and screaming.

"Where are we?"

"Times Square."

"New York City?"

Valthor nodded.

"What's all the screaming about? Are we under attack?"

"Far from it." Valthor gestured for Evans to head for the street and followed.

Nothing could prepare Evans for the sight that greeted him. Tens of thousands of people filled Times Square and flowed along 7th Avenue and 46th and 47th Streets. They cheered and danced. Many waved American flags or blew horns. News cameramen and photographers stood on the roofs of their cars or mingled among the crowd, taking photos. Evans stepped out of the alley, colliding with a young woman in a red dress holding a folded newspaper.

"Sorry, ma—"

The woman cupped Evans' cheeks in her hands and kissed him full on the lips for several seconds before hugging him. "Isn't it wonderful?"

"Yes, it is." Evans hesitated, not sure how to respond.

"It's over!" The woman handed Evans the newspaper, kissed him again, and raced off into the crowd.

"What's over?" Evans called after her.

"Read the headline," Valthor suggested.

Evans unfolded it to the front page. It was a copy of *The New York Times* dated 14 August 1945. The headline read:

JAPAN SURRENDERS, END OF WAR!
EMPEROR ACCEPTS ALLIED RULE

"What does this mean? We're not at war with Japan."

"Not in your current timeline. With the Soviet Union defeated, Japan invaded eastern Russia and obtained its needed supplies there. They never ventured into Southeast Asia or went to war with the Allies. In this multiverse, Germany did not have atomic weapons. Japan and Germany declared war on the United States in December 1941, and hostilities continued until 1945. The conflict between Germany and the Soviet Union lasted four years and devastated everything between Moscow and Berlin. America fought the Japanese on dozens of islands across the Pacific. It became known as World War II and cost nearly twenty-five million lives."

Evans stepped back and leaned against the front window of Bond Clothing, trying to wrap his head around this. "How did it all end? Did we invade Japan?"

Valthor shook his head. He made his way through the cheering crowds to a nearby newspaper stand and pointed to an older copy of *The New York Times* hanging on the outside wall. The newspaper was dated 5 August 1945. The headline stunned him.

FIRST ATOMIC BOMB DROPPED ON JAPAN;
MISSILE IS EQUAL TO 20,000 TONS OF TNT;
TRUMAN WARNS FOE OF A 'RAIN OF RUIN'

"Does this mean we… that America developed the atomic bomb?"

Valthor nodded. "America used it against two Japanese

cities, killing more than a hundred thousand people in a matter of seconds."

"Jesus, you mean we were as barbaric as the Nazis?"

"No. Truman made the decision hoping to force Tokyo to surrender without an invasion of Japan. It succeeded and probably saved a few million lives."

"And who the Hell is Truman? I've never even heard of him."

"In this multiverse, he's the President of the United States. He took over the office after Roosevelt died of a stroke in April 1945."

Evans raised his hands and waved them in frustration. "What do you mean? Roosevelt refused to run for re-election and Dewey became president in 1944."

"Not in this multiverse." Valthor moved closer to the major. "The Allies won the war and defeated Nazi Germany and Imperial Japan. The cost in human lives was tremendous, but evil was defeated. Here humanity has the potential for a great future. In your multiverse, the world is still under the influence of Hitler."

Evans closed his eyes and massaged his temples. All this information was too much for him to process at once. He felt overwhelmed.

"I know this a lot to take in," comforted Valthor. "May I suggest you focus on the task at hand and gather the necessary evidence for Colonel Blanchard and those in Washington?"

That snapped Evans back to reality. "You're right."

He grabbed a dozen copies of *The New York Times* off the stand. "How much?"

The clerk counted them. "Thirty-six cents."

"How much for *The Times* on the side of your stall?"

"You mean the one about us nuking them Japs?"

"Yeah."

"Sorry, it's not for sale."

Evans pulled his money from his pocket. "Would you sell it

for five dollars?"

"Make it ten and you got a deal."

Evans pulled off two fives and passed them to the clerk.

"It's yours, buddy."

Taking the newspaper from the side of the stall, he handed them to Valthor. "Could you hold these a minute?"

"Of course."

Removing the camera from its pouch, the major took four photographs of the newsstand, one of it in relation to the rest of *Times Square*, a close-up of the newspapers, and finally a shot of today's edition with enough background to prove it came from that stand. The rest of the images were of the celebration, including landmarks within the square for ease of verification. The last photo was of a sailor bending a nurse over and kissing her.

"I've got everything I need." Evans rewound the film into its roll and returned the camera to its pouch. "Let's go."

"Are you sure?"

"Yeah."

Winding their way through the crowd, the two made their way back to the alley. As they entered, something caught Evans' attention. "Hold on. I have to do something."

"Take your time."

Evans walked to the phone booth he had spotted on the corner of 7th Avenue and 46th Street. Closing the door barely diminished the noise outside, but it would be enough. He lifted the receiver and waited for the operator to answer.

"How may I help you?"

"I need to make a long-distance call."

"What's the number, please?"

"PENnsylvania four one three two."

"That'll be seventy-six cents, please."

The major inserted the proper amount.

"Thank you. Just a moment, please."

A moment later, the telephone on the other end began to

ring. Evans took a deep breath. After the third ring, someone picked up.

"Hello?"

Evans' heart skipped a beat at the sound of this familiar voice. The major lowered his tone so as not to be recognized.

"I'm sorry to bother you. I served with Bucky a few years back. I wondered if he made it home yet?"

Anguish filled the woman's voice. "I'm sorry. My son died at Omaha Beach."

"Thank you." Evans hung up and placed his forehead on the receiver. This entire situation was spiraling out of control, and he found himself in the middle of the God damn vortex.

Evans rejoined Valthor.

"Are you okay?"

"I'm fine," Evans lied.

Valthor did not believe him but offered him the courtesy of not pushing the issue. "Should we head back?"

"Yes, please."

Chapter Eleven

Washington D.C.
4 July 1947

EVANS WAS NOT easily intimidated. It came with being an intelligence officer. Over the years, he had been in many a situation that would have unsettled, often putting his life in danger. It came with the job. He had debriefed many sources of information and had been grilled a few times by his superiors. However, this was different. He never expected to be questioned by twelve of the most brilliant and influential men in Washington.

After returning from 1945 New York City, Evans had placed the camera back in the briefcase along with the newspapers he had collected. Blanchard closed and locked the briefcase and put five pieces of electrical tape across the opening, two across the locks, one beneath the handle, and one across each end. He then ran one long segment of electrical tape around the length so it overlapped the first five. Evans and the colonel initialed the overlaps of each piece of tape. All the while, the movie cameraman filmed the entire procedure. Evans, Blanchard, Valthor, the cameraman, and the MP who had witnessed the initial procedure immediately boarded a B-29 that flew them to National Airport in Arlington, Virginia. Brigadier General George C. Marshall, his aide, and two staff officers met the group at the airport. The aide took possession of the briefcase and the movie camera, took numerous photographs of both, and departed to develop both sets of film. The staff members escorted the MP and cameraman to the

Pentagon where they would be officially debriefed. Marshall's aide took Evans and Blanchard to the Washington Arsenal on Greenleaf Point to freshen up and rest before their noon meeting.

Evans expected the meeting to take place at the White House or the newly constructed Pentagon. Instead, it occurred in a nondescript red-brick three-story building at 2430 E Street NW. Only after being checked in did Evans realize the building housed the headquarters of the Central Intelligence Group, the successor to the Office of Strategic Services.

Now he sat in a large conference room. The shades had been drawn, with the only illumination coming from three strings of lights stretching across the ceiling. They sat at four tables, three in a U-shape at one end of the room, and the last six feet away and facing them. Evans, Blanchard, and Valthor sat at the fourth table from which they briefed the committee and answered questions. Valthor had gone first and took more than three hours. Evans followed, reporting on Valthor's landing at Roswell and their trip to the past. That portion of the questioning had lasted two hours and, considering the stature of those on the committee, would probably go on indefinitely.

Secretary of War Major General William "Wild Bill" Donavon chaired the committee. When war with Nazi Germany seemed imminent, President Roosevelt had requested Donavon set up the Office of Strategic Services, more famously known as the OSS, America's first intelligence service. He had created the foundation for an effective analysis and covert action operation, recruiting some of the best and the brightest. When the war ended, Donovan returned to private industry. When Dewey became President, he asked Donovan to take over as Secretary of War. The chiefs of staff of the Army and Navy reported to Donovan, and he reported directly to President Dewey. The President trusted Donovan's judgment, so his authority carried more weight than anyone else on the committee. Donovan had to buy into this theory otherwise the entire operation would be stillborn.

General Marshall sat on Donovan's right. As Secretary of the Army, Marshall was the highest-ranking military member, responsible for the ground forces and the Army Air Corps. To his right sat Doolittle, commander of the 768the Bomb Squadron. Admiral James Forrestal, Secretary of the Navy, sat on Donovan's left. Forrestal brought two factors to the table that made him invaluable—years of expertise as a naval officer and being one of the most brilliant scientific minds in the military.

Seated at the table along the right were other members of the intelligence community. When Donovan retired in 1944, the government downsized the OSS and morphed it into the Central Intelligence Group. Rear Admiral Sydney Souers, the assistant director of Naval Intelligence, accepted the position of Director of Central Intelligence (DCI). Army Air Corps General Hoyt Vandenburg, who temporarily replaced Souers in 1946, sat to his left. Rear Admiral Roscoe Hillenkoetter, the current DCI, occupied the last seat.

Across from the heads of the intelligence community were the scientific leaders. Vannevar Bush took the center seat. An engineer from the Massachusetts Institute of Technology and one of the most brilliant men in America, Roosevelt had appointed him chairman of the Office of Scientific Research responsible for leading six thousand PhDs and engineers in applying science for the upcoming war with Germany that never occurred. Jerome Hunsaker, an aeronautical engineer from the Massachusetts Institute of Technology, designer of the first airship in the United States, and chairman of the National Advisory Committee of Aeronautics, sat to Bush's right. Beside Hunsaker was Donald Menzel, an astronomer from Harvard University, one of the first theoretical astrophysicists and a consultant to the CIG. Detlev Bronk, an aviation physiologist, chairman of the National Academy of Sciences, a member of the National Research Council, and president of Johns Hopkins University, sat to Bush's left. Beside him was William McPherson Allen, chairman of the Boeing aircraft company.

Donovan thumbed through the photographs of Times Square from the alternate universe and the newspapers Evans had brought back. "General Marshal, do you believe these are legitimate?"

"I do. Colonel Blanchard has maintained an impeccable chain of acquisition from the moment Major Evans left for the alternate universe to his return. The evidence was properly sealed and transported. My aide took possession of it at National Airport and had the film processed and analyzed. You also have the sworn testimony of the MP and cameraman who witnessed the event, both of whom were debriefed by members of my staff, as well as the sworn testimony of the chief engineer at Roswell who examined Mr. Valthor's craft. My staff has studied the evidence Evans and Blanchard have provided and have concluded that it's legitimate. I agree with their assessment."

"Jesus Christ." Forrestal massaged his forward. "This can't be happening."

Valthor leaned forward. "As difficult as it is to comprehend, it is happening. You are living in a multiverse, an alternative timeline than the one you originally experienced, because the Nazis went back in time and altered the flow of history to their advantage. I am here to offer you the opportunity to correct the change."

"Can you explain to us how time travel works?" asked Bush.

"Of course. There are cylinders throughout the universe composed of hundreds of neutron stars, the collapsed remnants of regular stars that have burned out and imploded on themselves. These neutron stars are extremely dense. A thimble full would weigh one hundred million tons. The cylinders encasing them are forty kilometers wide and two hundred kilometers long and spin along the time axis at half the speed of light. The mass and density they create warp the surrounding space-time continuum, creating time cones that lead to the past and the future."

"That sounds like something from a science fiction novel," snorted Menzel. "Besides, the centrifugal force would be two billion times Earth's gravity. Nothing could survive that."

"In 1974, one of your scientists, Frank Tipler, will deduce the possibility of these cylinders based on Einstein's theory of general relativity. As for the issue of centrifugal force, we developed a way to compensate for that, but the technology is way beyond your current level of understanding. We moved one of these cylinders near the planet you call Neptune. It was originally constructed eight thousand years ago and is an early model, but created long enough ago to send your team back to Ancient Egypt."

"How come our scientists have never seen it?" asked Menzel.

"It follows the same orbit as Neptune and is behind it, making it impossible to see from your planet. If I may proceed." Valthor focused his attention back on the others. "The major's team will travel close to the cylinder and enter a clockwise circular orbit around it until his craft finds the time cone leading to the period he needs to travel to. The craft will enter the cone, emerge on the other side, and land in Ancient Egypt for Major Evans to complete his assignment. To return, he will initiate the same procedure in reverse."

"I have a question," said Hillenkoetter. "Assuming everything the three of you have told us is true, and assuming we agree to allow Major Evans to travel back in time to correct the past, doesn't the possibility exist that they could do more damage than the Nazis?"

"It is possible but unlikely," answered Valthor. "The time they will be returning to is early in your recorded history. If they limit their interactions only to the Germans who traveled there, the repercussions should be minimal. However, they should have no interaction with the locals, and under no circumstances must they kill any Egyptians, even if it means sacrificing their own lives."

"Why is that?" asked Hillenkoetter.

"The law of infinite ancestors." When no one understood what he meant, Valthor explained. "Suppose one of your team accidentally kills a small boy. That means all his future ancestors will not exist. Nearly one hundred and fifty of his generations would be erased from existence. Not knowing ahead of time what those future generations will contribute to society, that could irreparably alter the future timeline."

"What if we have to kill the Germans?" asked Evans.

"That will have limited effect. Their generations up to May 1945 are already in place. All you will do is stop future generations of those Germans from procreating, which will not affect the past."

"This is too dangerous," protested Vannevar.

"I would not have proposed this solution if I thought the risk of allowing the Nazis to continue in this multiverse did not outweigh the potential changes in the timeline that Major Evans might cause."

"I have a question." Bush leaned forward. "What happens to this timeline if Major Evans is successful?"

Valthor paused. "I admit I cannot say with full confidence. If Major Evans stops the Germans and does nothing to alter the future, this timeline will cease to exist."

"And us along with it?" asked Donovan.

Valthor nodded. An awkward silence descended over the room.

Donovan finally broke the silence. "Does anyone have any further questions?"

"I have one," said Hunsaker. "If time travel is so easy, how come no one from our future has visited us up until now?"

"Because it is dangerous. Fifty-five thousand years ago,

some of the civilizations that possessed such technology waged a Time War that caused considerable damage to their societies. To avoid the devastating effects of time travel, they agreed not to use it in any form. You see that by the results of the Anunnaki's interference in your past."

Forrestal shook his head. "The entire concept of time travel seems so bizarre."

"It shouldn't be. Your own Albert Einstein predicted it. In the 22nd Century, Earth will develop the ability to travel through time. At that point, other planets will make first contact and ask you to regulate its use."

"But you've already made first contact with us," said Donovan.

"True. But if Mr. Evans is allowed to go back and correct the timeline, none of this will take place."

The rest of the committee remained silent until Bush finally spoke.

"Colonel, Major, Sergeant, Mr. Valthor. Thank you for briefing us this morning. If you'll now excuse us, we need to discuss our options."

Evans waited for the others to stand before doing so himself, being the last one out of the room. He took a quick view of the committee as he passed through the door, wondering what fate they would decide for him.

✦　　✦　　✦

DONOVAN WAITED UNTIL the committee was alone.

"Before we begin our discussions, does everyone here concur with what we heard today? Show of hands, please."

Donovan raised his hand along with ten others. Only Souers held out.

"You don't believe what Valthor told us?" asked Donovan.

"No…." Souers. "I mean, I don't know. It sounds unbelievable." He looked across the room at the scientists. "Does any of this make sense to you?"

"Very much so," said Bush. "The scientific community has been proposing ideas like this for years. Valthor confirmed many of our hypotheses and opened up new avenues of potential research."

"Then why don't we have any aircraft like his?" asked Doolittle.

"Because their level of technology is centuries ahead of ours," answered Bronk. "Our B-29s are as primitive to their craft as DaVinci's helicopter designs are to us."

"From the few photographs I've seen of Valthor's craft," added Allen, "his planet has mastered technologies and materials we haven't even conceived of."

"I know," admitted Souers. "I believe it, yet it's still so...."

"Astounding?" offered Hillenkoetter.

"I was thinking more along the lines of incomprehensible. You heard what Valthor said. If we approve this operation and Major Evans is successful, all of us cease to exist."

"In this timeline," corrected Donovan.

"Doesn't that bother you?" asked Souers. "We'll be voting ourselves out of existence."

"We're aware of that," said Bush. The others murmured their agreement.

"There's another timeline, the original timeline." Souers struggled to find the proper wording. "Why do we have to erase ours?"

Donovan flashed him a disapproving glare. Marshall started to respond, but Bush beat him to it.

"We all feel the same way. None of us want to pass out of existence. Consider it this way. In one scenario, we correct the timeline and all of this goes away, us along with it. In the second scenario, Captain Evans succeeds with only minor changes to this timeline and we stay alive, hopefully in a world that's better than this. The last scenario, which in my opinion is the worst case, is we do nothing and this timeline remains.

Hitler controls all of Europe and the Middle East, Japan controls Asia, and millions of civilians are slaughtered in isolated corners of the world while we sit here and enjoy our lives, praying Hitler doesn't do anything to disturb our peace, all the while knowing war with Germany is inevitable. I couldn't look myself in the mirror every morning if I chose the latter. I vote to approve this operation."

"So do I," Marshall responded.

"Same here," seconded Forrestal.

"Ditto," added Hillenkoetter.

"Count me in," said Bronk.

Allen murmured his ascent. Vandenburg and Hunsaker nodded theirs. Doolittle raised his hand off the table. Menzel offered a thumbs up. All eyes fell on Souers.

Souers sighed. "I'm not going to be the asshole of the group. I vote yes."

"Then it's settled. We proceed with the operation." Donovan leaned back in his chair. "I'll inform the president of our decision. General Marshall, you'll oversee the preparations. If you need anything, let me know and I'll make certain you get it."

"Yes, sir."

"All we need now is to choose a code name."

"What do you call such a plan?" asked Hunsaker. "Operation Grandiose?"

Forrestal shook his head. "Too cumbersome."

"How about majestic?" suggested Bush.

"Operation Majestic it is," said Donovan. "And we'll call ourselves the Majestic Committee."

Chapter Twelve

Roswell Air Force
6 July 1947

THE LAST DAY and a half had passed in a blur. After returning to Roswell from Washington, Evans and Colonel Blanchard had only twenty-four hours to make all the preparations for the travel back in time. Luckily, others were handling the most difficult parts. Valthor had remotely brought down from his mother ship orbiting Earth the vessel that would transport the team back in time. Marshall had flown in from Fort Benning a squad of twelve Rangers from the 3rd Ranger Battalion led by Lieutenant Francis Dawson to provide military support as well as Nigel Davenport, a noted Egyptologist from the London Museum on assignment to the Smithsonian. Forrestal sent Lieutenant Commander Tobey, an officer from the Office of Naval Intelligence team, proving that military service rivalry always took center stage even in times of crisis. Evans and Kerdoshian rounded out the sixteen-man team that would save the world or change its history.

Evans stared at his image in the mirror. He would never admit it to Blanchard, or anyone for that matter, but he was apprehensive about this mission. The idea of combat did not bother him. He had geared up for battle when war with Germany seemed inevitable and had maintained that level of readiness. This was different. He didn't fear the possibility of death but its inevitability. Success would have consequences he could not avoid.

A knock sounded on his door. "Come in."

Kerdoshian stuck his head inside the room. "Are you ready, major? We're running late, and they're already waiting for us at the airfield."

Evans averted his gaze from his reflection. "Yeah."

Kerdoshian had parked his jeep outside the quarters. As Evans slid into the passenger's seat, he noticed a footlocker resting in back. "What's that for?"

"I'm taking it along." Kerdoshian started the jeep.

"We're not going on vacation."

"I have things in there we might need." The sergeant pulled away and headed for the airfield.

It took only a few minutes to arrive at Building 18. A chain-link fence had been hastily erected around the front of the hanger and covered with tarps so no one could see inside. Half a dozen MPs guarded access to the area, preventing any authorized personnel from entering. A young corporal saluted and waved them through.

As Kerdoshian passed through into the secure zone, he muttered, "Now I've seen everything."

The time travel device was a flying saucer. An actual flying saucer, like those made popular in science fiction magazines and serials. Only this was not the stereotypical disc that resembled two plates glued together. The bottom was flat with three tripod-shaped landing gear extending from the chassis, the struts resting on the tarmac. The top was layered, resembling a smaller plate stacked on a larger plate and topped with a bowl. It measured fifty feet in circumference and stood twenty-five feet in height, including landing gear.

Valthor emerged from the craft. Upon seeing the others, he descended the access ladder and joined them. "Gentlemen, I am ready to proceed when you are."

A private with the name CRANE embroidered on his uniform leaned forward so he could see Evans. "Major, you said you've done this before?"

"Yes."

"However," added Valthor, "Not in this craft. We used a wormhole to visit another multiverse. Time travel on the scale we are talking about is an exceedingly more complicated concept. Everything is pre-set. Once on board, you'll travel to Neptune, meet the cylinder positioned there, and travel back to Ancient Egypt."

"It'll take forever to get to Neptune," said Toby.

"It will take you approximately five hours at the speed of light, which is what you will be traveling."

The officers looked at each other, amazed at the possibility.

"You keep on saying 'you,'" began Evans. "Aren't you going with us?"

Valthor shook his head. "I cannot. My leaders will not allow me to. That would be a direct violation of the accord we have with the Anunnaki. Assisting you in correcting your timeline is as far as I am authorized to go."

"None of us know the first thing about your technology. How are we going to operate that thing?"

"You are not. I have already programmed into the onboard navigation system the coordinates to the cylinder." Valthor handed Evans his calculator/watch. "When you are ready, press the green button and the craft will automatically transport you to the cylinder, enter the proper time cone, and land you safely at your destination. When you are ready to return, press the green button again and the craft will return you here."

"It's as easy as that?" asked Blanchard.

"Yes." A slight hesitation entered Valthor's voice.

"Is there something you're not telling us?" asked Kerdoshian.

"I cannot guarantee how your species will react to time travel. The process affects different civilizations in different ways."

Tobey huffed. "You're saying we could all die out there."

"It is a theoretical possibility. I cannot say without additional empirical evidence."

"Shit." The lieutenant commander turned his back and took a few steps from the others.

Blanchard stepped forward and faced the rest of the team. "In light of this new information, if there is anyone who wants to back out, no one will think less of you."

No one took the colonel up on his offer.

"Thank you." Blanchard nodded. "Major, proceed."

Evans slipped the calculator/watch onto his wrist. "Is everything on board?"

"Yes, sir." A corporal saluted. "We secured the sergeant's footlocker."

"Thanks." Evans returned the salute. "The rest of you, mount up."

One by one, the Rangers, the naval officer, and Nigel climbed aboard the craft, followed by Kerdoshian.

Blanchard offered Evans his hand. "Best of luck."

"Thanks." Evans shook it. "We're going to need it."

Valthor stepped up to the major. "Are you certain you want to go through with this? I know what a moral dilemma it represents for you."

"What do you mean?" asked Blanchard.

"In the original timeline, Evans is killed during the invasion of France. It is why I chose him to go back to Times Square. I knew there was no way he could accidentally run into himself. If the major is successful in restoring the original timeline, he will die in 1944."

The colonel glanced over at Evans. "And you knew about this?"

Evans nodded. "While in Times Square, I called my mother and pretended I was an old army buddy. She confirmed it."

"And you still want to go?"

"I don't have much of a choice, do I?"

"You're an honorable man." Valthor offered his hand. "I think this is the proper gesture."

"It is." Evans shook it. "Thank you. For everything."

"You are welcome."

"Hopefully, we'll see each other again."

"We will not."

The statement caught Evans by surprise.

"If you are successful, this timeline will no longer exist, I will not have come to your planet, and we will have never met." Valthor expressed what passed as a smile. "I wish you success."

"Thanks."

Evans climbed aboard the saucer, retracted the access ladder, and closed and secured the hatch. The rest of his team had already strapped in. The interior contained a raised platform at the front with two seats and a control panel. Four rows, each with four seats and an aisle in the center, sat behind the cockpit. The saucer had no windows or viewports, only a monitor mounted on the console.

Evans ascended onto the platform, took what would be the pilot's seat on a human aircraft, and strapped himself in. He pressed the green button on the calculator/watch. A background hum emanated from the saucer. At first, Evans barely noticed because the sound was so soft. It slowly increased in intensity until it filled the cabin, reminding him of the noise inside an aircraft in flight, only not as intense. The monitor on his console came to life, showing the tarmac and Building 18.

Evans felt a barely noticeable jolt as the craft lifted off. It hovered ten feet above the ground for several seconds, the hum increasing in speed. On the monitor, Blanchard and the others stepped back, heading for the safety of the hanger. Only Valthor seemed unfazed.

Concern grew in Evans. Before he could do anything, the ship propelled forward. One moment he stared at the hanger and, the next, they entered outer space. Motion sickness washed over him. He leaned to the right and vomited, heaving until his stomach was empty. Glancing into the cabin, every member of his team had passed out, even Kerdoshian. Some had also puked on themselves.

Evans closed his eyes and leaned back against the headrest, struggling to stay conscious. His efforts failed and he blacked out.

He regained consciousness, though he had no idea how much time had passed. His stomach still felt nauseous. When he opened his eyes, the dizziness resumed. Evans closed them again, squinting and swallowing, although he found it difficult to keep even his saliva down. As his senses settled, a new sensation vibrated through the saucer. Despite his better judgment, Evans opened his eyes and focused on the monitor. The clock indicated more than five hours had elapsed.

Ahead of him, the time cylinder hovered in space.

The saucer entered its gravitational pull. Evans could not take the pressure. He dry-heaved again. Thankfully, nothing came up, or he might have choked to death. His vision spun despite his eyes being shut.

Evans passed out again as the saucer entered one of the cones and traveled through time.

BOOK TWO

Chapter Thirteen

?????
?????

EVANS REGAINED CONSCIOUSNESS slowly. The last thing he remembered was the high-pitched whir of the engines and the acceleration that caused him to pass out. Now silence and stillness dominated his senses. He attempted to move but could not. Evans thought he might be disabled, then realized he could move was unable to go anywhere. He opened his eyes. A bolt of agony shot through his senses, making him cry out. Once the pain lessened to a dull throb, he tried again, this time opening them slowly. Only then did he realize that most of the lightning in the craft had been extinguished except for a few fixtures, including one above the console that provided the barest illumination. The aching resumed, though not as much as before. After several moments, the pain ceased and his vision focused.

Evans remained strapped into the pilot's seat, only now he dangled against the restraining straps. From what he could determine, the saucer rested at a forty-degree angle, with the front pointed down. Except for the emergency lights, everything on the control panel had gone dark. Cracks extended across the service of the monitor. He shifted to his left, trying to see what had happened to the rest of the craft and his team. When he did, the restraints pressed against his bruised shoulders, sending more bolts of pain through his body.

"Fuck!"

A strained voice called out, "Is that you, sir?"

"Kerdoshian?"

"Yes, sir."

"Are you okay?"

"I feel like someone kicked the shit out of me but, other than that, I think I'm okay."

Evans leaned as far left as he could but could not see into the interior of the saucer.

"Tobey, are you awake?"

No response.

"Commander Tobey," Evans called out more loudly.

"I think he's dead," a strained voice answered.

"Who am I talking to?" Evans asked.

"It's me. Nigel."

"Are you all right?"

"I think so," replied the Egyptologist. "I ache and my muscles are stiff, but nothing's broken, and I don't think there are any internal injuries."

"That's good," said Evans. "Why do you think the lieutenant commander is dead?"

"His chest is caved in. It looks like his entire ribcage collapsed."

"Shit," Evans mumbled under his breath. "Is anyone else alive?"

"I don't know. No one is moving, but they could be unconscious."

"One of the Rangers is still alive," added Kerdoshian. "He's moving his head back and forth."

"Let's check out the rest of the crew," said Evans. "Be careful when you get up. We're at a horrible angle, and I don't need anyone getting hurt."

Evans braced his feet on the edge of the console, leaned back against his seat, and wrapped his left arm around the arm of his chair. With his right hand, he unbuckled the restraints, falling three inches before catching himself. Despite the pain in his muscles, he lowered himself down from the flight deck onto the slanted floor of the saucer. Half a dozen dim emergency lights lined the circumference, with three more mounted in the ceiling, providing barely enough light for him to see. The interior of the saucer seemed intact, with no signs of extensive damage. No one else moved except for Kerdoshian, Nigel, and the lone Ranger rocking against his seat belt. Once free of his seat, Kerdoshian slid along the saucer's deck to Evans.

"Any idea what happened?" asked Nigel, who struggled to unbuckle himself.

Evans shrugged. "I'm not sure. We definitely crashed."

"But where?" asked Nigel.

"I think the better question is when?" added Kerdoshian.

"First things first." Evans maneuvered past them to the closest seat occupied by a Ranger. "Let's find out who survived."

It took longer than expected to check on the others because of the angle of the saucer. Besides themselves, the only others who survived were Lieutenant Dawson and two Rangers. Evans felt heartsick. Ten members of his team died before the mission began, and he did not even know most of their names. For those who had survived, getting them down without injury proved more difficult than initially thought. Evans and Nigel woke them and, when they were aware enough to function, unstrapped and slowly lowered them to Kerdoshian, who helped them to the floor. The only one who did not regain consciousness right away was Dawson, who had a bruise on his temple that Evans feared might be a concussion. Naturally, they all had questions, few of which the major could answer, at least until they got outside.

The team gathered around the circular hatch on the bottom of the craft. Evans ran his hands along the rim, trying to find a switch that would open it. After his second attempt, he slammed his hand against the surface.

"Damn it. I can't open the hatch."

"Does that mean we're trapped in here?" asked the Rangers with CRANE embroidered on his tunic.

"No, it means we have to figure another way out."

"Sir," began Kerdoshian. "What about the remote Valthor gave you."

Evans had forgotten about that. He checked the calculator/watch on his wrist and studied it. Valthor had told him how to start the saucer but had not given him any other instructions. He would never know if it worked unless he tried. Evans raised the remote toward the hatch.

"Here goes nothing."

"Please don't hit the self-destruct button," joked Kerdoshian.

Evans glanced at his friend, surprised by the unusual display of humor.

The sergeant grinned. "Sir."

The first two buttons had no effect. The third activated something on the control panel because it hummed for a moment before shorting out. When Evans pressed the fourth one, a whir emanated from the hatch. It moved a few inches and stopped. Evans continued pressing the button until the hatch opened a foot. Sand poured through the opening.

"Are we buried?" asked Crane.

Evans shook his head. "I see daylight about six feet above us. There's sand blocking the opening."

Kerdoshian moved alongside Evans, using his hands and arms to shovel sand away from the hatch and into the saucer. When a two-foot-deep pile formed around his feet, the sergeant nodded.

"Try it again."

This time the hatch opened halfway before sticking.

The older Ranger raced up and helped Kerdoshian clean sand away. After a minute, the sergeant told Evans to try one more time. The hatch fully opened, allowing a waterfall of sand to cascade into the saucer. It stopped after a few seconds. The two men leaned forward.

"We're definitely near the surface." Kerdoshian climbed into the opening and began pushing sand behind him. As he did, the Ranger pulled it into the saucer where Evans and Crane spread it around. They continued for several minutes until the sergeant called down. "I made it. Come on up."

The youngest Ranger looked worried, "What about the lieutenant?"

"Leave him here for now." When Crane started to protest, Evans cut him off. "Let's first figure out where we are, and then we'll come back for him."

One by the one, they climbed up the tunnel, Evans leading the way. When he reached the surface, he saw that they had crashed in a desert. The saucer lay half-buried in the sand at a forty-five-degree angle, providing the only shade for miles around. Evans walked around to the other side of the saucer, the sun's heat feeling like a furnace on his face. He scanned the area, hoping to find a city, a landmark, anything that would offer a clue to their location. Instead, it was nothing but flat sand from horizon to horizon.

Kerdoshian stepped up beside him. "There's nothing to pinpoint our position."

"I know." Evans wiped the sweat off his forehead. "We could be anywhere."

"Once the stars come out, we'll be able to get our bearings."

"We can't afford to wait around here. We have a mission to accomplish."

"With all due respect, sir, we don't have any alternatives. We don't know when or where we are. If we head in the wrong direction, we'll die in the middle of nowhere. Besides, the lieutenant is still unconscious, and none of us are in any condition to go marching through the desert."

"You're right." Evans patted Kerdoshian on the shoulder.

"That's what I'm here for, sir."

"I'll check to see if our weapons are still working. You examine the rest of the team, especially Dawson, to make sure we're not dealing with anything more serious than a few scrapes and sore muscles."

"Roger that." Kerdoshian paused. "What should we do about those who didn't make it?"

"We'll bury them tonight after the sun goes down and we've rested a bit."

Kerdoshian went off to get the medical kit. Evans stared out across the desert, hoping those who died in the crash weren't the lucky ones.

Chapter Fourteen

Egypt
2557 B.C.

MARIA STOOD BY the open flap to the tent, preferring the shade to the blaring sun. She wore a white sun dress and matching low-heeled shoes. A pair of sunglasses hid her eyes. An occasional gust of hot air blew across the desert, rustling her auburn hair. She barely noticed, overcome by wonderment. She had dreamed of moments like this, fantasized about such experiences, yet never really believed they would come true. Yet here she was, witnessing one of the greatest moments of history.

Half a mile away, the first and most prominent of the three pyramids, the one the world would eventually know as the Pyramid of Khufu, stood half erected, the top two hundred feet yet to be built. For centuries, historians and archaeologists theorized how ancient Egypt could build structures as detailed and massive as the pyramids. Maria no longer had to wonder. She witnessed the moment first-hand.

"It's a magnificent sight, isn't it?"

The voice snapped Maria back to reality. She suppressed a sigh as Kammler moved up beside her, a glass of wine in his hand. Even in the broiling heat of the Egyptian desert, he wore a full uniform, his only concession to the climate being the tan-colored uniform of an *Afrika Korps* officer, yet still bedecked with SS insignia.

"It is," Maria responded without commitment. "We're witnessing history."

"No, my dear. We're *altering* history."

That's what bothered Maria.

Before the awkward conversation could continue, an SS *rottenführer* entered the tent from the entrance on the other side. "Excuse me, *Herr Obergruppenführer*."

"Yes?"

"One of the Anunnaki is here to see you."

"Thank you. I'll be out in a moment." Kammler crossed over to the table, set down his glass, and put on his service cap.

"Are you coming, *Fraulein* Orsic?"

"I'll stay here."

"That wasn't a request."

Maria crossed the tent and exited, followed by Kammler. She cringed as the *rottenführer* led them to the Anunnaki. Maria reasoned her disgust for the aliens resulted from her prejudices. She had telepathically communicated with them for years, all the time assuming they were like us. When she finally had the opportunity to meet them, she anticipated beings that appeared humanoid. The Anunnaki were anything but. They looked like insects, only more abominable. Each stood upright, stretching eight feet in height, with only four appendages, two prothoracic legs that served as arms and two metathoracic legs. Their thoraxes were slim and elongated. Their heads were nearly identical to those of a praying mantis, with the only difference being the placement of the eyes halfway down the skull rather than at the top. Unlike a mantis, these things possessed no wings and had a light greyish hue. Maria could have looked past the physical appearance if the Anunnaki did not act like insects, lacking emotion, sympathy or empathy, and restraint. After watching these aliens in action for the past two weeks, she understood why they had accepted Kammler and the SS as one of their own.

Of course, Gudrun conversed with the alien. The Anunnaki's language consisted of various clicks and buzzes, nothing translatable into any form of human communication. However, once in contact with them, Gudrun's ability to telepathically correspond increased. The bitch used this to her advantage. Gudrun sensed Maria's growing regret over enabling this meeting and, with her ability to communicate directly with the Anunnaki, had begun supplanting Maria as the scientific head of the mission. Gudrun had used her finely skilled talents, both in telepathy and in the bedroom, to worm her way into Kammler's graces and make Maria irrelevant. Once good friends, since arriving in ancient Egypt the two women had become rivals.

Kammler walked up to Gudrun and the alien. The *obergruppenführer* extended his right arm in a *Heil* Hitler salute. The Anunnaki, mistakenly believing it to be a universal human greeting, responded as best it could with its insect arm. Kammler faced Gudrun.

"What's the problem?"

"They came to report an anomaly."

"What type of anomaly?" Kammler made no attempt to hide his annoyance.

"That's what we were discussing when you arrived." Maria detected a tinge of fear in Gudrun's voice.

Gudrun closed her eyes and re-established contact with the alien. It clicked and buzzed, gesturing with its arms and pointing northeast. After a few minutes, Gudrun opened her eyes.

"Their ship detected the arrival of another alien vessel about an hour ago."

"One of theirs?" asked the *obergruppenführer*.

Gudrun shook her head. "It didn't have the same signature. He thinks it might belong to the Golden Sun."

"Isn't that their rivals?"

"It is."

A surge of hope rushed through Maria.

Kammler thought for a few seconds. "Do they know where the other ship landed?'

Gudrun closed her eyes and the Anunnaki resumed clicking.

"They can pinpoint where it landed within a five-mile radius."

"Ask them to send out a search party. They can do whatever they want to the Golden Sun but, if there are any humans on that craft, I want them brought back here for questioning."

Another brief exchange with the Anunnaki and Gudrun said, "He'll let you know what they find."

Kammler bowed a few inches to acknowledge his gratitude. The Anunnaki turned and lumbered away. Gudrun waited until it was out of earshot.

"Do you think it's a coincidence?"

"That their enemy shows up within two weeks of our arriving here?" Kammler headed back to the tent with Gudrun behind him. "Not likely."

Maria followed. "Maybe the Allies found out what we're doing."

"Not that it matters. We're less than a week from achieving what we came here to do. The Anunnaki will take care of the threat posed by the Golden Sun. We'll take care of the Allies if they're here." Entering the tent, Kammler stepped over to the table and held up the open bottle of wine. "Want some?"

"Of course." Gudrun joined Kammler as he poured wine into a fresh glass and handed it to her. He offered more to Maria.

"No, thank you. The heat is getting to me. I'd like to head back to the compound."

"Of course. Have Gunther escort you."

"Thank you, *Herr Obergruppenführer*."

As Maria left the tent, she heard Gudrun say, "To the success of our mission."

Kammler replied, "To a Thousand-Year *Reich*."

Maria prayed they were wrong. She also prayed the arrival of the newcomers would be her opportunity to correct the nightmare she had created.

Chapter Fifteen

EVANS ESTIMATED IT to be around midnight. He had no idea of the actual time but based his assumption on the fact the sun had set several hours ago.

They had crashed sometime in the morning, allowing them plenty of daylight to get everything done. They checked their supplies, which had survived the crash. Blanchard had thought ahead and packed the explosives with plenty of padding, otherwise none of them might have made it. Evans issued everyone a primary weapon, either an M1 Carbine or a Thompson sub-machine gun, plus a Colt .45. Explosives, grenades, bayonets, and rations were distributed in backpacks and stored near the saucer in case they had to move quickly.

Next was to honor their fallen comrades. They buried the dead one hundred from the saucer, covered them in sand, and used helmets as grave markers. Evans spoke a few words in Memorium. He also remembered the site's exact location in relation to the saucer if the opportunity arose to return and retrieve them.

With those tasks completed, the two Rangers built a camp-fire as dusk closed in, initially to provide light. When the cold desert night swept over them, Evans appreciated the warmth. His team sat around the flames eating K-rations except for Kerdoshian and Dawson. Kerdoshian had removed a bag from his footlocker an hour ago and wandered into the desert. Dawson had been slipping in and out of consciousness for the last two hours. The other ate, but none of them were hungry. They did it only to keep their strength up. Evans had been nursing along his can of food for thirty minutes and eaten less than half.

Evans studied the rest of his team. Nigel appeared the more collected of the group, probably because of his age and experience. Evans assumed him to be in his mid- to late twenties, although he still had a boyish face, round cheeks offsetting two brown eyes, and a crop of dark hair. The two surviving Rangers, on the other hand, were kids. Crane could not have been more than a year out of high school, at most, and the corporal was not much older. They had trained to be among the best, and back at Roswell had displayed that cocky confidence all soldiers do before going into battle. Right now, they looked like a pair of frightened schoolboys who wanted to be home with their mothers. Evans could not blame them one damn bit.

The major placed his K-ration can on the sand. "It's Nigel Davensworth, correct?"

"Nigel Davenport, sir."

"Sorry. Where are you from?"

"Liverpool, England, sir."

"Stop calling me sir. Considering our circumstances, I think we're beyond that."

"Okay."

"What made you want to study Egypt?"

Nigel opened the pack of cigarettes from his K-ration and placed one between his lips. "I wanted to see the world and have some adventure. At the time, the best way to do so was to become an archaeologist. In college, I fell in love with Egypt. Ancient Egyptian civilization lasted three thousand years and survived many hardships, yet so much of its past is still an enigma to us. During my sophomore year, Carter found the tomb of King Tutankhamun. After that, I became an Egyptologist."

"Why did you leave?"

Nigel held out the pack of cigarettes to Evans, who declined. He slipped them into his pocket. "Got more than I bargained for. I was in Cairo on an archaeological expedition when Rommel invaded North Africa and was I forced to return to London."

"You're kidding?" asked the corporal, speaking for the first time since they crashed.

Nigel shook his head as he lit his cigarette with a match.

"How did you wind up on this mission?"

"Since I was the foremost expert on Ancient Egypt and can speak Egyptian and Yiddish, General Marshall ordered me to be at Roswell by 0600 this morning."

Evans motioned to the private. "What about you?"

"What do you mean?"

"What's your name? Where are you from? How'd you wind up here?"

"I'm Richard Crane from West Virginia, a town so small I doubt you've ever heard of it. I'm the oldest of seven kids. There were no jobs in my county, so I joined the army for three hots and a cot and sent my folks all the money I could. When the lieutenant asked for volunteers for this mission, I stepped forward, figuring there might be some extra money in it." The corporal laughed derisively. "Got screwed on that one, didn't I?"

"Not necessarily. At least not yet."

"After everything that's happened, do you think we have a chance of completing our mission?" Crane asked without being sarcastic.

"Yes."

The corporal, who sat facing away from the others, snorted.

"You have something you want to say?" asked Evans.

"Why bother? You're doing all the talking."

Nigel bristled. "Corporal, that's no way to talk to a super—"

Evans held up his hand, cutting off the doctor, his gaze fixed on the corporal. "Go ahead. I'll give you a chance."

"No thanks. I don't feel like being court-martialed."

"You won't be."

"Have it your way." The corporal shifted in his seat so he could make eye contact with Evans. "We get sent on a mission that goes FUBAR at the beginning, and you have no way of getting things back on track, so now you're trying to be our friend. I don't need a friend. I need a commanding officer. For Christ's sake, this whole fucking thing is cloaked in so much secrecy none of us except you know why we're here."

Nigel cleared his throat to get their attention. "He's an asshole, but he is right about one thing. None of us are aware of what's going on."

"Fair enough."

Evans spent the next thirty minutes briefing them on everything that had transpired from Valthor's landing at Roswell Air Field to the covert meeting in Washington and why they had been sent back in time. Nigel remained stoic throughout the explanation. The corporal stared, incredulous. Crane glared at the corporal with disdain. When he finished, Evans leaned back against the saucer.

"You now know as much as I do."

None of them spoke for several seconds. Nigel broke the silence.

"To be honest, if I hadn't been on that saucer with you, I'd think you were bucking for a Section 8. Still, it's so… so…."

"I know what you mean," admitted Evans. "I thought the same way at first. You have to either believe it's happening or that you've gone off the deep end."

"I hear you there."

"This can't be happening," stammered Crane. "Flying saucers. Aliens from another world. Be truthful. This is all some type of fucked up exercise to test our loyalty. Right?"

The corporal snorted. "It's fucking bullshit, that's what it is."

"Belay that, private." The order came from Dawson, who rested on one elbow, staring down his subordinate.

"I didn't know you were awake," said Evans.

"I've been awake since you began filling the others in on what's going on. And I can testify that everything the major has told you is true."

"How do you know?" asked Crane.

"General Marshall filled me in and showed me the evidence before I left for Roswell. The Pentagon accepts as true the events the major has described and believes in this mission enough to send us along to support him. And corporal."

"Yes?"

"You ever talk to a superior officer like that again, I'm going to leave you in the desert to rot. Is that understood?"

"Yes, sir." The bluster deflated from the corporal like air from a balloon.

Nigel went over to check on Dawson. "How are you feeling?"

"Like someone hit me from behind with a baseball bat. At least nothing's broken."

"Take it easy for a day or two until you feel well enough to move."

"We don't have that much time." Dawson sat up, paused for a moment, then cautiously rose to his feet. He staggered for a moment but did not fall over. "If we're in the right place and time, we have to stop the Germans before they return and start a nuclear war. I suggest we leave before sundown tomorrow. We should be able to make good time at night when it's cooler."

"I agree," agreed Evans.

Dawson pointed to his Rangers. "You two are with me. I want to pay respects to those who didn't make it and then make plans for tomorrow."

Both Rangers got to their feet and followed Dawson. As the corporal passed by Evans, he paused. "Nelson."

"Excuse me?"

"Richard Nelson from Tucson." He extended his hand.

Evans gave it a firm pump. "Good to meet you."

Nelson forced an embarrassed smile and ran off after the lieutenant.

Nigel stood. "I'll see if they need any help."

"Go ahead."

As Evans policed the camp site, Kerdoshian emerged from the dark.

"I was beginning to worry about you."

"I'm fine. Just needed to get as far away from light as possible."

"What were you doing?"

Kerdoshian sat beside Evans, opened the bag, and removed a sextant and a compass. "I was getting our bearings."

"You know how to use that thing?"

"Not by choice." The sergeant slid the sextant back into the bag and pocketed the compass. "My father was a college professor at Lincoln University and wanted me to be a Renaissance Man, so in addition to my regular studies, he made me learn a bunch of esoteric stuff, most of which has never been of any use. Until now."

"What else did you learn?"

"Latin. Poetry. Art history. Hieroglyphics. The only one I enjoyed was playing the piano." Kerdoshian broke into an uncharacteristic grin. "It made me popular with women."

"When we get back to our timeline, I'll be sure and thank him."

"You'll have to go back earlier." Kerdoshian's grin faded. "Cancer took my father in 1940."

"I'm sorry." Evans changed the subject. "Where are we?"

"Exactly where Valthor said we would be. The pyramids are approximately twenty miles to the southwest."

"Do you know what year we're in?"

"I can't be certain, but there was enough of a shift in the position of the stars to indicate a time variation of a few thousand years. Valthor got the location correct, so I'm willing to bet we're at the right moment as well."

"At least something's gone right."

Kerdoshian opened his footlocker. "What's our next move?"

"Dawson wants to head out before sunset tomorrow."

Kerdoshian placed the bag with the sextant inside and removed another item. "Is he up to it?"

"He should be by tomorrow."

"Good to hear."

Kerdoshian sat beside the fire. He held the reddish-tan diary. Pulling aside the clothed-covered elastic cord, the sergeant opened the book and began to write.

"Isn't that the book you took notes in when we questioned Valthor?" asked Evans.

"It is."

"What are you doing with it? I figured you'd have to turn it in."

"I will eventually." Kerdoshian passed the book to Evans. "Once we get back, we'll have to draft a report about what happened here. Might as well keep it all in one place to make it easy."

Evans thumbed through the pages. It contained detailed notes of the first interview with Valthor, the multi-verse experiment to New York City, the meeting in Washington, everything. He handed it back to Kerdoshian.

"Blanchard agreed to let you take it along with us?"

"I never asked." The sergeant grinned. "But he never said I couldn't bring it with me."

Chapter Sixteen

EVANS WOKE UP from a fitful nap, surprised he slept at all in this heat. Even though his team rested in the diminishing shadow of the crashed saucer, the temperature had to be well over one hundred. As the sun set, its rays encroached on the underside of the craft, heating the air around them. Even though none of them moved, sweat drenched their uniforms. Once dusk arrived, they would head out for the pyramid. If Kerdoshian's calculations were correct, they should arrive at their—

Crane raced around the corner of the saucer into the shaded area. He had been on the other side, keeping watch in case anything approached from the west. Fear shone in his eyes.

"What's wrong?" asked Nelson.

"They're approaching from the west."

"Who's approaching?"

"I have no fucking idea." Crane struggled to find the right words. "There's three of them. They gotta be aliens."

"Why?" asked Evans.

"Because they look like bugs, but they're walking on two legs. And they're carrying weapons."

"What type of weapons?"

"I don't know." Crane took a deep breath and pulled himself together. "They're carrying staffs about five feet long with glowing blue orbs on the end. I assume they're weapons."

Dawson turned to Evans. "Do you think they're from the Golden Sun here to help us?"

"I doubt it. They usually take human form."

"And Valthor said the Anunnaki were monstrous," added Kerdoshian.

"What do you suggest?" Nelson asked.

"Whatever you're going to do, do it quickly." Crane, who had been peering around the edge of the saucer, joined the others. "Those things are only a hundred yards away."

Evans calculated his options. He felt sure his team could get a jump on them. However, he had no idea how vulnerable the aliens would be to their weapons, the power of the aliens' weapons, and whether any more were nearby. Their mission was to stop the Nazis, not kill Anunnaki. The major scanned the surrounding area, his eyes settling on the graves one hundred feet away.

"We have to avoid combat. Fall back behind where we buried the others and take cover. If those things are hostile, then we'll give them Hell. Come on."

Evans led the way across the small strip of desert to the make-shift cemetery, making sure to keep the saucer between them and the aliens. Nelson and Crane brought up the rear, running backward and ready to fire if necessary. Only then did Evans realize the Rangers and Kerdoshian were the only ones to bring their backpacks. In their haste, they also left behind the footlocker. When they had gathered behind the grave site, each pushed themselves low in the sand and hid behind the mounds, their weapons trained and ready.

A moment later, the three aliens cautiously moved around either side of the saucer, two on the right and one on the left. Valthor had not been exaggerating when he said these things were hideous. They reminded Evans of a praying mantis, only these creatures were eight feet tall. They held the staffs horizontal in a threatening manner, scanning the sand and the backpacks. After a few seconds, the alien in charge communicated with the others via a rapid sound, halfway between a buzzing and a clicking, then squeezed through the hatch into the saucer. With their leader inside, the other two examined the items left behind, one poking the two backpacks with its staff, the other lifting the lid to Kerdoshian's footlocker. It rummaged around inside, finally picking up the sextant in its claws and examining it. Dropping the sextant back in the footlocker, it peered out over the desert. Evans felt his body tense when the alien's head stopped moving, its compound eyes focusing on the grave markers.

"Shit," whispered Nigel.

"Stay calm." Nelson tilted his head almost imperceptibly to the right, lining up his shot.

A tense moment followed. The alien clicked and raised its staff.

Two gunshots rang out, one from Nelson and one from Crane. Nelson's bullet struck between the alien's eyes, lodging in its brain. It collapsed, screeching, but it did not die. It thrashed about, trying to aim its staff. Nelson fired two more shots in rapid succession, shattering the exoskeleton and splattering a viscous, yellow-green substance across the saucer's exterior. Only then did it stop moving.

Crane would have struck the other alien between the eyes, but it moved aside at the last moment, the bullet nicking its thorax and ricocheting off the saucer. The alien raised its staff. The orb on the end glowed a brilliant blue, like a sapphire, spiking in intensity. Kerdoshian pushed himself to his knees and aimed his Thompson. Both weapons fired at the same time. The alien's staff emitted a sound like an electronic puff as a dozen .45-caliber rounds slammed into its abdomen, tearing out chunks of meat. The concussion threw the carcass against the saucer where it lay in a heap in the sand, its wounds oozing yellow-green fluid.

The shot from the staff hit the graves in front of Evans' team. Rather than exploding on contact, the mound of sand and markers glowed, radiating a bright blue that matched the orb's color. The molecular structure of the helmets broke down, losing their forms and turning to dust as the surrounding sand crystalized. A vortex formed in the center, the dust and sand swirling into the opening. Seconds later, the glowing segment imploded, creating a shock wave that threw the team back five to ten feet.

Though half-conscious, Evans felt around for his Thompson. One alien was still alive and, if it attacked them with its disintegrator, this mission would be over before it began. His hand swept back and forth, his fingers digging through sand. Goddamn it, where is it? Panic replaced his training as he faced imminent death. Then his fingers touched metal. Evans pulled the Thompson toward him, grabbed the stock, and struggled to his knees. His vision remained blurred, yet he saw well enough to notice that the alien inside their saucer had crawled out and aimed at them. Evans raised the Thompson to chest level and emptied the magazine, hoping a few rounds would hit their target. None did. A string of .45 caliber bullets went over the alien's head, ricocheting harmlessly across the underside of the saucer. Seeing what this weapon did to its comrades, the alien opted to escape. It raced behind the saucer and out of the line of fire.

A hand patted Evans' shoulder. The major jumped until he realized it was Kerdoshian.

"Good shooting, sir."

At the far end of the line, Nelson stood and motioned for Crane to follow. "Come on. Let's stop it before it warns the others."

"Wait," ordered Evans. "We need to grab the rest of our gear and get out of here."

"What if there are others nearby?" Nelson protested.

"If there are, we'd never fight them off," said Kerdoshian. "Our best bet is not to be here when they get back."

Nelson shook his head. "I can take it out from here so it'll never—"

The argument ended with an electronic puff. They ducked, afraid the shot had been directed at them. Instead, the saucer was the intended target. A flash erupted from the other side of the craft, expanding around the circumference and engulfing the underside. The vehicle's outline became distorted, the sharp edges and straight lines falling apart as the ray tore apart its molecular structure. Their means of escape transformed into a cloud of dust. A vortex opened, sucking in the saucer's remains, the two backpacks, and the footlocker.

"Get down!" ordered Evans.

As the cloud imploded, everyone dropped onto the sand. The shockwave shot out sand for several hundred feet. As the dust settled, Evans lifted his head. The alien scurried away, traveling much faster than he thought a two-legged insect could. Around him, the others rose to their feet and brushed themselves off.

Nigel stared at the crater left in the desert. "That's bloody great. Now how are we supposed to get home?"

"Stow it," ordered Dawson. "We'll worry about that later. Right now, we have a mission to accomplish."

"What happens when we're done? We have no way of getting home."

"Yes, we do," Evans lied.

Dawson turned to the major. "Are you serious?"

"Valthor knew losing our saucer was a possibility, so he had a backup plan."

"Which was?" Nigel seemed skeptical.

"It's irrelevant." Dawson slung his M1 over his shoulder. "If the major says there's a way back, you'll believe him."

"What now?" asked Crane.

Kerdoshian removed his compass from his backpack and studied it. "Our friend is heading southwest at a bearing of two hundred and eighteen degrees. I'm assuming he's heading straight to the pyramid. I suggest we head that way." Kerdoshian pointed to the southeast.

Nelson shook his head. "Won't that take us away from the target?"

"For a while. If we head in the direction they came from, we'll run right into the next search mission the Germans send out, and this time we probably won't fare as well. My way will still take us to the Nile north of our target. Then we can follow the river south and sneak up on them from behind."

"I'm in," said Dawson.

The others agreed.

"What about them?" Crane motioned toward the destroyed gravesite. All but two of the bodies and the upper portion of a third had disintegrated in the attack. The three corpses lay in awkward positions on the sand.

"We don't have time to rebury them." Evans hated the idea of not giving them a proper resting place. "Straighten them out and lay them side by side."

"Yes, sir." Nelson and Crane went to carry out their morbid task. Nigel and Dawson helped.

When the others were out of earshot, Kerdoshian moved alongside Evans. "That's a pretty good lie you told back there. I almost believed it."

"As long as they did." Evans forced a smile. "How far do you think it is to the Nile?"

Kerdoshian shrugged. "Fifteen miles, twenty at most. We should be there by morning."

"Good. I don't want to be caught out in the middle of the desert in this sun." The major paused. "Do you have your sextant in case we get lost?"

"No. Everything was in the footlocker. All I have is the compass."

"You lost your notebook, too?"

"That doesn't leave my side." Kerdoshian unlatched the outer pouch of the backpack and lifted the flap, revealing the notebook resting inside.

The rest of the team joined them. "We're all set," said Dawson.

"Good. I'll take point. Dawson, keep an eye on our left

flank so we don't set ambushed. Crane, you do the same for our right. Nelson, keep the doctor safe. Kerdoshian will bring up the rear and watch our backs. Stay at least fifty apart. Any questions?'

There were none.

"Then let's head out."

Chapter Seventeen

KAMMLER RARELY DINED with his troops. Not that he felt superior to them, but boundaries needed to be maintained between officers and enlisted men. It had been a rule he had followed his entire career until traveling to Ancient Egypt. Part of the reason for his change in policy centered around the need to inspire camaraderie and keep morale high during such an unusual and dangerous operation. Tonight's meal was sumptuous as all the others since their arrival—geese, duck, and fish followed by grapes, figs, and dates.

However, the decision boiled down mainly to the sparsity of accommodations. Due to space limitations aboard the *Haunebu II*, they brought only two large tents, one for the *Vril Damen* and one for Kammler, which doubled as his command headquarters. A smaller tent had been set up near the pyramid for when they visited the site. The *Waffen* SS originally were going to sleep outside until the Anunnaki provided three mud buildings for their use, one of them large enough to serve as both the troops' quarters and dining hall. Kammler allowed it because using the structures would leave no trace of their presence. For the same reason, everything they brought from Germany would be stored for the return voyage, including their trash. Nothing would be left behind for the locals to find that could alter the future. The only exception Kammler made to this rule was allowing Jochen, who had been a sculptor before joining the SS, to carve a *Reichsadler* into the lintel above the doorway of the largest building. The Germans would even take that down before they departed.

The only expedition member who did not belong to the SS contingent or the *Vril Damen* was a last-minute addition personally requested by the *Reichführer*—Doctor Kurt Meissner, an Egyptologist from Leipzig University. The academic appeared to have come directly from central casting, either from Hollywood or the Ministry of Propaganda. A man of average height and build, his black hair tinted with streaks of white and gray, a pair of circular-rimmed glasses hanging halfway down his nose, he would have fit in non-conspicuously at any college campus in the West. Out here in the desert, adorned in his typical sweat-soaked white shirt and pith helmet, he did not present the proper image of Aryan racial superiority. Though demure, his one outstanding personality trait, a habit that annoyed everyone on the expedition, was his incessant blabbering.

Himmler had asked that Meissner join Task Force Kammler to bolster Germany's standing within Europe's academic community. Before Hitler's rise to power, Germany was a respected center of Egyptology. The Ministry of Foreign Affairs even financed an archaeological institute in Cairo. German scholars had made essential contributions to the field, including helping to understand ancient grammar and art. However, during the 1930s, German Egyptologists formulated a theory that the Ancient Egyptians were more north European in their genetic make-up than North African, an idea adopted by a few racist American and European Egyptologists. As such, Egypt adopted the racial collective that became essential for shaping their culture, indicating the pharaohs understood and developed the ethnic forces lying dormant in the national mindset waiting to be freed, a reiteration of the *Volksgemeinschaft* theory proposed by Hitler. Kammler had no issue with adding Meissner to the roster so long as he did not get in the way of the mission.

Halfway through the meal, a pair of Anunnaki approached the building and stood at the entrance. The one Kammler recognized as the leader bent over and peered inside. The alien drew its claw toward its chest when it saw him, a poor imitation of a human waving for someone to join it. Kammler acknowledged the alien with a nod and leaned over to Gudrun.

"Go see what it wants."

Gudrun rose from the table, leaving her meal unfinished, and crossed the dining hall. Once outside, Gudrun and the lead alien spoke, if you could call that incessant clicking a conversation. After a few minutes, Gudrun stepped inside and motioned for Kammler to join them. As Kammler rose from his chair, Gudrun mouthed, "And bring Fuchs."

Seeing his commanding officer heading to meet with the Anunnaki, Fuchs fell in behind to offer protection if needed. Kammler suppressed a smile. Such loyalty was hard to come by, especially so late in the war.

Unfortunately, Maria also joined them. As the head of *Vril Damen*, she was entitled to be there, though he found her presence tiresome. Though an advocate for this mission initially, Maria's enthusiasm had declined since arriving in Egypt. She was not a liability yet. The first chance he got, Kammler would replace Maria with Gudrun.

Kammler nodded to the Anunnaki and turned to Gudrun. "What's going on?"

She gestured toward the second alien. "They found that anomaly reported yesterday. It was a spacecraft belonging to the Golden Sun. Earthlings... I mean humans, manned it."

"How many?"

"Five or six. He's not sure. The humans attacked them while they were checking out the Golden Sun's ship. The other two with him were killed."

"What type of humans were they?"

Gudrun telepathically communicated the question to the alien. It responded with that damnable clicking. "They looked like us, except for the tallest seemed Egyptian, whatever that means. They wore what I assume are uniforms. That part was difficult to translate. From what I can deduce, they were military but not German."

"Were any of the humans killed?" asked Fuchs.

Again, a telepathic exchange. "He doesn't think so. He fired back to distract them, destroyed the Anunnaki ship so they could not escape, and raced back here to inform us."

"Would it be willing to take us there?"

Gudrun nodded. "I think so."

"Good. *Standartenführer* Fuchs?"

Fuchs snapped to attention. "Yes, *Herr Obergruppenführer.*"

"Take nine of your men and follow this thing back to the site where the others landed. Try to figure out who traveled back in time to stop us. We need to know as much about them as possible to prevent them from interfering with our mission. Gudrun will go with you to translate."

"Shouldn't I go along, too?" asked Maria. "I am in charge of the *Vril.*"

"You're needed here," Kammler lied without making eye contact. "Gudrun can handle this."

Maria was not happy with the answer. *Screw her*, Kammler thought. *He's accountable to the Führer, not her. So long as he is successful, it does not matter which Vril Damen he relied on.*

"I'll leave right away," said Fuchs, breaking the awkward silence.

Kammler shook his head. "Wait until morning. I don't want you ambushed in the dark. They can't escape and they're probably not equipped to survive in the desert. Just to be safe, starting tonight post an around-the-clock guard on *Haunebu II* and *Die Glocke*, two men on four-hour shifts until we head back."

"Any idea how long that will be, sir?"

"Soon, *standartenführer.*" *Sooner than you think.* Kammler switched his attention to Gudrun. "Tell them what our intentions are and thank them for warning us about the other humans."

"I'll take care of it."

"Good. Afterward, report to me in my quarters and let me know what these things say." Gudrun nodded, a seductive look in her eyes. "My pleasure, *Herr Obergruppenführer*."

Kammler made his way past the aliens and headed for his tent, making a detour out into the desert to *Haunebu II.*

Climbing inside, he maneuvered to the center of the craft where six wooden storage containers were bolted to the main deck. Five of them were latched shut. The sixth was empty. Kammler went over to the closest container, undid the latch, and raised the lid. Nestled inside within a wooden frame sat a spherical device a meter in circumference, the perfect size to fit inside the bay of a bomber or the nosecone of a rocket. The exterior surface was smooth. Inside, thirty-six hexagon-shaped plates were arranged in such a manner that, when detonated simultaneously, they would compress together a critical core of atomic material that would start a chain reaction, generating an explosion equivalent to hundreds of thousands of tons of TNT. Heisenberg had called them atomic weapons. His team failed at developing them, but he would have created a weapon capable of destroying Moscow or London if he had. The ones used by the Anunnaki were of superior technology, much more reliable than anything the *Reich* could produce, and, most importantly, far more destructive. With these weapons, Germany would win the war.

Kammler closed the container and secured the lid. His team had been here for just over two weeks. In that time, the Anunnaki had provided five devices, one every three days, which was the amount of time it took to construct one. They had loaded the fifth aboard the *Haunebu II* this afternoon. The last would be ready in three days. Once delivered, they would return to Germany, this time landing in early 1941 just long enough to drop off their cargo and change history in Berlin's favor. The task force would then proceed ahead to 1 May 1945, their original departure time, to ensure their presence did not create a causality loop. Kammler hated the idea of missing the four most glorious years of the Reich's history.

The arrival of these other humans was merely an inconvenience. Six people could not stop this mission, especially since their means of travel were destroyed. They would probably die in the desert before they got anywhere near the pyramid. Worst case scenario, Kammler would return to his own time with only five weapons, which would still be more than enough to ensure victory.

Departing *Haunebu II*, Kammler headed back to his tent, feeling confident about the future. Tonight, he planned on taking advantage of Gudrun's willingness to get ahead.

Chapter Eighteen

TRAUTE SAT IN front of the mirror inside their tent, animated in her emotions. "I can't believe we're going to see the pyramid tomorrow."

"For God's sake," teased Sigrun. She held Traute's knee-length hair in her left hand and brushed it with the right. "You're acting like a schoolgirl on her first date."

"It's better than a first date. We're about to experience one of the great mysteries of the ages. How the pyramids were built."

"Pyramid," corrected Sigrun. "The other two won't be built for another hundred years."

Traute shifted her gaze to her friend. "Aren't you excited?"

"I am." Sigrun made Traute face forward. "Just not as much as you."

"You're impossible." Traute glanced in the direction of her other friend, who lay in a hammock off to the right, thumbing through an issue of *Signal* magazine. "Heike, aren't you excited?"

"Of course." Heike turned the page. "I'm more thrilled that Fuchs assigned Werner to be my escort."

"Isn't he the tall one with the dueling scar on his left cheek?" asked Sigrun.

"And the tight trousers?" added Traute. Sigrun gently yanked her friend's hair.

Heike looked up and smiled. "Yes, to both."

"You know we're not supposed to get too close to the SS," Sigrun reminded the others. "Kammler ordered his men not to get too familiar with us. They'll never disobey him.'"

"I know. But a little flirting never hurt anyone." Heike went back to reading.

"What about you, Maria?" Traute tried to catch her friend's reflection in the mirror.

Maria sat at the table, not listening to the conversation. Only when she heard her name did her ears perk up.

"I'm sorry. What was that?"

"I asked if you're looking forward to tomorrow."

"Sure," Maria responded with no emotion.

"You don't sound it."

"She's right," added Sigrun. "You've been morose the past few weeks. Are you okay?"

Maria would never admit she wasn't. Exactly the opposite. She had set out on this expedition with high hopes, with dreams of achieving what no other human had ever accomplished before while saving Germany, her Motherland. She had visited Hamburg and Dresden a few days after incendiary bombings had incinerated those cities. Had observed hundreds of charred and still smoldering bodies lining the rubble-strewn streets. Had gagged on the stench of burnt flesh that still hung in the air. And had witnessed the shock of the survivors and the heartbreak of those who had lost loved ones in the cataclysm. As she and the *Vril Damen* had maneuvered across the countryside to avoid advancing Allied forces, she had seen how around-the-clock bombing raids had turned her beloved Berlin into a wasteland. She had witnessed firsthand the devastation that had befallen Germany at the hands of the Soviet barbarians invading from the east. Maria would never erase from her mind that horrifying image of a German settlement on the border with Poland the day after a Red Army raiding party had stumbled across it. Every male, regardless of age, lying on the ground, his hands tied behind his back and a single bullet to the back of the head, the bodies resting in a large pool of congealed blood. The village women, ranging from toddlers to the elderly, lined up in a row within view of the men, their skirts pushed up around their hips and undergarments torn off. Rumors had been passed around of the Soviets raping their way across East Europe, but she had refused to believe them until that day. Maria could barely comprehend the nightmare those innocent people had suffered. Those villagers did not start the war, participate in atrocities, and murder innocent Russian civilians. Yet, their lives, souls, and probably their sanity were torn from them for the sin of being German.

Maria knew they had traveled back in time to Ancient Egypt to procure a weapon that would defeat the Allies, allow Germany to win the war, and prevent this mass slaughter. She assumed Hitler would use the weapons against Russian, British, and American soldiers. That was acceptable, in her eyes and the eyes of the other *Vril Damen*. Only after they had arrived did she learn that the weapon the Anunnaki would provide was the most destructive device ever created, even in an era when total warfare had been considered the norm. She had heard Kammler explaining to Fuchs they were retrieving atom-initiated bombs, a weapon with incredible firepower. Only these weapons would not be used against troops in the field but against civilian population centers, inflicting considerably more damage on London and Moscow in a matter of seconds than Hamburg and Dresden had suffered after hours of bombing, and with a much higher casualty rate. The major difference, though, was while those who survived Hamburg and Dresden only had to contend with psychological and emotional wounds, most of those who would survive the attacks using these weapons would suffer the effects of radiation poisoning for years to come. Her efforts to prevent an Allied victory had merely given Hitler and the Nazis a means to inflict mass destruction on innocent civilians. In Maria's eyes, that made Hitler no better than those war criminals Stalin, Churchill, and Roosevelt.

All thanks to her.

"Maria?" prodded Sigrun.

Hearing her name snapped Maria back to reality. "I'm sorry. What do you say?"

"I asked if everything is okay?"

"I'm fine."

Heike chuckled. "You may be the best psychic in Europe, but you're a poor liar."

"What do you mean?"

"You've barely spoken to anyone in the past few days."

"And rather than enjoying the greatest adventure of our lives," added Sigrun, "you seem like you want to be somewhere else."

Traute smiled. "That's because she has to spend tomorrow with Kammler."

"Don't even say that in jest." Sigrun gently tapped her friend's head with the brush. "You know what'll happen if Gudrun hears you."

Traute swiped her hand above her head. "She's not here, though, is she?"

"I wonder where she is?" Heike asked with heavy sarcasm.

"We all know the answer to that." Traute grinned.

"Doesn't it bother you?" Sigrun asked Maria.

"Please." Maria grimaced. "I have no interest in that ass-hole."

"That's not what I mean. Doesn't it bother you that Gudrun is trying to push you out of the picture and take over the *Vril Damen*?"

She's welcome to it, Maria thought. Instead, she responded with, "Not at all."

"I *know* it bothers you." Heike tossed the issue of *Signal* onto the sand and swung her legs out of the hammock. "But you have nothing to worry about. Gudrun can suck up to Kammler all she wants."

Traute giggled. Sigrun yanked on her hair just enough to warn her to behave.

"We're all behind you," continued Heike. "And so is the *Führer* and Himmler. Kammler may not like you, but he doesn't have enough pull within the party to replace you."

"She's right," agreed Traute. "All of us are in your corner. We won't let that bitch push you out of the way."

"Thanks." Maria swallowed the lump in her throat.

"It'll be the new motto of the *Vril Damen*," joked Sigrun. "All for one and one for all."

"And Gudrun for herself," added Heike.

The women laughed, even Maria. It was the first time in weeks that she had. Sadly, she knew the happiness would not last.

✦   ✦   ✦

GUDRUN LAY NAKED, clutching the silk sheet over her body. As always, after making love, she felt unsatisfied and used. Making love. What an inappropriate term for what they did. To Kammler, she was nothing more than a convenient fuck, what the troops in the field called a mattress—something you sleep on. Kammler did not even show a pretense of intimacy. For him, it was the satisfaction of a primal need, like eating, drinking, or taking a piss. When finished, he would get out of bed and go about his business, leaving Gudrun to take care of herself. She could never bring herself to do it, instead of dressing and excusing herself, making an excuse about having business to attend to and skulking away to sulk in her humiliation.

Humiliation. Gudrun had felt that way before this. For the past two weeks, she had been behaving like a camp follower, like a cheap slut using her body to get what she wanted. She was so much more than that. Gudrun had been raised in an upper-middle-class household, received the finest education possible, and been allowed to explore her psychic gifts. Gudrun was every bit as talented as Maria, probably more so. Luck had propelled Maria to the head of the *Vril Damen* when the Anunnaki reached out to her. It could have as easily been any of the women who they contacted, someone like herself who would have taken the responsibility more seriously.

For all her maturity, Maria acted like a teenager when it came to her talents. Maria had seen the opportunity to travel to the past and acquire weapons that would defeat Germany's enemies as an adventure, a fantasy from a Jules Verne novel. Once she realized the magnificent potential of these weapons, Maria failed to see how they would ensure the *Reich*'s survival, focusing more on their inhumanity. She seemed to ignore or had forgotten the horrors the Allies had put Germany through. The woman was too emotionally weak to head the *Vril Damen*. On the other hand, Gudrun appreciated why they were in Egypt, understood the importance of what the Anunnaki had provided them, and had no moral qualms about using them against Germany's enemies. In a cruel twist of fate, Maria led the Vril Damen with all her frailties while she had to whore herself to gain what should rightfully be hers.

Kammler stood ten feet away getting dressed, his back to Gudrun. "You should get up. You have a big day ahead tomorrow."

"About that." Gudrun sat up, still clutching the sheet in front of her chest. "I wanted to see how the pyramids were built. Why do I have to miss it to go on this recon mission?"

"I need someone who can communicate between Fuchs and the Anunnaki."

"What about the others? They can translate as well."

"Maria is the only one who can communicate with them as well as you, but I need someone I can trust to go with Fuchs." Kammler turned around as he finished knotting his tie. "End of discussion."

"Yes, sir." Gudrun made little attempt to hide her displeasure.

"I know I'm asking a lot of you." Kammler showed uncharacteristic sympathy. "But no more than the *Führer* has asked all of us by sending us on this mission. In a few days, we'll be back in our own time and, shortly after that, we'll turn this war around. Once the timeline has changed, the *Führer* can concentrate on expanding and fortifying the *Reich*, and I'll be a major part of that effort, as will you. Besides, Maria has proven she's not up to this. She'll either distance herself from the *Vril Damen* or will do something stupid to get on the *Führer*'s bad side. Once she does, I'll make sure you take over."

"Do you mean that?" Gudrun's spirits rose.

"Of course. As long as you're the most qualified person for the position."

The comment cut Gudrun deep.

Kammler did not seem to notice or did not care. He walked around Gudrun and headed for the tent opening. "I have to make final preparations for tomorrow. You should get dressed and rest up."

After Kammler left, Gudrun stood, wrapped the sheet in a ball, and threw it into the corner. She dressed as quickly as possible to get out of the tent before he came back. If only she could run from her humiliation as easily.

Chapter Nineteen

"**H**OW MUCH FARTHER do we have to go?" panted Hans.

"Ask her." Fuchs nodded toward Gudrun, who walked one hundred yards ahead of them with the Anunnaki. "Are you warm?"

"Warm? It has to be over a hundred degrees out here."

"I'd say closer to one twenty in the shade."

"Where the hell will we find shade out here?"

"Cut him some slack," chided Dietrich. "He spent two years on the Eastern Front. He's used to cooler weather."

"I always get the shitty assignments." Hans wiped the sweat from his brow. "How come I never get France or Italy?"

"If you did, you probably would have been killed at Falaise or Monte Casino." Fuchs changed his tone. "Keep alert. We should be nearing the location."

As if on cue, the Anunnaki stopped, pointed ahead of them, and began clicking. Fuchs stepped aside and looked ahead. He saw craters in the sand that could have been made by explosives and, farther beyond that, three mounds in the sand. Waving for the others to follow, Fuchs joined Gudrun.

"What's up?"

"This is where they found the Golden Sun's ship and destroyed it." Gudrun pointed to the mounds. "That's where the other humans were when the attack began."

Fuchs faced his men. "Dietrich, you're with me. The rest of you search this area for any clues that might tell us who the intruders are."

Dietrich led the way, veering to the left toward a piece of

debris jutting out from the ground. He bent over, picked it up, and used his hand to brush off the sand. "Check this out."

Fuchs stepped over. The object was a charred helmet distorted from heat.

"Maybe those things killed some of the intruders," suggested Dietrich.

"I doubt it. This looks like it was destroyed in battle. My guess is that whoever arrived lost some of their people during the trip." Fuchs gestured toward the bodies.

The two men walked over. The three bodies were left unburied. Sand had blown over them, covering segments of the corpses. An olive-drab collar stuck up from the sand. Fuchs grabbed it, pulling free the garment. He shook it several times. As the sand cascaded back onto the desert, it revealed the three stripes of a sergeant on the right sleeve and, on the left, a black banner outlined in red with 1ˢᵗ Ranger Bn sewn in white in the center.

"Americans," said Dietrich.

"Shit." Fuchs had been hoping the intruders would be anyone except Americans. The Russians were fanatical but not imaginative. They preferred a mass assault that would suffer massive casualties but eventually overwhelm the *Waffen* SS by sheer numbers. The British, French, and other European units in exile were highly predictable. The Americans, on the other hand, never obeyed their manuals. They were cowboys, rogues whose unorthodoxy could not be anticipated, making the Americans more dangerous than any other adversary Germany faced. Fuchs draped the jacket over his shoulder to show Kammler.

Gudrun approached with the Anunnaki. "What did you find?"

"Our intruders are Americans."

"Is that bad?"

"It's not good," Dietrich answered.

"It gets worse." Wilhelm came over and handed Fuchs a

brick-sized block of C-4 explosives. "Looks like they might be on to us."

"We've got problems now," Dietrich mumbled.

"It's a glitch, that's all." Fuchs tried to reassure himself as much as the others.

Gudrun translated for the Anunnaki. The tone of its clicking left little doubt as to its displeasure.

"Should we go after them?" asked Dietrich.

Fuchs thought for a moment and shook his head. "The Americans have more than a twelve-hour start on us. Our best bet is to head back and inform Kammler. We need to prevent the Americans from destroying the atomic weapons or stealing the craft."

Gudrun's eyes scrunched. "Why would they steal them?"

Fuchs pointed to the larger of the craters. "Because your bug friends here destroyed their means of traveling back to our own time. If it were me, I'd do anything I could to get away from this shithole."

The others nodded their agreement. Without saying another word, Fuchs led the way back to the pyramid.

Chapter Twenty

EVANS DOZED BY the river half a mile from his childhood home. He could almost hear his father teaching Jimmy, his youngest brother, how to fly fish, praising Jimmy when he did it correctly and lovingly correcting him when the kid made a mistake. And his two older brothers, Clark and Franklin, a hundred feet upstream arguing because they both tried to catch the same bass. And his Pitbull Smokey running through the woods chasing squirrels. When they got home, his mother would gut, clean, and prepare the fish while a homemade apple pie cooked in the oven. Then they would all eat dinner around a picnic table outside. Those were some of the best memories of his life.

"Shit. Don't we have to be concerned about alligators?"

Then reality set back in. Evans opened his eyes. Nelson and Crane checked to make sure their M1s were handy. Kerdoshian wrote in his red notebook.

"The Nile has crocodiles, not alligators." Nigel sat facing the river. "And I wouldn't be concerned. They won't come ashore during the day because it's too hot."

"What if they're hungry?"

Nigel pointed to the herd of sheep drinking along the opposite bank. "If there are any crocodiles in the area, they'll feed off them first."

"If you say so."

It did not matter if there were crocodiles nearby. Evans would have risked it for this little patch of good luck.

An hour before dawn, his team had stumbled upon this

plush, tiny oasis along the western banks of the Nile. Nelson and Crane went ahead and checked the area. Since there were no signs of others present, Evans decided to set up camp for the day. It provided everything: fresh water, fruit from the trees, cover, and, most importantly, shade. He scheduled someone to stand guard every four hours and told those not on watch to get as much rest as possible. After today, he doubted any of them would sleep until this mission was over, one way or the other.

Evans sat up and admonished his friend. "Sergeant, I thought I told you to rest."

"I'm too excited to sleep." Kerdoshian closed the notebook and returned it to the backpack. "Besides, when do I ever listen to you?"

"That's probably why we're still alive."

"We're better off than you think." Kerdoshian picked up a pair of binoculars from the sand and headed for the edge of the river. Evans and Nelson followed. When they reached the waterline, Kerdoshian handed Evans the binoculars and pointed south along the same bank as they were. "A few miles down there is a settlement. I studied them earlier this morning. It's not large, no more than one hundred people if that many. What's interesting is they have a dozen wooden boats tied up along the river."

The scene was as Kerdoshian had described. Two good runs of luck in one day. Evans only hoped their luck would hold. He passed the binoculars to Nelson.

Kerdoshian stepped back into the shade. "I figured we'd wait until tonight when everyone has gone to sleep, then sneak down and take two boats."

"You mean steal them."

"Requisition," Nelson corrected with a chuckle.

Evans grinned. "Looks like we'll be doing a lot of rowing tonight."

"Not necessarily. I saw that several of them had sails."

"Do you know how to sail?" Nelson handed back the binoculars.

"I do," said Dawson as he and Nigel joined the others. "They should be easy to navigate. How far upriver do we have to go?"

Nigel thought for a moment. "Three or four hours at most."

"Any chance we'll sail right by them?" asked Nelson.

"We'll see the pyramid from the river miles before we get there."

"That settles it," said Evans. "Everybody rest up. By this time tomorrow, we'll be on target."

Chapter Twenty-One

KAMMLER, THE *VRIL Damen*, Dr. Meissner, and their SS escorts strolled up the ramp stretching to the top of the half-constructed pyramid. Three Anunnaki walked to their right, ensuring no contact occurred between them and the Egyptians or workers. Once at the top of the ramp, one of the aliens ushered the group to the southwest corner of the pyramid where they could observe everything without being in the way or in danger.

Maria watched this marvel of ancient engineering but took in little of it. Her mind raced. Not only could she not come to terms with her participation in… no, her enabling of Nazi Germany in the acquisition of weapons of devastating capability, but now she had to be worried about her girls and their SS escort. Maria carefully watched them. Heike posed no problem. She was the most mature of the group and could easily handle herself. In fact, she had her SS escort eating out of her hand. He walked beside her, holding an umbrella to provide shade. Heike kept him distracted, asking him questions about the construction process and responding to his answers with a coy smile. Traute and Sigrun, on the other hand, made no attempts to curb their flirtatious behavior. Traute wrapped her left arm through her escort's right, standing beside him hip to hip. Whenever he said something funny, she would laugh and place her right hand on his upper arm. Sigrun was only slightly more refined, constantly leaning in closer to her escort whenever she spoke to him. If her girls continued this behavior, they would return to their own time with more people than when they arrived.

"This is amazing," said Meissner as he focused his gaze on the construction efforts. "We are not only witnessing history in the making, but we're also observing an activity lost for millennia. Once we return with this knowledge, Germany will become the leading voice in Egyptology."

"Just remember, *Herr Docktor*," Kammler stated cautiously, "everything you discover must be proven archaeologically. No one can ever know about this expedition."

"Of course, of course." Meissner stepped over to the edge of the white limestone exterior and peered down into the tunnel where workers hauled a block of marble weighing well over ten tons to the top. "Now that I know what to look for, I can make astounding finds."

Kammler chuckled at the doctor's pomposity. "I wish Gudrun was here to see this. Don't you agree, Maria?"

"I guess."

Kammler faced Maria. "Aren't you intrigued by all this?"

"I am. Though I'm concerned."

"Over the intruders."

Maria shook her head and glanced over at the *Vril Damen* and their escorts.

Kammler chuckled. "You do not need to worry. Despite your girls teasing my men, they will not take advantage of the young ladies or tarnish the *Vril Damen*'s reputation."

"How can you be so certain?"

"Because I told them not to, and my men follow orders." Kammler turned back to watch the workers. "Perhaps you should advise your girls to show similar restraint."

Maria seethed at the remark and held back saying what she honestly thought. She knew Kammler did not like her and probably had no qualms about leaving her behind and making Gudrun the head of the *Vril Damen*.

A commotion at the bottom of the ramp caught Maria's and Kammler's attention. The workers stopped and watched the Anunnaki escorting Fuchs and Gudrun to ensure they had no contact with the Egyptians. Kammler stepped over to the top of the ramp to meet them, with Maria following a few feet behind. Fuchs reached the top of the ramp, panting from the heat.

"*Herr Obergruppenführer.*" Fuchs paused to inhale.

"Relax. Take a deep breath."

Fuchs removed his cap, used his palm to wipe the sweat off his brow, and placed it back on his head. "We just came back from where the Anunnaki found the Golden Sun's spacecraft. The intruders are Americans. Rangers. And they have explosives with them, I assume to stop us from taking the wonder weapons back to Germany."

Gudrun's gaze bore into Maria. "I wonder how the Americans found out what we're doing?"

"Most likely the Golden Sun," answered Kammler. "The Anunnaki warned us they might interfere to prevent us from tampering with the timeline."

Gudrun backed down but maintained her glare on Maria.

If Kammler noticed the hostility between the two women, he ignored it. "Did you find the Americans who survived?"

"No, *Herr Obergruppenführer*. A sandstorm had blown through last night and covered their tracks."

Kammler huffed in frustration.

"We've already posted my men around the *Haunebu II* and *Die Glocke* to make certain the Americans don't get near them. They'll do round-the-clock shifts until we depart."

"I doubt the Americans will pose much of a threat since there's only a few of them and most of their weapons are destroyed."

"With your permission, *Herr Obergruppenführer*, I'd like to ask the Anunnaki to patrol the western banks of the Nile."

"Do you think that's necessary?"

"Better safe than sorry. The Americans will probably die in the desert but, in case they don't, our best chance of catching them will be along the Nile."

Kammler nodded. "I agree. Be sure to let the Anunnaki know that I want at least a few of the Americans captured alive. I want to find out what they know and what they planned on doing."

"Of course, *Herr Obergruppenführer.*" Fuchs headed back down the ramp, escorted by the alien.

Gudrun stayed behind. Maria distanced herself from the woman.

"What are we going to do now?" Gudrun asked.

"Nothing." Kammler had an air of confidence that bordered on arrogance. "Even if they're still alive, the Americans pose no immediate threat. When the Anunnaki go out, I want you with them to make certain my orders are carried out. Right now, I plan on finishing our tour. Will you join me for dinner?"

Kammler bent his right arm at an angle. Gudrun slid her hands around his arm, moved in close, and followed Kammler back to where they had been watching the construction.

✦   ✦   ✦

HEMIUNU GLARED DOWN at the outsiders from the top of the site, a look of dissatisfaction distorting his usually handsome features. He wore only a loincloth wrapped around his waist, a *khat* made of white linen on his head to deflect the sun from his face and neck and let everyone know who was in charge, and sandals, his traditional outfit when overseeing the project. As every other Egyptian had done, he had shaved his head to prevent getting lice but forewent his wig since he was outdoors. The afternoon sun glistened off his arms, chest, and back.

The heat bothered him less than the presence of the outsiders. The men and women milled around as if leisurely strolling along the Nile rather than parading through a dangerous work site. Their presence disgusted him. Granted, the outsiders did not interfere with or delay the project. Yet their presence served as a distraction, not only among the workers but the Star Travelers. What infuriated him most, the Star Travelers allowed this interruption despite his protests.

As the man charged with overseeing the project to build the pyramid in honor of the Pharaoh Khufu, Hemiunu deserved more respect than he was being shown.

As one of the highest officials in the royal court to serve the pharaoh, Hemiunu garnered considerable respect as represented through his titles: king's son of his body, chief justice, and vizier, greatest of the five of the House of Thoth. He was responsible for keeping the kingdom running efficiently. Yet all that paled in comparison to the honor that befell him nearly ten years ago when the Star Travelers arrived. They came not to conquer humanity but to praise it, to help build a monument that would withstand the test of time and forever tout the glory of the pharaoh and the kingdom. The pharaoh had bestowed upon Hemiunu the responsibility to oversee this grand project, an honor he wished his father Nefermaat could have witnessed. At first, Hemiunu had feared the Star Travelers would utilize their advanced technology to build it. Instead, they showed Hemiunu how to complete the project using the means available at the time, merely providing insights on how to complete such a monumental undertaking. The last decade had been the proudest years of his life, only now it was tarnished by the presence of the outsiders.

Hemiunu felt insulted that he could not speak with the Star Travelers directly, though through no fault of his own. Their languages were incompatible. They communicated through Ain, a sixteen-year-old girl who could speak with them through her mind. He did not mind that Ain had the ability to talk with the Star Travelers. Her special gift had proven invaluable to the building of the pyramid. Hemiunu's displeasure came from his injured pride at not being able to converse with the Start Travelers in person. It provided little comfort that the outsiders could only communicate with them through two females within their group.

The outsiders. Their presence did not bother him as much as how the Star Travelers catered to them. They had arrived two weeks ago and immediately received preferential treatment. Most of the Star Travelers diverted their attention from assisting in building the pyramid to working on something for the intruders. He knew that because he had observed the Star Travelers moving objects from their vessel and storing them in the outsider's ship. When Hemiunu asked what they wanted, the Star Travelers politely but firmly informed Hemiunu he should not ask questions and the building of the pyramid remained their top priority. However, the outsiders had come requesting special assistance, and the Anunnaki were obliged to help.

What perturbed Hemiunu most was that the Star Travelers refused to allow his workers, and even himself, to mingle with the outsiders. The Star Travelers offered an excuse he could not understand about not altering the timeline and asked Hemiunu to trust their judgment. As vizier, he knew such requests were a normal aspect of diplomacy and thought nothing of it. As a man, he felt slighted, as if his workers were not good enough to meet the outsiders. They were supposed to leave in a few days and, as far Hemiunu was concerned, the sooner they did, the better off everyone would be.

"Vizier, are you listening?"

The question snapped Hemiunu back to reality. Ankhmare, the foreman overseeing the pyramid's construction, stood beside him. Hemiunu had not even heard him approach.

"I'm sorry. What did you say?"

"We're still ahead of schedule, but our progress has slowed slightly."

"Why is that?"

"We've had questions with some of the new building techniques the Star Travelers have taught us. Since the outsiders arrived, it's been difficult to get the Star Travelers to focus on the project."

Hemiunu sighed.

"Not to worry, vizier. The workers are experienced enough they were able to figure it out on their own."

"Are you certain?"

"Yes, vizier. They brought the solution to my attention and I approved it."

Hemiunu faced his foreman, not attempting to conceal his displeasure. "It's presumptuous of you to approve something that I'll be held responsible for."

Ankhmare struggled to find the words that would not get him into deeper trouble. "I assumed that with... with you having to deal with the outsiders... I meant no disrespect. S-sorry, vizier."

"I'm the one who should apologize." Hemiunu regretted having snapped at Ankhmare. "You've done your job well despite the intrusion. I should not have taken out my frustrations with the outsiders on you."

"No need to apologize," said Ankhmare, visibly relieved. "Their presence has been disruptive."

"I've been assured they'll be leaving in a few days, then work on the pyramid will resume as normal."

"Did you ever find out where the outsiders came from and what they're doing here?"

Hemiunu shook his head. "The Star Travelers won't discuss them with me."

"That isn't right. You're in charge."

Not really, Hemiunu thought. That was another aspect of this relationship that bothered him. Though they never said as much, it was clear the Star Travelers had thought of them as inferior, which they were. It was a reality he could accept so long as the pharaoh did. He had put up with the presence of the outsiders for this long, so another few days would matter little. Just so they were out of here as soon as possible.

Something about their presence foretold doom.

Chapter Twenty-Two

EVANS WAITED UNTIL the fishing village went dark before leading his team from the grove along the river down to the boats. They needed to be especially careful not to be detected. In their uniforms and carrying 20th-century weapons, they stood out from everyone else. He had no idea if being seen would create a ripple effect in the timeline, so he opted to play it safe than be sorry.

When a hundred feet from the village, Evans signaled for the others to stop. He leaned in and spoke softly.

"Kerdoshian and I will recon the area. You wait here. If anything happens, head back to the grove."

"Roger that," whispered Dawson.

The two men crouched and made their way along the riverbank.

The Egyptians left their boats unguarded on the sand bordering the Nile, one of the few breaks they had gotten on this trip. The first two they came to were small, large enough for only three occupants.

"Should we search for a larger one?" asked Kerdoshian in a hushed voice.

Evans shook his head. "I'd rather take two smaller ones. It doubles our chances if—"

Footsteps crushing against the sand interrupted them. Whoever drew near came from the nearby village. Evans fell prone and moved against the side of the boat. Kerdoshian knelt by the bow. Neither went for their weapons. If spotted, they could not fight back, only run away.

The footsteps drew closer. An awkward shadow emerged from the night. The intruder stopped fifteen feet from them. Its large head scanned the bank. *Shit*, thought Evans. *It must be one of the Anunnaki.*

It took another step forward and brayed.

"What the hell?" whispered the major.

"It's only a donkey." Kerdoshian chuckled and slowly stood. "Hey, boy."

The donkey brayed a second time.

"It'll bring the whole village out."

"No, it won't." Kerdoshian slowly approached, his left hand extended. With his right, he slipped off his shoulder the pouch containing their K rations and raised it to the donkey's nose. It stepped forward and sniffed the bag. Kerdoshian petted its head.

"Good boy. You want something to eat?"

The donkey nuzzled its nose against the pouch. Kerdoshian opened the flap, removed a pack of crackers, and unwrapped it. Pulling one out, he offered it to the animal. The donkey sniffed the cracker once before taking the piece in its mouth. He enjoyed it.

"Get the others while I keep our friend distracted."

Evans rose and waved. Dawson, Nelson, Crane, and Nigel rushed over.

"Where did you find that thing?" whispered Dawson.

"He found us," answered Evans. "Let's move."

"Hurry up," added Kerdoshian, feeding the donkey another piece. "He's almost through the bar."

The five men commandeered the two small boats and pushed them into the Nile. Dawson, Nigel, and Crane took one boat and rowed out into the river. Nelson jumped into the other and picked up an oar. Evans followed.

"Come on. We're ready."

"Just a second."

Having finished the chocolate bar, the donkey stepped

forward and stuck his nose in the pouch, sniffing around for another treat. When he withdrew his head, he had an apple clutched between his teeth. Dropping it into the sand, the donkey bent his head and began eating. Kerdoshian rubbed its side.

"You enjoy that and be quiet."

Kerdoshian slowly made his way over to the boat and climbed in.

Several minutes later, the team raised the sails and slowly made their way down the Nile.

Chapter Twenty-Three

I T HAD TAKEN Evans' team longer to travel down the Nile than expected, mainly because no one on their boat knew how to work a sail, even Kerdoshian. After nearly capsizing twice, Dawson pulled alongside so Nigel could switch places with Evans. After the Egyptologist put the rigging back in order, they set off again down the river.

The other delay came from the number of vessels navigating the Nile, more than anticipated for night travel. It started with an isolated few here and there but, the longer Evans' team continued south, the more numerous they became. The boats sailed along the center of the river heading south, each burning a torch for illumination, making them easy to avoid. Dawson and Nigel maneuvered theirs closer to shore, slowing down so as not to create a wake and hugging the banks to stay concealed. They had been traveling like this for three hours when the clouds on the eastern horizon began to glow orange-red from the rising sun.

"You have any idea where they're heading?" asked Dawson.

Evans shrugged. "My guess is the pyramids. If we're going in the right direction, it shouldn't be too far ahead."

"There's another oasis along the river bank a few hundred yards ahead of us. We should pull in there for the day."

"Let's try to get a little closer."

"I wouldn't advise it." Dawson motioned with his head toward the boats in the center of the river.

Evans glanced over. The approaching dawn made it easier

to see the people in the other boats, their darker features toned from living in the Mediterranean, their chests bare from wearing minimal clothing in the intense heat. One older man stared back, squinting to see the strangers in the dim light better, bewilderment in his eyes.

"We don't blend in," added Dawson to emphasize his point.

"You're right. Head for the clump of papyrus along the riverbank."

From behind him, Evans heard Kerdoshian quietly calling. He shifted in his seat. Nigel had drawn his boat closer.

"Do you see it?" said Kerdoshian.

"I know," Evans replied, motioning toward the river. "We're getting under cover."

"That's not what I'm talking about." Kerdoshian pointed inland. "Look at that."

The first rays of sunlight cresting the horizon fell on the uncompleted pyramid. The structure stood only a few miles away. God damn, they made it after all.

Chapter Twenty-Four

TEN ANUNNAKI MADE their way along the banks of the Nile, one group of five on each side. Gudrun accompanied the team searching the western bank.

Gudrun marveled at how the situation had changed since the Star Travelers, as the locals referred to the Anunnaki, first arrived years ago to assist in building the pyramid. In those first few weeks, the people feared the aliens. The Egyptians had come to know them well since their arrival and no longer felt intimidated by them. That did not prevent her from being unnerved every time she was close to them. How could anyone not with aliens that looked like insects that towered over you? At least Gudrun felt safe with them.

After a few hours of scouring the riverbank and finding no signs of the Americans, a young boy in his pre-teens ran toward the search team. The boy, who only wore a white linen loincloth, yelled something and waved his hands. The lead Anunnaki stepped forward. The boy spoke to the alien, gesturing with his hands and pointing north along the river. After a moment, he stopped and stood by as the leader turned to Gudrun.

"What's up?" she asked telepathically.

"Boy says strangers with light skin and strange clothes hiding in trees along river. Strangers stole boats from village. Boy agree to take us there."

Gudrun smiled. They had found the Americans, and she would get the credit. This should make her even more valuable to Kammler.

"Ask the boy to take us to them."

The leader nodded.

"And be sure to tell the others that we want them alive, if possible."

The Anunnaki leader nodded its head and clicked its agreement.

✦　　✦　　✦

EVANS' TEAM HAD set up camp near a grove of palm trees along the Nile protected by a large patch of ten-foot-tall papyrus running along the river. After pulling the boats out of sight, the men napped under the shade of the palm trees. Nelson had this watch and was several hundred yards away on the western edge of the grove where he could see clearly to the north and south. Evans had the next watch and should be resting but couldn't. The fate of the future rested on him and the decisions he would make. One wrong choice and his team could irreversibly alter the timeline. Damn, he wanted more than anything to complete this mission, despite the cost to himself.

Dawson slept against the trunk of a palm tree off to Evans' right. Kerdoshian sat against the tree by his commanding officer cleaning his Thompson. Crane sat opposite them, doing the same to his M1. Nigel curled up in the shade of the papyrus to Evans' left, sound asleep and completely oblivious to the heat and what lay ahead in the next few days. In a way, the major envied the Egyptologist's naivety.

Once finished cleaning his weapon, Crane shouldered the Garand and joined Evans.

"Sir, can I ask you a question?"

"Only if you stop calling me sir."

"What happens to us when this is over?"

Evans sat up. "We'll find a way to return to our timeline."

"I'm not referring to how we get home." Crane almost

added 'sir' to the end of his sentence, stopping himself at the last second. "I'm talking about if we change timeline back to normal. My understanding is that, in the original timeline, America goes to war with Germany and Japan. All of us except Nigel are soldiers. Does that mean we'll wind up fighting in that war? And do any of us get killed?"

Evans thought for a moment. "How old were you in 1945?"

"I'll turn... I mean, I turned seventeen that September."

"You should be fine. Probably Nelson, too. I can't be certain about Dawson. He's been in the army for a while."

"What about you?"

Evans met the kid's gaze. "I die at a place called Omaha Beach."

Crane blanched. "So, if we succeed...."

"When I go back, I'll cease to exist."

"Shit."

As Crane tried to take in what he had heard, Nelson burst into the clearing.

"We got trouble."

"What?" Evans moved into a crouching position and reached for his Thompson.

"Five of those insect things are heading this way from the south with a boy and a woman leading them."

"Damn." Evans took the binoculars from Nelson and used them to scan the southern horizon.

Five Anunnaki approached the grove. Each carried the same type of orbed staff used to destroy their ride home. Of the two humans, one was an Egyptian boy who pointed in their direction. The other was a woman with short-cut dark hair who wore tan slacks and a long sleeve shirt designed for desert wear.

Dawson, roused by the commotion, knelt beside him. "Can I see?"

Evans handed over the binoculars then turned to the others. "We have five Anunnaki approaching accompanied by two humans. The aliens are armed."

"The odds are even," said Crane. "We can take them out before they can attack."

"We might hit the humans."

"Does that matter?" asked Nelson, incredulous.

"We have no idea what role that boy plays in the future. Killing him could alter the timeline in ways we can't imagine."

Crane moved closer. "What do we do?"

"We fall back." Dawson handed the binoculars back to Evans. "We can regroup and approach the pyramid from another direction."

"We'd be exposed if we tried to escape via the river or into the desert."

"We won't survive in the desert," added Dawson.

Nigel joined them. "If I may interject, but maybe we're not meant to succeed. It's possible we fail in our mission and never change the new timeline."

The others stared at him.

Shit, thought Evans. *I never considered that possibility.*

Kerdoshian broke the silence. "If you ask me, we have only one option."

Dawson glared at the sergeant. "Are you suggesting we give ourselves up?"

"We have no way of completing the mission if we're dead. So long as we're still alive, there's hope."

As much as Evans hated to admit it, Kerdoshian was right. Besides, with luck, the Anunnaki would take them inside the Nazi encampment.

Shouldering his Thompson, Evans stood, raised his hands above his head, and left the grove. The rest of his team reluctantly followed.

✦   ✦   ✦

Upon seeing the humans emerge from the grove, the Anunnaki clicked furiously. One of them raised its staff.

"Don't shoot," Gudrun telepathically warned the leader. "They're surrendering."

The leader clicked an order to the others who lowered their weapons.

"*Bist du Amerikanischer?*" yelled Gudrun.

"*Wir sprechen keine Deutsch,*" Evans called back.

"Place your weapons on the ground and approach slowly. You won't be hurt."

The Americans complied. One of the Anunnaki circled the outsiders and retrieved the weapons. Evans' group stopped a few feet from the aliens.

"You are prisoners of the Third *Reich*," said Gudrun.

"I'm Major Matthew Evans, U.S. Army Air Corps."

"I don't care about any of that. Kammler will ask you the questions. My job is to take you to him."

The Anunnaki motioned with their staffs to proceed. With their hands still raised, the group headed in the direction the Anunnaki indicated. Only Nelson hesitated. One of the aliens shoved him in the back to move him along. The corporal spun around.

"Keep your hands off me, you overgrown cockroach."

The Anunnaki bared its mandibles in a threatening manner, leaned closer to Nelson, and clicked menacingly.

"Don't provoke him," warned Gudrun. "His orders are to bring some of you back alive. You're expendable."

"Fall in line, soldier," snapped Dawson.

Nelson obeyed. The Anunnaki shoved him again, this time with no response.

Gudrun turned to the boy and rubbed his bald head. "*Viele dank.*"

Even though the boy did not understand her, he knew the gesture. He smiled, bowed slightly in appreciation, and ran off.

Gudrun fell in behind the group as the Anunnaki led the prisoners back to the pyramid.

Chapter Twenty-Five

KAMMLER SAT AT the table inside his tent, nursing along a glass of wine as he feigned interest in Meissner's discussion on Egypt and all the discoveries this expedition had unearthed. Not that it was difficult. The Egyptologist had prattled on for over an hour as if he were giving a lecture to himself, barely noticing the *obergruppenführer*. All Kammler had to do was smile and occasionally nod or listen in for a few moments and ask a question or comment that would send Meissner down another rabbit hole. The only reason he tolerated the insufferable academic was that Himmler had chosen Meissner personally to represent the SS. As much power as Kammler possessed, he knew better than to say no to the *Reichsführer*.

No, Kammler's thoughts focused on something more important than Meissner's ramblings—the completion of the mission. That morning, the Anunnaki had informed Maria that they would deliver the last of the devices within forty-eight hours. Once safely aboard the *Haunebu II*, the expedition would return to May 1941. In a few weeks—or a few millennia, depending upon how you viewed it—the *Wehrmacht* would use the atomic devices during the invasion of Russia, quickly ending the war against the Soviet Union and establishing the *Reich*'s dominance over all of Europe. Kammler still remembered the nightmare of those last few months from the old timeline and pondered what Germany's new future would be like.

The *obergruppenführer* had resumed listening to Meissner

when someone knocked on the wooden support holding the entry flap.

"Come in."

Fuchs pulled aside the flap and centered him in the opening. "Sorry to bother you—"

"That's fine."

"The Anunnaki and Gudrun have returned with the prisoners."

"Excellent. How many?"

"Six, *Herr Obergruppenführer*. Five Americans and one Brit."

"Bring them here. And have Maria join us."

"Yes, *Herr Obergruppenführer*."

"And post six of your men outside as guards."

Fuchs offered the *Heil* Hitler salute and departed.

Kammler turned to Meissner. "You're welcome to stay."

"This is a military matter. I'll leave you to it."

As Meissner headed for the exit, Gudrun escorted the prisoners inside and handed Kammler the pouch that Kerdoshian had been carrying. Meissner's eyes lit up. "Dr. Davenport?"

Nigel was confused. "Do I know you?"

"Not personally. I'm Dr. Reinhard Meissner, an Egyptologist at Leipzig University. I attended your lecture in London before the war on the significant social findings from King Tut's tomb. Brilliant presentation. And fascinating."

"Thank you."

Meissner followed the prisoners. "Is the invitation to stay still open?"

"Of course." Now someone else would have to listen to Meissner. Kammler turned to Gudrun. "Please bring us three more bottles of wine and seven more glasses."

"You speak English?" asked Evans.

"Of course," acknowledged Kammler. "Many of us in this expedition do. It's the universal language. For now."

As Gudrun went off to get the items, Evans snapped to attention. "I'm Major Matthew Evans of the U.S. Army Air

Corps. Serial num—"

Kammler waved his hand. "Please, gentlemen. You're not prisoners, merely unexpected guests. Have a seat and enjoy a glass of wine as we celebrate our success."

Evans nodded to the others who sat. Kammler motioned for the major to take the seat beside him. Evans sat as Gudrun returned, placed a glass in front of each seat, and opened the wine bottles.

"You're not going to interrogate us?" asked Dawson.

"There's no need. You have no information of value to me. Your presence here is all I care about."

Evans and Dawson cast glances at each other. "How so?"

"You're here to stop me from altering the timeline, which means this mission will be a success." Kammler waited for Gudrun to fill everyone's glass then motioned for them to pick up their drinks. "A toast. To the Thousand-Year *Reich*."

None of the Americans drank. Nelson poured his wine onto the sand, a stunt that irked Kammler. Nigel partook, but only out of professional courtesy.

Meissner took over the conversation, chatting excitedly. "The discoveries I've made are groundbreaking, Nigel. May I call you Nigel?"

"You may."

"The insights I've gained on how the pyramid's construction are fascinating."

"Aren't the aliens building it?" asked Crane.

"Dear boy, your mind has been muddled by all those pulp fiction magazines you Americans read." Meissner returned his attention to Nigel. "The Anunnaki showed the Egyptians the best way to use their limited technology to improve the process."

"I saw the ramp coming in."

"That's only the tip of the iceberg. I'll show you the series of internal ramps built inside the pyramid…."

At that moment, Maria entered the tent, pausing when she

saw the Americans.

Kammler waved her over. "Please join us. Gentlemen, this is Maria Orsic, the young lady that made all this possible. Maria, this is Major Matthew Evans of the U.S. Army and... I'm sorry, but I didn't get your names."

"Lieutenant Dawson."

"David Crane, ma'am. From West Virginia."

"Staff Sergeant Allen Kerdoshian." He stood and bowed slightly.

Nelson folded his arms across his chest and remained silent.

Maria sat opposite Evans, eyeing him warily. Gudrun joined her, a smug expression on her face. Kammler rummaged through the pouch, removing the diary and thumbing through it.

As the two Egyptologists engaged in their private conversation, Evans faced Kammler.

"What happens to us?"

"Nothing." Kammler leaned back in his chair. "In this timeline, America is not our enemy. But I'm afraid I will have to detain you until we return in three days."

Gudrun's eyes widened. "Three days?"

"Yes. The Anunnaki informed me this morning that they will deliver the last device tomorrow evening. We depart the following day." Kammler shifted his attention to Evans. "Of course, you'll accompany us back. I'll ask the Anunnaki to return you to the time and location from which you left so there'll be no causality loop."

All Evans could think to say was. "Thank you."

"My pleasure. You'll see we Germans are not as—"

An Anunnaki stuck his head past the flap and clicked. A second stood outside the tent. Gudrun rose and went over to communicate with it. A moment later, she walked back to Kammler.

"The Anunnaki are demanding that we give them one of the... guests... so they can gather information on the Golden

Sun."

Kammler bristled. "Demand?"

Maria leaned close. "There's no word in the Anunnaki language for request. Remember, they're an aggressive race."

Kammler nodded his understanding. "They can have the Negro. He's of no use to me."

Gudrun relayed the message, followed by another round of clicking.

"They refuse to take him," Gudrun responded hesitantly. "They say he is of the same color as the Egyptians and they do not want to make them angry."

"Fine." Kammler brushed away the inconvenience with a wave of his hand. "Take the quiet one."

Nelson jumped up, knocking over his chair. He grabbed the closest wine bottle by the neck and smashed the bottom against the edge of the table, shattering the glass. He brandished the weapon like a knife, threatening the alien. "Come on."

The Anunnaki grew agitated. It stepped into the tent. The other from outside joined it. Nelson clasped the makeshift weapon in his right hand and urged the alien to attack with his left. The Anunnaki raised its staff.

"Enough!" barked Kammler.

Everyone stared at the *obergruppenführer*.

"Need I remind you that you are here as my guests. I could just as easily have you executed or leave you behind."

Evans' gaze flashed between Kammler, Nelson, and the alien. "They want to take him away."

"To ask him some questions about the Golden Sun. He'll be fine," lied Kammler. He had no idea how the Anunnaki would interrogate the American. Nor did he care. "Any of you are welcome to take his place."

"I'll go," offered Dawson.

"No," countered Evans. "That's my job."

Nelson tossed the broken wine bottle on the table. "Sirs, I'll go. You're too valuable."

He raised his hands and slowly approached the Anunnaki, which lowered its staff.

Gudrun stepped beside Nelson. "I'll go with you to interpret."

The alien shook its head and clicked. Gudrun stiffened.

"What's wrong?" asked Kammler.

Gudrun spun around, her face quivering in fury. "They requested Maria accompany the American instead." She practically spat the woman's name.

Kammler looked over at Maria. "Do you mind?"

"Of course not." Maria stood and headed for the exit, pausing by Evans. "I'll make sure they don't harm him."

Evans smiled and whispered, "Thank you."

Fuchs entered the tent as the others left.

Kammler stood. "If you'll excuse me, gentlemen. I have things to attend to. *Standartenführer* Fuchs will take you to your quarters. Even though we won't treat you as enemy combatants, for security reasons I must place you under… how do you Americans call it… oh yes, house arrest. If you need anything, just ask."

"How about letting us go?" quipped Crane.

Kammler laughed. "You Americans do enjoy your humor. Please go with Fuchs. He'll show you to your quarters for the next few days. And don't try anything foolish. My men have orders to kill you if necessary."

The *obergruppenführer* watched as the prisoners stood and Fuchs escorted them away. When they left, he poured himself another glass of wine.

Gudrun sat beside him. "Do you think it's wise to let them live?"

"Are you questioning me, *fraulein*?" Kammler purposefully said it so Gudrun remained unsure if he was serious or kidding.

"They pose a threat to our mission."

"Not since you captured them. I'm keeping the Americans alive for propaganda purposes."

"What type of propaganda value can they have?"

"The best kind. When they get back to Washington, they'll report to their superiors, like dutiful soldiers. They'll tell the president about what they observed and how we've strategically adapted the use of time travel and made allies of an alien nation. By then, we'll have destroyed Moscow and Leningrad and defeated the Soviet Union. It'll instill in the Americans fear about what we're capable of. So, you see, they are a valuable propaganda tool." Kammler sipped his wine. "Much better than anything that crippled misfit Goebbels can come up with."

✦ ✦ ✦

"WHERE ARE YOU taking us?" asked Evans.

Fuchs did not bother to make eye contact. "You and your men won't be harmed."

"Reassuring words coming from a Nazi," muttered Dawson.

The *standartenführer* turned his head and nodded to Wilhelm, who drove the stock of his *Mauser* into the lieutenant's back. Dawson stumbled and fell to his knees.

Crane spun around to confront the German only to have three *Mausers* aimed at him.

"You said we wouldn't be harmed," snapped Evans.

"As long as you don't give us shit." Fuchs got into the major's face. "You mouth off to my men or try anything stupid, and you won't live to return to your own time. Is that clear?"

"Yes." Evans practically growled the word.

"Now that we understand each other, follow me."

They came to two mud huts side by side. The hut to the right had a metal grate covering the entrance. Several SS soldiers finished moving crates of ammunition from that building to the one on the left. An *obersturmbannführer* saluted Fuchs. The two spoke in German.

Fuchs turned to Evans. "These are your quarters for the next few days. My men will bring you sleeping bags and food in a little while. Even though you are guests of the *obergruppenführer*, you will be under guard. I suggest you relax unless we have any more incidents."

Evans entered, followed by the others. Once inside, Fuchs closed and locked the gate. He issued an order to the *obersturmbannführer* who stood guard out front as Fuchs led his men away.

The major checked out their prison. The walls were a foot thick with no windows or skylights. It had been built as a storage facility and not for comfort.

Kerdoshian walked around, scuffing his foot across the sand floor. "I don't suppose they left anything behind like a rifle or a hand grenade."

"I doubt it," Nigel answered. "One thing Germans are notorious for is their efficiency."

Dawson sat and leaned against the wall, wincing when his bruised back touched the surface. "What now? Do we sit around and wait for Kammler to shoot us?"

"These walls aren't solid." Crane chipped away at the dried mud with his fingers. "We could dig our way out."

Evans shook his head. "The guards would hear us. Then they'd tied us up and we'd never get out."

"Or worse," added Kerdoshian.

Crane tossed the mud onto the sand and wiped off his hands. "So, we're going to sit here and do nothing?"

"Of course not." Evans laid down on the sand beside Dawson. "We're going to figure out a way to stop the Nazis and then wait for our chance to escape."

Chapter Twenty-Six

THE TWO ANUNNAKI led Maria and Nelson north across the desert, one leading and the other following. Neither appeared aggressive. Still, something about the situation did not settle well with her. She had promised Evans no harm would come to his friend and hoped she would be able to keep that commitment.

Nelson walked beside Maria. She glanced at him out of the corner of her eye. He met her expectations of an American, or at least one of those portrayed in Goebbels' propaganda movies. Tall and muscular with rugged good looks and a stern yet handsome face. Nelson carried himself with the composure of a typical soldier, strong and quiet. However, he did not present the pomposity and arrogance of those Americans portrayed in German films, probably because they were meant to inspire fear among the populace toward their soon-to-be conquerors. This one seemed polite enough, though Maria harbored no illusions he would kill her if necessary.

"Do you know where they're taking me?" asked Nelson.

"I don't. Sorry." Maria glanced over at him. "I've never been to the Anunnaki's base camp."

"Really?"

"That surprises you?"

"These things seem to like you, at least better than they do Gertrude."

Maria snickered at the mispronunciation of the bitch's name.

"What's so funny?"

"Nothing." Maria composed herself. "In answer to your question, the Anunnaki are particular about their level of contact with humans. Only a few of their race are allowed to interact with us. We're forbidden to talk with the Egyptians. If we need to talk with the Anunnaki or want to leave the compound, we reach out to one of the guards."

"How do you talk with them?"

"Telepathically. Originally, I was the only one who could communicate with them, but now Gudrun has developed the ability."

"You don't like her, do you?"

Maria hesitated before answering. The truth might get her killed, but it could also present an opening to stop this nightmare.

"No one does except Kammler, and that's because she has aligned herself with him. She'll do anything, including betrayal, to see this mission through and remove me as the head of the *Vril Damen.*"

Nelson stared at her. "You don't know what the future holds, do you?"

Maria shook her head. "I only know the previous timeline, the one we're supposed to change. America, Britain, and the Soviet Union destroy Nazi Germany. Tens of millions of people die. I can only assume things are worse now that Hitler won."

"Why did you go along with all this?"

"At the time, it seemed like the right thing to do to save my nation. Now I regret my actions."

Nelson stopped and turned to Maria. "Then why don't you stop it?"

"Because I can't do it alone. But now that you're here...." Maria hesitated, knowing what she was about to say could easily get her killed. "Do you think the major will help me end this?"

Nelson smiled. "That's why we're here."

The Anunnaki behind them clicked and motioned for the humans to continue.

A few minutes, they topped the crest of a dune. Nelson said, "You gotta be fucking kidding."

Though a bit crass, Maria agreed with the sentiment.

The Anunnaki spaceship hovered in front of them. It was huge, twice the size of the pyramid, and tear-shaped. It sat on its side, the pointed end horizontal to the desert. The vessel remained elevated twenty feet above the ground with a slight hum emanating from it. A ramp extended from an opening in the center down to the sand.

Nelson whistled. "It doesn't look like anything I read about as a kid."

"We're both about to witness something no other human ever has."

The Anunnaki led them up the ramp. The interior was pristine. A shiny metal corridor ran the length of the vessel. No light fixtures were visible, yet an aura filled the corridor, much brighter than the desert outside. Maria noticed no doors along the walls. Other Anunnaki scurried about like in an office, presumably performing routine tasks. One stopped and waved its tibial spines across the surface. Two sections of the wall slid aside, allowing the alien access to another room, then closed, leaving no visible trace behind.

Their escorts walked them part way down then stopped. A swipe of the lead's tibial spines and another opening appeared. Maria stepped inside what seemed to be an elevator. The others entered and the sections closed. The lead Anunnaki clicked and the elevator rose. Maria studied the red-colored display. She did not recognize the symbols but assumed by the number of times the image changed that they had ascended at least ten levels before stopping. The wall slid aside again, revealing another corridor like the previous one. They walked for a few minutes before the lead Anunnaki swiped the wall again. Another opening appeared and it ushered the humans inside.

The chamber was massive. Maria estimated it to be fifty feet across and several hundred feet in length. Pods in the shape of capsules, each large enough for the Anunnaki, lined both walls. The first five pods on the left contained motionless Anunnaki floating in a yellowish-green liquid with tubes and wires attached to their bodies. A sixth alien stood outside the third pod and studied a computer display. The scene reminded her of the covers of those science fiction magazines from America.

Nelson became agitated. "Why did you bring me to a morgue?"

"Where are we?" Maria telepathically asked the lead Anunnaki.

It turned its head and continued walking. "We're in the recovery chamber for those of our kind ill or injured."

"It's a hospital," she informed the American.

"It's still as creepy as shit."

At the end of the chamber, another opening appeared in the wall. They entered a brightly lit room. Instruments well beyond the technological level of Germany lined the walls, with two Anunnaki standing in front of them. A white slab large enough to hold one of their kind sat in the center of the room at a forty-five-degree angle. A footrest extended from the bottom.

The lead Anunnaki stopped, turned to Nelson, and motioned for him to lay on the slab.

A wave of discomfort washed through Maria.

"No fucking way I'm getting on that," protested Nelson.

"Relax." Maria tried to console him despite her concerns. "They're probably going to inject you with a drug to make you talk."

"Screw that, lady." Nelson spun around and headed for the exit.

The Anunnaki to their rear touched Nelson with its staff.

The corporal's body stiffened then went limp. The other two aliens came over, lifted him off the floor, and placed him on the slab.

"Did you kill him?"

"We stunned him to make him cooperate."

"What is this place?"

"It's where we extract information?"

"You mean ask questions?"

"We use other methods to acquire knowledge."

The lead Anunnaki clicked a command to the others who moved over to one of the instruments.

Nelson slowly came to, shocked to find himself on the slab. He glanced over at Maria for guidance. She mouthed a single word.

Run.

Before Nelson could respond, one of the Anunnaki waved its tibial spine across a console. A loud electronic hum filled the room. Nelson was drawn against the slab, his body stiff and motionless.

"I can't move!"

"What are you doing to him?"

The lead Anunnaki glared at her. "Do not interfere."

A whir sounded from above. A white metal shaft lowered from the ceiling, heading toward Nelson. He tried to break free, but something held him in place.

"Get me out of here!"

The shaft stopped nine inches from his head. The end opened and a drill one inch in diameter extended out. When three inches away from Nelson, it switched on.

"I'll cooperate."

The tip of the drill touched Nelson's forehead. He screamed in agony as it bore its way through his skin. Bits of flesh and blood poured from the groves as the drill penetrated deeper. Maria's disgust turned to nausea when the pitch changed and chunks of skull spilled out down Nelson's face.

After a few anguished moments, the drill stopped and retracted. His eyes locked on Maria's, pleading for mercy.

Maria lowered her head.

She looked up upon hearing a second whir. A metal arm the same size as the drilled hole lowered from the shaft. Before connecting with the wound, a large needle several inches in length emerged and entered the hole. Nelson cried out, stiffened as the needle penetrated his brain, then passed out.

The four Anunnaki gathered around the console. Despite her desire to vomit, Maria joined them.

Images flashed across the console, presumably from Nelson's point of view. Scenes of the man's life flashed across the screen, thousands playing themselves out. They went by so rapidly Maria could only pick out a few. Swimming with young boys in a river. An elementary school classroom. A fistfight in a school yard. Awkwardly making love to a young teenage blonde in the back seat of an old car. Boot camp. An assignment to a military base. A briefing with Evans and the others captured. Their travel through time and crashing in the desert. Being taken prisoner by Gudrun and the Anunnaki. Finally, their walk to the spaceship.

The scenes came to an end. One of the aliens swiped the console. The needle withdrew from Nelson's head and retracted into the shaft, which pulled back into the ceiling.

The lead Anunnaki turned to Maria. "We successfully obtained the information required. My superiors will be pleased."

Maria raced over to Nelson and checked his pulse. He was still alive, but his eyes had a soulless quality to them.

"What did you do to him?"

The lead Anunnaki stepped over. "His mind was not as strong as ours. When we gathered information, we wiped it clean in the process. He lives but has no brain function."

"What'll happen to him now?"

"Since he is no longer viable as a species, our scientists will dissect him to acquire knowledge of its biology. It will assist us greatly in understanding these primitive life forms."

Maria stepped back as the two Anunnaki that had all but killed Nelson came forward, released the force holding his body in place, and moved him to the chamber where they placed him in one of the pods. The other two Anunnaki surrounded Maria.

"We'll escort you back to your camp."

A sense of uneasiness settled over Maria as they made their way out of the spaceship and across the desert. She expected at any moment to be dragged aside and executed so Kammler would never know what the Anunnaki had done to their fellow human, not that the *obergruppenführer* cared one way or the other. She doubted the asshole would be upset if the Anunnaki eliminated her. Her death would provide the perfect opportunity for Gudrun to take over the *Vril Damen*.

The Anunnaki returned her to the compound, thanked her for her cooperation, and returned to the mothership. Maria stood stunned as the realization slowly dawned on her. Ever since first conversing with the Anunnaki in September 1917, she had viewed the relationship as two intergalactic species making first contact as equals, even though the Anunnaki were far more advanced technologically than humans. She also assumed assisting the Egyptians in building the pyramid had been done to allow this civilization to achieve its greatest potential. Only now did she realize she had grossly misunderstood their intentions. The Anunnaki did not view humans as a species equivalent to their own but as a primitive society to study with wonder, like an entomologist observing a colony of ants. Their total disdain for what they did to Nelson and how they intended to dissect his body proved that.

And she had fallen for it. She had seen their relationship as a way to better humanity. Kammler viewed the Anunnaki merely as a means to an end, a way to ensure the survival of a Thousand-Year *Reich*. Gudrun saw the aliens for what they were and leveraged that knowledge against her, slowly replacing her as leader of the *Vril Damen*. Maria had hoped to make the world a better place but instead had allowed her misguided desires for a utopian future to benefit the Nazi takeover of all of Europe.

Maria had to end this nightmare before it embraced the world. And she knew the person who could help.

Chapter Twenty-Seven

HEMIUNU STOOD ON the surface of the pyramid facing south as Ankhmare, his foreman, briefed him on the progress of its construction. The workers completed the burial chamber two days ago, the project's most intricate and time-consuming portion. This morning, they had dismantled the counterweight and pulley system, clearing the way to complete the top third of the structure.

Hemiunu felt both pride and contentment. Pride that his workers had masterfully constructed the most perfectly built pyramid in all of Egypt for Khufu. Contentment that the project was ahead of schedule by several years. As much of a nuisance as the Star Travelers had been, their advice on how to best utilize the current means of production saved years of labor. This masterpiece would be the glory of Egypt for centuries to come.

The approach of one of the workers and the expression of concern on his face warned Hemiunu that his moment of happiness would soon be over.

The worker raced up to them, pausing to catch his breath. "Vizier, two of the outsiders are on the work site."

"The females?"

"No, vizier. The curious one and one of the outsiders brought in the other day."

"Have they bothered any of our workers?'

The man shook his head.

"Ankhmare, stay close to them. If they interfere in any way, have Ain inform the Star Travelers."

"Of course, vizier."

The two men bowed and raced off.

Hemiunu sighed. He could tolerate the Star Travelers, but the outsiders were a nuisance. Thank God they would be gone soon.

✦　✦　✦

MEISSNER HAD ARRANGED to give Nigel a private tour of the pyramid early that morning. Kammler agreed, primarily to get rid of Meissner for a few hours so he could get a respite from listening to the doctor talk incessantly about the wonders of Ancient Egypt. Jochen accompanied them, more to appease the Anunnaki and Egyptians than as a guard. At first, Nigel refused the invitation until Evans convinced him to get on Meissner's good side and maybe gather information of intelligence value.

Nigel's reluctance changed to exuberance as the two men drew nearer to the pyramid. His eyes widened at the site of the half-constructed structure towering above him.

"This is...." For a moment, words failed Nigel. "Magnificent."

"I knew you would appreciate this," Meissner responded with child-like excitement. "Only a true Egyptologist can understand the wonders we're witnessing. The *Vril Damen* view this as a sight-seeing tour. The SS doesn't care. They're more interested in those devices the Anunnaki are giving us."

Nigel saw his opportunity. "What type of devices?"

Meissner brushed away the question with a wave of his hand. "The ones we're going to use on the Soviets. Kammler calls them atom weapons, or something like that. They don't interest me. I'm a historian, not a scientist. Look."

Nigel focused his attention on where the doctor pointed. A cedarwood sled passed by carrying one of the two million, three hundred thousand two-and-a-half ton yellow limestone blocks used to build the pyramid. It was similar to a wooden sled without runners but large enough to carry the stone. Thirty-six men pulled the cart using strands of heavy rope, eighteen on each side. Two others walked in front of it, wetting the sand with buckets of water constantly replaced by a string of workers carrying water from the Nile. A man stood on top of the stone, directing the operation.

"Where are the logs?" Nigel asked in bewilderment. "I thought the Egyptians used logs and rolled the stones on top of them."

"So did I." Meissner practically squealed with excitement. "We were wrong. The Egyptians figured out a way to wet the sand enough so the carts glide along it like on snow. It's ingenious. Think of the time and manpower they save."

Meissner raced for the ramp leading to the top of the pyramid, waving for Nigel to join him. The doctor's enthusiasm was contagious. Nigel ran after him. Both men made their way up like two excited schoolboys running around a toy store. Once at the top, Meissner led him to the northwest corner where a group of workers maneuvered stones into position using wooden levers and dolerite carved into ball bearings. He pointed to an outer layer of angled white stone casing running along the exterior.

"We've always wondered how the Egyptians built the pyramid so perfectly. Here's the answer. They construct the exterior walls first. Once certain the angle is a perfect fifty-two degrees, they build the next layer of the pyramid starting from the outside and working in."

Nigel ran his hand across the smooth, angled surface of the white stones. He rested his head on the slab, his eyes level with the surface, and peered down. The slope extended perfectly down to the sand below.

"Amazing," Nigel mumbled.

"It is."

"And the aliens are not helping them in any way?"

"Not at all." Meissner corrected himself. "They showed the Egyptians how to use their technology to achieve such progress, but that's where their help ended. Something about not wanting to influence ancient civilizations. I'm not sure. You have to see this."

The men crossed over to the opposite corner. Meissner directed Nigel to look over the side. The Brit did, fascinated by what he witnessed.

An internal ramp several feet from the inside of the exterior, one and a half meters wide and at a seven-degree angle, ran the length of the pyramid. They used wooden rails to pull the block up from one level to another. A stone block sat at a notch at the end of the tunnel. Workers used levers and pulleys to lift the block, spin it ninety degrees, then lower it onto the wooden rails of the next internal ramp where more workers proceeded to drag the block to the next level.

Nigel was awestruck. "This is remarkable."

"Isn't it? I assessed that the Egyptians kept lengthening the ramp during the construction, but the flaw in that thinking is that to keep the ramp at a constant seven-degree angle, it would extend into the Nile and use more stones than required to build the pyramid. Any ramp greater than seven degrees would require too many workers to pull it."

"It's groundbreaking."

"I know. Wait until you see this. Follow me."

They made their way to the center of the structure where two dark granite slabs sat on top of a granite cantilevered arch, forming a roof.

Nigel crouched and ran his hand along the surface. "Is this what I think it is?"

"Yes. It's the Pharoah's burial chamber."

"Amazing."

"That's nothing. I've saved the best for last."

Meissner led the way down the main ramp and past the smaller one leading to the internal tunnel system. He approached the pyramid from the south. A ladder placed against the surface led to an opening several meters up in the facade. Meissner climbed the ladder and motioned for Nigel to follow. At the top, they entered a corridor eight meters high and forty-eight meters in length.

Nigel whistled. "I can't believe I'm standing in the Grand Gallery."

"You're not." Meissner stated it smugly, like a university professor revealing an enlightening truth to his pupils. "That's what we always believed. But the gallery makes no sense from a ceremonial point of view. Unless you look at it from another perspective." He pointed to the limestone protrusions that ran the length along both sides of the gallery. "We always assumed these were benches, but they're not. There are twenty-eight notches evenly spaced in them. These notches contained logs, logs used to guide the counterweight for the granite stones hauled up to the burial chamber."

"Impossible."

"It isn't." Meissner bent over and wiped his hand along the bench, scooping up a sticky brown substance that he ran between his fingers. He passed it to Nigel. "Feel this. It's a lubricant. Plus, look at all the scratches along the wall. And up there."

Nigel shifted his gaze. Wooden beams ran along the upper wall the length of the gallery.

"So? The wood rotted over time."

"Those beams are the stabilizers for the trolley to keep it from shifting when moving. Those groves are pristine. The ones we see in the pyramid from our time were chiseled out, probably because the Egyptians re-used the wood. This is how the Egyptians maneuvered the large marble stones to the top. Rather than using six hundred men, which would be impossible, they used this counterweight system and hauled the granite up the ramp with only one hundred. I have more proof. Let me show you."

The men climbed the Grand Gallery that led up to the King's Chamber. The final step had a V-shape cut in it.

"See. This is for the ropes for the counterweight system."

Nigel was convinced.

The two men continued to the top of the tunnel, emerging in front of the Pharoah's burial chamber. Nigel peered back down the Grand Gallery. "This is fantastic."

"I know."

"We'll change Egyptology forever."

Meissner's demeanor became harsh. "*We?*"

"Of course. With what we've learned, we can advance the study of Ancient Egypt by a hundred years. We'll be famous."

"You're right, *meiner Freund*." Meissner forced a smile. "If there's nothing else you want to see, let's head back to camp for lunch."

Chapter Twenty-Eight

MARIA ARRIVED AT the former arsenal now used as the prisoner compound. She mentally breathed a sigh of relief to see Jochen on duty rather than Fuchs. Summoning her courage, she approached the guard who stepped away from the structure to meet her.

"I'd like to speak with the Americans," she said in German. "I need to ask them a few questions."

"Go ahead." Jochen returned to his shady spot in front of the mud house.

Maria stepped up to the gated door and spoke in English. "Major Williams, can I talk to you?"

The four Americans appeared out of the shadows. Maria became nervous when she didn't see the Egyptologist among them.

"Where is your British friend?"

"He's out getting a private tour of the pyramid with your German doctor," answered Dawson, his tone dripping with disdain.

"Is he safe?"

"Why wouldn't he be?" asked Evans. His tone became serious. "Where's Nelson?"

Maria took a deep breath and lowered her eyes. "He's dead."

"You killed him?" yelled Dawson.

"No. The Anunnaki did.

Dawson approached the bars. "How did he die?"

The commotion attracted Jochen's attention. He came over

to protect Maria, but she waved her hands, indicating things were all right.

"It's okay. They're upset because I told them their friend was dead. I'm fine."

"Are you sure?" Jochen's finger hovered near the trigger of his MP40 submachine gun.

"Yes."

"As you wish." Jochen stepped to the end of the building, removed a cigarette from his pocket, and lit it.

Maria switched back to English. "I thought the Anunnaki were going to ask him questions. Instead, they attached him to a machine that wiped his mind clean and stored his memories."

"What did they do with his body?"

"They're going to dissect it."

"And you allowed that?" snarled Dawson.

"I tried to stop them, but when I did, they got angry. I'm sorry."

Kerdoshian quieted Dawson and stepped closer to the bars. "Did they get the information they needed?"

"I don't know. Why?"

Kerdoshian glanced over at the major. "If they didn't get what they wanted from Nelson, there's a good chance one of us might be next."

"Shit." Evans stepped away to process what he had heard.

"May I ask you something?" said Maria. "What's the future like, if Kammler succeeds."

"He does succeed," Kerdoshian answered. "He returns to May 1941 and Germany uses the atomic weapons to defeat the Soviet Union. Britain sues for peace and America never enters the war. Hitler eventually takes over all of Europe and half the Middle East. Germany becomes the most powerful nation in the world."

"What about the Jews?"

"Do you care?" blurted Dawson.

Kerdoshian ignored him. "Every Jew in Europe, Siberia,

and those areas in the Middle East under German control are rounded up and exterminated. Close to nine million in total. And that doesn't include Gypsies, Slavs, and every Communist in Russia."

Maria closed her eyes and fought back the tears. So many lives would be lost because of her.

Evans returned to the others. "Maria, can you help us break out of here?"

"Now?"

"Tomorrow. We need time to plan out a course of action. Will you help us?"

"On one condition."

"What?"

Maria stiffened her resolve. "You have to help me stop Kammler from succeeding."

Chapter Twenty-Nine

"D EAL." EVANS EXTENDED his hand.

Maria ever so slightly shook her head. "Yell at me."

"What?"

"I don't want the guard to think we're conspiring. Pretend you're mad at me."

"I wouldn't be pretending."

"Just do it."

Evans charged the bars, making a show of shaking them. "You bitch! Why did you let them murder our friend?"

Maria jumped back. "I'm sorry. I didn't mean to."

Jochen rushed over and slammed the stock of his MP40 against the bars, barely missing Evans' hands. Maria stepped over to the guard and pulled him away.

"It's alright," she said in German. Then, turning to Evans, she shifted back to English. "I said I was sorry."

Maria spun around and headed back to her tent.

Jochen watched her leave, glanced over his shoulder at Evans, and growled, "*Arschloch.*"

As Jochen moved back to the shade, Evans watched Maria until she disappeared behind a sand dune. He admired her, and not only for her beauty. He could tell that the death of Nelson upset her, which meant she was not like Kammler and the others. And her regret over what she had caused seemed genuine. Evans sensed it eating away at her soul.

Kerdoshian stepped up beside him. "Do you trust her?"

Evans considered it for a moment. "I do."

"I don't," spat Dawson. "She's a Nazi like the rest of them."

"Right now, she's the only hope we have for getting out of here," replied Kerdoshian.

Evans changed the subject. "We need a battle plan."

"That's easy," chuckled Crane. "We kill all the Germans."

Kerdoshian shook his head. "That's not enough. We have to destroy the atomic devices as well."

"If Kammler and the others are dead, how will they get them home?"

"Kerdoshian's right," said Evans. "The Anunnaki put a lot of time in developing those devices. Nothing is stopping them from using the *Haunebu II* and *Die Glocke* to send them back to Hitler without the Germans. We have to make sure their mission is a total failure."

Kerdoshian motioned to the mud hut beside them. "There's probably explosives in there along with the ammunition. We could use that to destroy the ships."

"Agreed." Dawson made eye contact with Evans. "But how do we get back, or was that spiel about having a way home just bullshit?"

"We don't," Evans admitted. "We'll be stuck here."

"That's what I thought."

"Sorry."

"Don't worry about it. We all knew it could happen."

An uneasy silence passed between the four men.

"What if we steal *Die Glocke*?" asked Crane.

The other three stared at him.

"Think about it a minute. Valthor pre-set the instruments on our ship to return to the future. The Anunnaki probably did the same thing for the Germans. Once we destroy the *Haunebu II*, we can take *Die Glocke* and return to our own time."

"Right into the middle of Nazi Germany?" asked Dawson.

"It's better than staying here," said Evans.

"Not if they hand us over to the *Gestapo*."

Kerdoshian raised an eyebrow. "We might have a better chance of survival if we take the *Vril Damen* with us. They don't deserve to be left behind."

Dawson disagreed. "They'd be a liability."

"It's still a shot."

"A long shot."

"I agree with Kerdoshian. It's our only chance." Evans paused. "But we have to leave Gudrun behind."

"Why?" asked Kerdoshian.

"The other ladies might support us. I'm sure Maria would. But Gudrun would throw us under the bus to save herself."

"No fucking loss," Dawson chuckled again. "That bitch deserves what she gets."

"So, we're all in agreement?" asked Evans. "We break out, kill the Germans, destroy the *Haunebu II*, steal *Die Glocke*, and escape back to our own time with the *Vril Damen*."

Kerdoshian nodded.

"I'm in," said Crane.

"Why not?" said Dawson.

Kerdoshian examined the walls of the hut. "Now we have to figure out how to get out of here."

"I already have that planned. We do it the next time Maria visits us."

Chapter Thirty

MARIA SPENT THE next few hours sitting in a shaded location absent-mindedly watching the pyramid's construction, trying to reconcile herself to committing treason. Not that she harbored any second thoughts. Kammler needed to be stopped at any cost. The ramifications of his returning to their timeline with atomic weapons would be devastating for Europe, at least according to the Americans.

She vividly remembered the last six months of the war before they jumped back in time. The constant bombings by the Allies. The devastation of almost every major city in Europe. The brutality of the Russians. The drafting of old men and young children to fight a war already lost. Only in those last months had she contemplated what had befallen those countries invaded by Germany and the destruction and inhumanity they must have endured. When she volunteered the *Vril Damen* for this mission, she thought it would be for the betterment of Germany. Now she realized her motives were misguided. Germany got what it deserved, having finally reaped what it had sown for so many years.

Maria's only regret focused on the fate of the *Vril Damen*. Except for Gudrun, the other ladies had willingly followed Maria, believing in her and their mission. She had led them astray. Now they would suffer for her arrogance.

Maybe the Americans would find it in their hearts to help her ladies. She sensed decency within them, at least in Evans and Kerdoshian. In the timeline she was helping to create, America and Germany were not enemies. Ironically, if

Kammler failed and events returned to normal, they would be again. The entire concept seemed so surreal.

Maria checked her watch. It was almost dinner. She should join the others and pretend she had not betrayed them.

✦   ✦   ✦

THE OTHERS HAD already gathered by the time she arrived at Kammler's tent. Gudrun sat to his right. Meissner and Fuchs also attended. She noticed two bottles of vintage French cognac on the table.

"Are we celebrating something?" she asked as she took the empty chair to Kammler's left.

"We're celebrating the success of our mission." Kammler poured cognac into her glass. "The Anunnaki confirmed they'll be delivering the last device tomorrow afternoon. We'll be returning to Germany the next morning."

A flutter of excitement went through the *Vril Damen*.

Traute turned to Fuchs. "Does this mean we have to cancel our camel ride in the morning?"

Kammler raised an eyebrow. "This is the first I've heard of it."

"I was going to bring it up with you after dinner," said Fuchs. "The ladies requested they be taken on a camel ride into the desert before we depart. Four of my men agreed to escort them."

"Permission granted."

"Thank you, *obergruppenführer*."

Three SS soldiers arrived with their meals, placed the plates in front of those seated at the table, and then departed. Kammler motioned for them to eat.

Halfway through dinner, Kammler announced, "*Obersturm-bannführer* Fuchs, I think we should arrange a farewell party tomorrow evening for your men. They also deserve to celebrate."

"Thank you, *Herr Obergruppenführer*."

Meissner perked up. "May I invite Dr. Davenport?"

"Of course." Kammler switched his attention to Maria. "Would you like to invite the other Americans?"

"Why would I want to do that?"

"You seem to be friends with them. You visited them this afternoon."

Maria remained stoic. She cast a glance over at Fuchs who stared at her, measuring her response. She should have realized that Jochen would inform his commanding officer of the visit.

"I visited the Americans to tell them about the murder of their friend."

"I prefer the term 'untimely death.' I doubt the Anunnaki planned on killing him." Kammler cut off a piece of goose and stabbed it with his fork. "How did they react?"

"They weren't happy, but that's only to be expected."

"Jochen said they were upset on hearing the news." Kammler lifted the fork to his mouth and continued eating. "Is it true that Evans went after you?"

"Yes." Maria gulped a swig of cognac to settle her frayed nerves.

Meissner attempted to change the topic of conversation. "*Fraulein* Gudrun, will you be joining the other ladies tomorrow?"

Gudrun lowered her eyes to her plate.

"*Fraulein* Gudrun will be with me tomorrow," Kammler answered. "As the new head of the *Vril Damen*, I'll need her to communicate with the Anunnaki."

So, that bitch Gudrun had finally supplanted her. "Excuse me, but I'm the leader of the *Vril Damen*."

"Not anymore. Your dedication to the mission has slackened over the past few days. I need someone whose loyalty I can rely on."

Traute, Sigrun, and Heike appeared stunned. Traute spoke for the others. "You can't do that. None of us would be here if not for Maria."

"I'd advise you not to question my decision." The stern tone in Kammler's voice ended any further discussion. He turned to Maria. "As of now, you'll be confined to your tent until we leave. I trust you'll obey my orders. I'd hate to have to leave you behind."

Maria stiffened. "I'd prefer you drop me off in 1st Century B.C. Egypt. You can leave Gudrun to keep me company. Who knows, she might become Cleopatra. She's slutty enough."

"Fuck you." Gudrun grabbed her glass and threw the cognac into Maria's face.

The other ladies protested until Kammler raised a hand, silencing them. He focused his attention on Gudrun.

"You should be more discerning. This cognac is too expensive to waste."

Maria remained calm despite wanting to strangle the bitch. "May I be excused?"

"Of course. Fuchs will escort you back to your tent."

Fuchs came around the table, standing behind Maria. Maria stood, glared at Gudrun, then spun around and left. Fuchs followed. She did not look back.

Hans waited at the *Vril Damen*'s tent when they arrived. The bastard had planned this, and she had been too naïve to see it coming. She lowered her head as she approached. The enlisted man lifted the flap for her to enter and nodded as she passed.

Fuchs paused at the opening. "*Fraulein* Orsic. A word of advice. The *obergruppenführer*'s patience with you has worn out. I suggest you accept what has happened and gracefully bow out once we get back to Berlin."

"I will."

Maria knew it was a lie. Although she could not be sure if Fuchs' concern for her well-being was genuine or merely a ruse to keep her calm before disposing of her, it did not matter. No way would she sit back quietly and allow this nightmare to play out. Too much was at stake. She vividly recalled the original timeline in which Hitler devastated Europe and brought down *Götterdämmerung* on her homeland. It had been what the Buddhists called *karma*. She refused to allow that madman to devastate Europe again and then bask in his victory.

Tomorrow evening, during the celebration, she would find a way to sneak away, free Evans, and together they would stop this madness.

BOOK THREE

Chapter Thirty-One

FOLLOWING BREAKFAST, TRAUTE, Sigrun, and Heike gathered outside their tent. After last night's encounter at dinner, the *Vril Damen* had remained silent all evening. You could cut the tension with an ax. Thankfully, one was not available, otherwise either Maria or Gudrun might have used it on the other. Gudrun had risen before the others and slipped out before any of them woke up, not that anyone missed her. Traute hoped today's trip would brighten their mood.

Dietrich approached with seven one-humped camels, or dromedaries, that the Anunnaki had prepared to take them into the desert. Dietrich once served in the *Afrika Korps* and had experience with such animals. Fuchs had assigned Jochen, Hans, Wilhelm, and Dietrich to accompany them. The ladies had replaced their usual sundresses with tan slacks and military shirts, though they kept their sunhats.

Sigrun stepped up to her camel, admiring its size. "They're so much bigger than the horses I used to ride as a child."

"And smellier," chuckled Heike.

"I think they're special." Traute petted her camel and scratched the side of its head. It leaned forward and placed its nose against hers, then licked her with its massive tongue. Traute laughed.

"It reminds me of one of your boyfriends," teased Sigrun.

"Which one?" added Heike.

Traute hugged the camel around its neck. "But none of them have ever kissed me like that before."

Dietrich and his men joined the ladies. "Are you ready?"

"Where are the saddles?" asked Heike.

"You don't need them. We rode them bareback in North Africa all the time."

"There are no camel saddles," explained Hans as he placed seven blankets on the sand. "I asked Dr. Meissner about it last night. He spent an hour explaining that camels were not used as transportation by the Egyptians until the 6th Century B.C."

"It doesn't matter," Dietrich called Hans over. "I'll show you how to mount one."

Dietrich stood by the camel's head, talking to it. He gently pulled down on the rope jury-rigged as a rein. The camel crouched on its front knees. Hans threw one of the blankets over its hump, climbed on, and held the reins. The camel stood. Balancing himself, Hans reached forward and petted its neck.

Dietrich turned to the ladies. "The toughest part is keeping your balance while you mount. Other than that, it's like riding a horse bareback. Try it."

Dietrich, Jochen, and Wilhelm helped each of the ladies climb onto their camels. Sigrun could not get her camel to stand once on it.

"Am I doing it wrong?" she asked.

"No." Dietrich came over. "Sometimes they can be stubborn. Lightly but firmly pull back on the reins. Let him know who's in charge."

Sigrun yanked on the rope. "Come on, boy."

Still no response.

"Try a little harder. And be firm in your voice."

Sigrun yanked back on the reins. The camel finally stood. It turned its head toward her and snorted.

"Now that reminds me of one of my old boyfriends," joked Traute from her mount.

The SS soldiers mounted their camels and Dietrich led them off into the desert.

Traute enjoyed the ride. Well, at least the trek through the desert. While riding a camel was fun and adventurous, it proved far less comfortable than a horse. Nor did it make her comfortable that their escorts carried MP40s strapped across their backs, a discourtesy required by Kammler before he approved this jaunt. Eventually, Traute became used to the swaying and the weapons and relaxed, taking in the beauty of the desert.

Once away from the pyramid and the Nile, the desert presented itself in its pristine glory, a vast sea of sand stretching endlessly from one horizon to the other, interrupted only by sand-blown dunes that reminded her of waves on a storm-swept ocean. As barren and lifeless as it appeared on the surface, Traute knew the desert possessed a life all its own. The air above its surface constantly shimmered from the heat generated by the sun. And, unlike the oceans, which had remained static for millennia, the desert constantly changed shape, its sands driven by the wind. Five thousand years from now, the workers' village and the other structures around the pyramid would be buried, waiting to be discovered by future archaeologists. The desert would even claim most of the Sphinx in its mysterious grasp.

"What's that?" Sigrun pointed to the east.

Hans shaded his eyes with his hand. "It's a mud hut."

"Can we check it out?"

"I don't see why not. It looks abandoned."

Hans prodded his camel in the direction of the hut. The others followed. They stopped fifty feet away and dismounted. Wilhelm tended to the camels as the rest approached the structure.

It was abandoned. Sand piled three feet high along the east façade and stretched down the sides, partially burying the doorway. The wooden roof had collapsed.

Jochen stuck his head inside and peered around. "I wonder who it belonged to?"

"We'll never know," said Heike. "One of the many mysteries concealed by the desert."

The adventurers cooled themselves off in the shade and stretched their legs. Jochen removed a canteen from his belt, took a drink of water, then extended it to Traute. She gulped down a mouthful of water and handed it back.

"You're awfully young and handsome for an SS soldier."

Jochen blushed. "Thank you, *fraulein*."

"May I ask how old you are?"

"Eighteen."

"Have you ever seen combat?"

The young man became embarrassed. "Not yet. I lost a brother in the Crimea and another at Normandy. My parents and sister died in the fire-bombing of Hamburg. I enlisted in the SS on my eighteenth birthday and was assigned to the defense of Berlin. Kammler reassigned me to this unit in February."

"You're a brave man and we're glad to have you with us." Traute kissed Jochen on the cheek, smiling as he blushed. She turned to Dietrich. "How about you?"

"I served in the *Arika Korps* from the day Rommel landed in North Africa and was one of the last evacuated. Then I spent time in Italy until nearly being killed at Anzio. After nearly a year of rehabilitation, I ended up here. I have to admit, this North Africa is nothing like I experienced."

Traute smiled at Hans. "What about you?"

"I was there for the invasion of France. After the armistice, I was fortunate enough to be stationed in Paris. The French women were, how should I say it, accommodating. After General von Choltitz abandoned the city to the Allies, we fell back into the Netherlands. I saw action at Nijmegen, Aachen, and the Hurtgen Forest before being joining Task Force Kammler. No matter how it ends, I'll be glad once the fighting is over."

No one disagreed with that sentiment.

"And you, Wilhelm?"

Wilhelm grew sullen. "I joined the SS early in 1941 and saw combat on the Eastern Front non-stop for three and a half years. As bad as it was in Europe and North Africa, nothing compared to fighting the Russians. Warfare so brutal I'll have nightmares about it so long as I live. Men frozen alive due to the lack of cold-weather gear. German troops so hyped up on Pervitin that they could barely function. You'll never know the true feeling of terror until your positions are shelled for hours by thousands of artillery pieces before being overrun by Red Army soldiers whose only intent is to slaughter as many Germans as possible. And none of that compares to what the Russians did to our people trapped in Poland or east Germany. Using those alien weapons against the Soviets is preferable to what we experienced in Russia."

"Do you think the Russians deserve to be annihilated?" asked Traute.

"Yes." Wilhelm's emphatic response softened. "Neither side was innocent on the Eastern Front. But if a few hundred thousand have to die in the first few days to spare the nightmare that engulfed east Europe, then it's worth it."

A darkness settled over the group, eroding the gaiety of the past few hours.

Finally, Dietrich said, "We should get back. We don't want to miss tonight's celebration."

One by one, the group filtered back toward the camels. Wilhelm stopped halfway, turned around, screamed, and fired his MP40 into the side of the mud hut until the magazine emptied. The bullets had ripped open a hole in the wall.

Traute walked over and placed a tender hand on his shoulder. "Are you okay?"

"Sorry. Just releasing some tension."

"It's fine." Traute flirtatiously placed a hand on his shoulder and pointed to the submachine gun. "I've never fired a weapon before. May I?"

"Sure." Wilhelm smiled. He slipped the MP40 off his

shoulders then replaced the magazine. Handing it to Traute, he showed her how to hold it and stepped to the side.

Traute held the weapon by her hip like she had seen gangsters do in American movies and pulled the trigger. The first five rounds struck the wall in a tight pattern, with the remaining bullets striking it higher up and to the right.

"What did I do wrong?"

"You didn't compensate for the recoil. Here, let me show you." Wilhelm took the MP40, switched out magazines, and gave it back to Traute. He moved in close behind her, his left hand clasping hers and his right on her waist. "This time, hold her steady as you fire."

Traute pulled the trigger again. Wilhelm helped her keep the gun level. This time, her aim was improved, punching a second hole in the wall.

"See? You did much better."

"I want to try," Heike said excitedly and spun around to Hans. "Will you show me?"

"Of course." Hans handed his MP40 to the woman and cuddled her from behind as Wilhelm had done with Traute.

Not wanting to be left out, Dietrich volunteered to train Sigrun.

For the next fifteen minutes, the ladies practiced their firing skills until they could place their bullets in a tight circle, more than enough to defend themselves if need be, which was what Traute had wanted. Given the way things were going back at camp, she wanted the *Vril Damen* prepared for any eventuality.

With the training over and a sense of happiness restored, the group mounted their camels and began the long trek back to camp.

Chapter Thirty-Two

KAMMLER SAT AT the end of the table, reading through Kerdoshian's journal, enthralled by the details of the Golden Sun's alliance with the Americans. He found the entire scenario mind-boggling. A year ago, if anyone had told him that two alien races would be assisting the Germans and the Americans in fighting World War II, he would have committed them to an institution. Kammler chuckled to himself, wondering how future historians would record this moment.

Gudrun pushed aside the tent flap and entered. "Sir, the Anunnaki are here. They just loaded the last of the device aboard the *Haunebu II*."

"Excellent. I'll be right there."

Kammler tossed the diary on the table and exited the tent. Two Anunnaki stood behind Gudrun. Despite spending all this time with them, he could not read their emotions, assuming they had any. Emotionless, efficient, and loyal. These creatures would make perfect SS soldiers.

"Please express my gratitude for all they have done for us. Myself, Hitler, and the Third *Reich* owe them a debt of thanks. And tell them we'll be more than happy to share Earth's mineral resources."

Gudrun telepathically relayed the message. The two Anunnaki responded with a clicking noise. To the *obergruppenführer*'s surprise, the aliens straightened and extended their right tibial at a forty-five-degree angle. Kammler snapped to attention and returned the Nazi salute. Gudrun did the same.

"*Heil* Hitler."

The Anunnaki sauntered off.

Kammler and Gudrun re-entered the tent.

"You've done an excellent job, Gudrun. You seem to have won their confidence."

"Thank you, *Herr Obergruppenführer*."

"I'll have no trouble convincing the *Führer* that you're the prefect leader for the *Vril Damen*."

"I won't let you down."

"I'm certain of that." Kammler took his seat. "I trust everything ready for tonight's celebration?"

"The cooks are preparing dinner now."

"Are your ladies back?"

"Not yet, but they should be soon."

"Have them pack their belongings when they get back. We're leaving at 0600 tomorrow."

"I will. What about the Americans?"

"We'll be taking them with us. They'll prove to the world that we're telling the truth. One more thing." Kammler took the diary and handed it to her. "Give this back to the Negro."

"Is that a good idea?"

"Yes. Having this will only deepen the shame of losing to us so late in the war. And it'll serve as a warning to the Golden Sun not to interfere in our future affairs."

"I thought you might want to give it to Goebbels for propaganda purposes. He's been espousing the Frederick the Great outcome for a while now."

Kammler sneered. "That club-footed idiot deserves no help from me. He can make up all the legends he wants. The *Führer* knows who saved Germany."

"I'll take care of it." Gudrun started to exit the tent when Kammler called to her.

"One more thing. Meissner asked that the British Egyptologist join us for dinner. I agreed. Let the good doctor bore the hell out of someone else for the night. Please pass along the invitation."

"I will. See you at dinner."

✦ ✦ ✦

EVANS SAT WITH his back against the wall, trying to sleep. The heat and the dozens of thoughts racing through his mind made relaxing impossible. Kerdoshian, Dawson, Crane, and Nigel were in the same predicament.

A female voice came from outside.

"Get ready," warned Evans. "We're getting out of here."

Evans moved to the barred door. Instead of Maria, a brunette with short hair stood waiting for him. He did not know her name but recognized her as the one who led the search party that captured them.

"Well, to what do we owe this pleasure?"

"As you Americans say, cut the crap," Gudrun snapped. She held out the diary. "I don't want to be here, but Kammler asked me to drop this off."

Evans reached out and took it. "I thought Maria would be the one who delivered it."

"You can forget about her. Maria has been confined to her quarters until we leave in the morning, and I'm the head of the *Vril Damen*."

"I'm sure you worked hard to get that position," Dawson sneered. "Your back must hurt."

Gudrun bristled but said nothing.

Kerdoshian stepped forward. "What happens to us?"

"If I had my way, I'd leave you here. But Kammler wants to take you back with us. We're leaving at 0600."

Gudrun took a few steps before stopping. "Is Nigel there?"

Nigel stood and came over to the door. "Where else would I be?"

Gudrun ignored the comment. "Meissner wants you to join him at tonight's victory celebration."

"Of course. What time?"

"Six o'clock. Someone will come for you."

"Thank you."

Gudrun stormed off.

Nigel watched her leave. When she was out of earshot, he grinned. "What a charming young lady. A fine example of National Socialism."

"We know Maria won't be able to help us, so we're on our own." Evans moved inside the hut so the guard could not overhear him. He focused on Nigel. "An hour after you're gone, we'll break out and destroy the *Haunebu II*. Try to keep the Germans distracted. When the shit hits the fan, make your way to *Die Glocke*. With luck, we can use it to get back to our timeline. Any questions?"

No one had any.

"Good. All we can do now is wait."

✦   ✦   ✦

THE CELEBRATORY FAREWELL dinner started a little after six that evening. The cooks prepared goose, ox, fish, and bread and fruit. Kammler even broke out a case of Czech pilsner he had hidden aboard the *Haunebu II* for such an occasion. Almost the entire expedition attended except for Hans, who guarded the Americans, and Dietrich, Jochen, Wilhelm, and Erin who stood watch over their ships. And, of course, Maria. The event not only marked the success of their mission, it meant they would be back in Germany by this time tomorrow, a phrase that had lost much of its relevance when time travel was involved.

Halfway through the meal, Kammler stood and clinked his fork against the side of his glass. "Soldiers of the SS, ladies, and our esteemed doctors. Today is a special occasion for the Third *Reich*. What we have done here the past few weeks has ensured our victory will last a thousand years. Most of you have lost friends and family during the last four years of the war and witnessed the devastation that had befallen the Fatherland. Soon that path will be altered, and Germany will enter a future where we are victorious. The German people and our nation owe everyone on this expedition a debt of gratitude. Each of you should feel pride in what we have accomplished. A toast to our success."

Everyone except Nigel raised their glasses. "*Prosit.*"

"And to our *Führer.*"

Fuchs stood and extended his arm. "*Heil* Hitler!"

The other SS snapped to attention and joined in a chorus of, "*Sieg heil.*"

Kammler placed his glass on the table, leaned over to Gudrun, and whispered, "Meet me in my tent in ten minutes."

"With pleasure, *Herr Obergruppenführer.*"

Kammler left and headed for his quarters.

Meissner nudged Nigel. "Dr. Davenport, if you have a moment, I have one more thing I'd like to show you."

"What is it?"

"The preparation chamber used for mummification."

"Are you serious?"

Meissner nodded. "I discovered it while touring the construction site. You and I will be the only modern Egyptologists to see one in perfect condition."

"What about their others?"

"They don't care. All they want to do is get drunk and flirt with the *Vril Damen.* You and I are going to experience history."

Nigel could not resist such a discovery. He followed Meissner.

Chapter Thirty-Three

MEISSNER AND NIGEL crossed the work area to the opposite side of the pyramid then made their way toward the Nile where a stone structure sat isolated from the other mud huts. The doctor waved for his friend to follow. When Nigel entered, his eyes lit up in wonderment.

The chamber inside measured a hundred feet on all four sides, with each wall plastered over, painted in royal colors, and inscribed with hieroglyphics. The chamber was empty except for three tables positioned side by side in the center of the floor, each equidistant from the rest. The two nearest the rear wall and entrance were identical, each the size of a bed and made of wood, their legs ornately carved to resemble a lion. Gold accouterments covered the four corner posts, the two on one end formed into the shape of lion heads, and those on the opposite end curved into tails. Between them sat a granite table shaped more like a bathtub with the interior filled with sand. Four metal stands five feet tall stood in the corners and one against the walls on either end of the tables, their basins holding burning oil that provided the only illumination.

Nigel walked through the chamber, gawking at the sites. "This is amazing."

"Isn't it?"

Nigel placed his fingers on the surface of the closest table, running them from the lion's head, along the edge, and up the golden tail to the tip.

"We're inside the burial preparation chamber for the Pharoah." Meissner pointed to the table closest to the wall. "That is where the body is readied for embalming. The priest removes the brain and internal organs and cleans the interior. Once the body is sewn back up, it's placed in this basin." He stepped over to the tub-shaped table seated in the center. "It's covered with linen pouches filled with natron, a substance similar to a mixture of salt and baking soda that sucks the moisture from the body, which is then buried in sand. The body sits for thirty-five days until it's dried out. That's when the priest transfers the body to the last table." Meissner moved over to the closest wooden table and ran his hands across the surface. "Here it's washed, covered in resins and oils, and wrapped for burial. A month later, the Pharoah is moved to his burial chamber and proceeds into the afterlife."

"Fascinating."

"Wait until you see this." Meissner motioned for Nigel to follow. He led them to the rear of the chamber where a smaller table stood by the embalming table, each the same height as the larger one and covered with linen. The German lifted the cloth. Four white limestone jars, each a foot tall and with flat lids, rested in holes drilled into the tabletop. Each jar would contain a different set of internal organs—the liver, the lungs, the stomach, and the intestines. Nigel immediately recognized their significance.

"Are these canopic jars?"

"Unused ones, yes. The Egyptians won't use animal-headed jars for another thousand years."

Nigel ran his fingers across the limestone. "We're looking at something that one day may be an archaeological discovery."

Meissner approached the slab. "And check these out."

To the left of the jars sat a stone knife and a wooden adze-like tool for opening the chest and removing the internal organs, and a tall jar for oil.

"Dear God," whispered Nigel.

"I thought you might be impressed. These are the tools used to prepare the body for the afterlife."

"I would love to see the process first-hand."

"Funny you should say that."

"What do you—"

Something struck Nigel on the back of his head. He remembered falling to the floor before passing out.

✦　✦　✦

HEMIUNU TOURED THE top of the pyramid. This morning, the workers had started to place down the next layer of stones that would cover the Pharoah's burial chamber. With the more complex sections of the pyramid completed, the rest of the project could proceed rapidly. With luck, he would complete the pyramid ahead of schedule, which would please—

"Vizier."

Hemiunu turned to the ramp. Ankhmare reached the top and ran over, the expression on his face a mixture of anger and disgust.

"What's wrong?"

"The outsiders...." Ankhmare paused to catch his breath. "Two of them are in the sacred chamber."

"What are they doing in there?"

"I don't know, vizier. Some of the workers saw them enter a little while ago."

The outsiders had been a nuisance since arriving, both in distracting the Star Travelers and in their repeated requests to view the construction of the pyramid. Hemiunu had tolerated them up to now. He could not tolerate this defiling of the sacred chamber.

"Take four guards with you and bring them to me. They must pay for their defiance."

"Right away, vizier." Ankhmare bowed and ran off.

Hemiunu took a deep breath and tried to calm the fury welling up inside him. The Star Travelers had been precise in maintaining discretion between themselves and his people, but their uninvited guests had continually pushed the limit. This incident eroded the last of his patience. These two needed to pay for their arrogance.

✦   ✦   ✦

NIGEL SLOWLY CAME around. His head throbbed. For a few seconds, he could not recall where he was or what had happened. He had been in the burial preparation chamber when someone had struck him in the back of the head. That someone could only have been Meissner.

Nigel tried to get up but could not move. Not quite. He still had control of his body, but something held him in place. Opening his eyes, he was still in the chamber, only now his body had been lashed to the embalming table. Meissner stood beside him.

"I'm glad you're awake, my friend. Please forgive me for knocking you out. I had no other choice."

"What are you doing?" Nigel strained against the ropes. "Untie me."

Meissner grimaced. "You see, that's the problem. I can't. I've worked too hard on this expedition to discover the secrets of Ancient Egypt."

"What are you talking about?"

"The other day, while touring the pyramid, you said once we return to our timeline, we'll advance the field of Egyptology hundreds of years. I'm not about to let you share my findings with the world. That honor is mine alone."

"Is that what this is about?"

"I'm afraid so."

Nigel relaxed, trying to lull Meissner into a sense of security. "Don't worry about it. I'll let you publish your findings and will say nothing. You can have all the credit."

"I can't take that risk." Meissner bent over to pick something off the floor. "But I am going to allow you to participate in a major discovery that will change the way the world views mummification."

Meissner stood and placed three bronze rods on the table beside Nigel, each eighteen inches long and half an inch think with a hooked end. He picked up one of the rods and spun it between his fingers, examining it.

Cold fear ran down Nigel's spine. "Aren't those the tools used for extracting a body's brain?"

"Yes."

"Where did you find them? The Egyptians won't remove the brain for mummification until much later."

"I brought them with me from our timeline. Don't tell Kammler. He'll have a fit." Meissner chuckled. "By now, we're aware of the mummification process. The only aspect that remains a mystery is how the Egyptians extracted the deceased's brain. I've always thought the process too cumbersome and felt we must be missing something. With your help, I'll be able to see exactly how it works."

"You're insane."

"I understand your hesitation. Please try to be reasonable. Your sacrifice will be the greatest contribution you can ever make to Egyptology."

Nigel thrashed about, trying to loosen the ropes, but Meissner had tied them too tight. He screamed for help.

"No one can hear you." Meissner moved the hook closer to Nigel's face.

Nigel shook his head back and forth. Meissner grabbed the doctor by the hair and held him in place.

"Please stop making this more difficult for me than it already is." Meissner inserted the hook into Nigel's left nostril and pushed.

The pain was unbearable as the hook made its way through his nose. Being larger than the nasal cavity, the curved end abrased and tore the tissue. Having no flexibility, the staff distorted the cavity lining as it passed, increasing the agony. An uncontrollable urge to sneeze washed over Nigel, though not as disturbing as the sensation of blood flowing from the gashes down the back of his throat. Nigel repeatedly swallowed, preferring to drink his blood rather than drown in it.

The hook bumped against the bone at the top of the nasal cavity. Meissner pulled it back an inch and rammed it home, shattering the thin layer and driving the hook into Nigel's frontal lobe. Nigel screamed and thrashed his head, succeeding only in driving the hook deeper into his brain. Terror shut down his thinking and pain overloaded his senses. He tried to cry out but couldn't form the words.

Meissner turned the hook one hundred and eighty degrees and withdrew it. It caught on portions of Nigel's brain, shredding it. His body stiffened, momentarily paralyzed. The pain subsided as he felt the metal intrusion moving through his nasal cavity and exiting. Nigel watched as Meissner examined the hook. Chunks of brain hung from it. *My brain*, thought Nigel. Was it his brain, though? It had to be. Nigel felt the residue in the back of his throat.

Meissner tapped the hook against the oil jar until the grey matter fell away then reinserted it into Nigel's nostril. The pain continued, but not as bad as before. Nigel felt the metal enter his skull again and puncture his brain. He tried to move his head and stop the torture, but it refused to respond. Who was this man, and why did he torment me this way?

"Please, stop."

Only the words were not spoken. Or maybe they had been. Nigel realized his hearing had stopped functioning. He tried pleading again. His lips did not move. Nigel focused on the hook as Meissner rammed it further into his skull.

The metal passed through the frontal lobe, scraped against the top of Nigel's skull, and drove itself into his motor strip. Meissner twisted it several times. Agony wracked Nigel yet faded quickly, becoming an unusual sensation inside his head, almost like a headache. The left side of his body went limp. For some reason, the front and rear of his pants were wet.

Meissner withdrew the hook. Nigel felt a mass of something moving down his nasal cavity. He felt relief when the doctor raised the instrument. A glob of mass hung from the end. What was it? Meissner dropped the wad into the oil jar along with the other matter, then inserted the hook a third time.

Nigel felt an intense discomfort as the hook entered his skull again. It went farther back this time, pushing to the back of his brain. The chamber they were in suddenly changed size, becoming…. Smaller? Larger? He could not tell. When Meissner twirled around the hook, Nigel's vision blurred. His right leg twitched as the doctor pulled back. It stuck somewhere near the front of his head. Meissner yanked it several times.

An explosion of memories flashed through Nigel's thoughts. His boyfriend in college, a young rugby playing whose name escaped him. Ashley, his older sister, ten years old, picking on him for being smart. He as a small child lost in the woods crying for help. Two older boys beating him up in the bathroom, calling him names that made no sense to him now.

As suddenly as the influx of memories began, Nigel's mind went blank as the hook exited. Confusion filled his few remaining thoughts. What was happening to him? Who was he? Why was he here? Nigel involuntarily coughed, spewing up a red liquid on the man hovering over him. Maybe this man wanted to help him.

The man inserted the thing in his nose again. Or was it the first time? No, he recalled feeling the same sensation before. Only this time, the man spoke to him. Or did he? His lips moved, but Nigel could not distinguish the words. The man twisted the metal thing again. Nigel's brain exploded in a display of colors and sensations, overpowering what few senses remained before his mind went blank.

✦　✦　✦

MEISSNER PAUSED. THE last removal of the hook had dragged out remnants of torn brain matter that dropped across Nigel's jaw. He disposed of the tissue in the oil jar and examined his friend. Nigel lay motionless, his eyes open and vacant but still showing some semblance of life. Meissner hoped Nigel had not suffered too much.

He continued probing until the hook no longer came back with matter. What remained were the portions in the lower rear of the cranium where the instrument could not reach, the area that needed to be liquified and drained. A quick assessment of the contents of the jar indicated he had removed eighty percent of Nigel's brain. His research had been a success. He had removed the brain using the method performed during mummification in later dynasties and had witnessed the procedure first-hand. Kammler's expedition had allowed him to answer many mysteries about Ancient Egypt. Once the party had returned to their timeline, Meissner would undertake a few archaeological tours of Giza and "uncover" these secrets, advancing the world's knowledge about the Pharaohs by hundreds of years and allowing him to become the world's leading Egyptologist.

Meissner stepped over to Nigel's body and placed two fingers on the man's carotid artery. A weak pulse pumped through his veins. Meissner checked his eyes. They showed no signs of conscious thought. The man merely existed, every part of his brain that made him human removed. Only the primordial sections remained, keeping him functioning with as much rational thought as a vegetable. He had hoped Nigel would not survive the procedure. Well, without a means of life support, Nigel would not last much longer. At least in his current state, he would not suffer.

Five Egyptians burst into the chamber. Four surrounded Meissner as the fifth walked over to the table and examined Nigel. He spun around to face Meissner, fury in his eyes as he yelled in Ancient Egyptian, a dead language that Meissner could not understand.

"What have you done? You defiled the sacred chamber and killed a man while doing so."

Ankhmare seethed with rage. This time the friends of the Star Travelers had gone too far. "Take him away. Then have someone clean up this miss. I'll tell the vizier what happened."

Chapter Thirty-Four

MARIA PACED AROUND her tent. In less than twelve hours, the expedition would be back in Germany. If what the Americans told her was true, Kammler would be successful, the Third *Reich* would win the war, and evil would encompass Europe. She could not live with that on her conscience.

The victory celebration had begun half an hour ago and grew louder, meaning the SS soldiers had been drinking. Good. That would make them less capable of defending themselves. When Maria heard Kammler begin his speech, she realized this would be her best opportunity to free Evans and put an end to this.

Maria couldn't leave through the main entrance because someone would spot her. She walked over to the rear of the tent, lay prone, and crawled under the covering. Once outside, she made her way into the desert so no one would spot her and circled back to the mud hut used as their jail cell. Approaching from the rear, she made her way between the twin huts.

Hans noticed her immediately. A confused expression washed over his face. "*Fraulein* Orsic, what are you doing here? You're confined to quarters."

"I need to talk with the prisoners."

"I can't allow that without the *obergruppenführer*'s permission."

"Please, this will only take a moment." Maria moved toward the door.

"*Nein*." Hans jumped in front of her, his back to the prisoners. "I can't allow that. Go back to your tent now, or I'll have to report—"

Evans reached through the bars, grabbed Hans by the collar, and pulled him against the door. With the German pinned against the metal, Evans wrapped his arm around Hans' neck and choked him so the soldier could not yell for help. Dawson rushed forward and grasped Han's left arm, yanking it back so he could not use the MP40. Crane reached for the weapon, hoping to rip it out of the German's hand. Kerdoshian circled to the other side and reached for Han's right hand. Hans released the submachine gun, pulled the *Luger* from its holster, and aimed it behind him at Evans' head. Kerdoshian clutched the barrel and pointed it away from his commanding officer, holding the German's hand still. If the pistol discharged, it would bring the rest of the compound down on them.

Maria rushed forward and covered Hans' mouth with her left hand. With her right, she removed the SS dagger from its sheath on his belt. Hans' eyes widened in fear. He tried to plead with her not to do it. Maria plunged the blade into his abdomen and under his ribcage. The teenager stiffened. She withdrew the dagger and drove it under his ribcage three more times until Hans' body went limp. Stepping back, she dropped the bladed weapon onto the sand. Only then did she notice that blood covered her right hand and had splattered her clothes.

"Grab the keys," whispered Evans.

Maria yanked them from Hans' belt and unlatched the lock. Still holding the body, Evans pushed open the gate. Crane and Dawson ran out, took the corpse, and carried it back inside, placing it in the corner.

"Thanks," said Evans.

She threw her arms around Evans and hugged him tightly. "I can't believe I murdered a man."

Evans wrapped one arm around her back and cradled her head in the other. "It's okay. You had to do it."

Dawson exited with the *Luger* and MP40. He gave the latter to Evans along with the pouch of spare ammunition. Turning to Maria, he gently asked, "Can I have the keys?"

She broke her grip and handed them to Dawson, who closed and locked the gate to the hut.

"What now?" asked Kerdoshian.

"First, we have to destroy those atomic devices aboard the *Haunebu II.*"

Kerdoshian pointed to the adjacent mud hut that the Germans used to store their ammunition. "Maybe there's something in there we can use."

As Kerdoshian, Dawson, and Crane went to check, Evans used his foot to kick around the sand, covering the blood and signs of a struggle. Picking up the dagger, he held the blade and presented it to Maria.

"You might need this later."

She took the weapon and slid it between her back and her trousers.

They joined the others.

"What did you find?"

"Nothing." Kerdoshian shook his head. "They must have loaded everything aboard the saucer."

Evans thought for a moment. "Crane and I are going to take care of the SS. You three go to the ship and destroy the devices. We'll meet you there."

"You can't do it with just the two of you," protested Dawson.

"Stopping those ships from returning to Germany is the priority. The three of you have a better chance of succeeding."

"I'm going with you," said Maria.

"You stay with them."

"I have to save the *Vril Damen*. They're innocent. If we have a chance to make it out of here, they're coming with us." When Evans tried to argue, Maria cut him off. "This isn't up for debate."

Evans smiled and nodded. "Okay, you're with us. You two, destroy the *Haunebu II* at any cost."

Dawson saluted. "Yes, sir."

Kerdoshian reached out and took Maria by the hand. "Will you do me a favor?"

"What?"

He handed her the diary. "If anything happens to me, make sure this gets back. It details everything that has happened in the last few days. If we succeed in changing the timeline, this will be the only evidence of what occurred."

"I will." Maria slid it into the front pocket of her pants then zipped it closed. "Good luck."

Maria ran off after Evans and Crane.

Kerdoshian and Dawson headed for the time machines.

Chapter Thirty-Five

Evans, Maria, and Crane stayed low and circled the compound's exterior, approaching the celebration from behind the SS troop quarters. Evans hoped nobody would spot them. Their only chance of success rested in a surprise attack.

On reaching the building, they hugged the side wall and made their way to the corner. When three feet away, Evans motioned for the others to stop. He heard laughter and Germans talking. Inching his way to the edge, he peered around. Fifteen soldiers and three women sat at the benches. Evans took note of the fact there were numerous mugs of beer scattered around the table. Good. If the SS had been drinking, they'd be less efficient in fighting back.

Evans rejoined the others. "There are fifteen SS and three women. I didn't see Kammler or Gudrun."

"I know where they are." Maria's face crinkled in disgust.

"Nigel and Meissner weren't there either."

"Where are they?" asked Crane.

"I don't have a clue. As long as they're not there when we attack."

Maria clutched Evans' shoulder. "We have to safe the *Vril Damen*."

"How are we going to do that without alerting the SS?"

"Please, let me try. They don't deserve to be gunned down."

Maria had a genuine concern for her ladies. He found it admirable.

"Okay. But if the SS is tipped off, I have no choice."

"Thank you." Maria kissed Evans on the cheek then disappeared around the back of the troop quarters.

"I wish I had a weapon," said Crane.

"So do I, kid."

MARIA MADE HER way to the opposite corner of the building. If anyone spotted her, she would say she wanted to join the celebration. The worst they would do is send her back to her tent.

She peered around the corner. Fortunately, the *Vril Damen* sat at the last table, so she did not have to expose herself too much. She waited. After a few minutes, Traute glanced in her direction. Maria waved, catching her attention. She placed a finger over her lips, then held up her middle three fingers and waved for Traute to join her. Traute acknowledged with a slight nod. Maria ducked back behind the corner.

Traute stood and leaned in closer to Sigrun and Heike. "Come with me for a minute."

Herman, who sat beside Sigrun, playfully grabbed Traute's hand. "Where are you lovely ladies going? The party is only getting started."

"We're going to freshen up. Our SS soldiers deserve only the best." Traute leaned forward and flirtatiously kissed Herman's cheek, causing the *unterscharführer* to blush. "We'll be back."

Traute led the other women behind the quarters.

On seeing Maria, Sigrun asked, "What's going on?"

"I'll explain later. Trust me on this." Maria led the others back to Evans.

WHEN THE *VRIL Damen* turned the corner, Crane tapped Evans on the shoulder. "They're safe."

"Here goes nothing."

Evans stepped away from the building and raised his MP40.

FUCHS WATCHED THE three *Vril Damen* get up from the table together and leave the group. Something seemed off, though he didn't know what. Six years of combat had taught him to trust his instincts. He stood to check on them.

Out of the corner of his eyes, he detected movement at the opposite end of the building. One of the Americans emerged from around the corner, holding an MP40.

Fuchs dropped to the sand as the first rounds tore into the celebration.

A HAIL OF 9mm shells bore down on the unsuspecting troops. Those seated at the closest table with their backs to him died instantly. The rest stood and went for their weapons, only to be cut down by the gunfire. None of them had a chance to defend themselves. By the time Evans' ran out of ammunition, most of the SS had been killed or wounded.

As Evans switched out the submachine gun's magazine for a full one, Crane charged the tables, heading for the weapons left by the dead SS. Maria and the *Vril Damen* followed. Crane neared the closest table as a German soldier stood, holding a *Mauser*. Crane dived onto the sand and crawled toward an MP40.

WHEN THE FIRING stopped, Fuchs knew he had only a few seconds before the American reloaded. Grabbing the closest weapon, a *Mauser*, he jumped up and ran for the opposite corner of the quarters, firing indiscriminately at the Americans. They dove for cover, including the traitorous *Vril Damen* who accompanied them. He would deal with those bitches later.

Right now, he had to make certain *Obergruppenführer* Kammler was safe.

EVANS DOVE ONTO the sand when the German popped up and aimed. The first round missed his head by inches.

Crane picked up the MP40, stood, and fired back. Because his target was moving, his shots failed to hit home. The German fired a round that struck the table, ricocheting off and grazing Crane's right arm. Crane aimed and pulled the trigger. The German had already disappeared around the building. Crane succeeded in blasting away chunks of mud from the façade of the SS quarters.

Evans moved alongside the private. "Are you okay?"

"I'm fine, sir. The bastard caught me by surprise."

Evans glanced over his shoulder. Maria and the *Vril Damen* lay on the sand. Luckily, none had been hit.

"Should we go after him?" asked Crane.

"I will. I need you to take the ladies to *Die Glocke* and keep them safe."

"We can take care of ourselves," said Traute.

"Are you sure?"

Traute reached down and picked up an MP40. She withdrew the magazine, made sure it contained rounds, and reinserted it. She pulled back the slide and loaded a bullet in the chamber, then switched off the safety.

"I'm convinced." Evans smiled and turned to Maria. "How many more soldiers are there?"

"There were twenty in total. Fuchs escaped. The remaining four guard the time machines. And there's Kammler and Gudrun."

"Good. The odds are now even. Any idea what happened to Meissner and Nigel?"

"They headed off to the pyramid an hour ago and haven't come back yet," said Heike.

"Shit." Evans thought for a moment. He hated leaving the two men behind. God only knows how that would affect the timeline. "Crane, stay here. If they show up, send them to *Die Glocke*. After fifteen minutes, head for the *Haunebu* II and see if Kerdoshian and Dawson need help."

"Yes, sir."

"Maria, take your girls to *Die Glocke* and wait for us."

Maria shook her head. "I'm going with you. I want to save Gudrun."

"After everything she's done to you?" asked Sigrun.

"I have to try at least. We're better than the SS." She switched her attention to Evans.

He knew better than to argue. "Fine, stay close to me. Everyone, grab a weapon."

Heike took a *Mauser* and Sigrun an MP40.

"What about you?" Evans asked of Maria.

"I hate those things." She smiled at him flirtatiously. "Besides, you'll protect me."

"You're with me." Evans turned to the *Vril Damen*. "Will you be okay with the guards?"

"Don't worry," answered Traute. "We can sweet talk our way past them."

"Do you know how to operate *Die Glocke*?"

"There's a green button we push that will send us back to our timeline."

"If we're not there in thirty minutes, get out of here."

"We're not leaving you behind," Sigrun protested.

"If we're not there in thirty minutes, we're probably dead. Now go."

The three women headed off into the desert.

Evans walked over to Crane and leaned in, speaking softly. "When we're gone, dispose of the wounded."

"You mean kill them?"

"I know it sounds cruel, but if any of them survives and are taken prisoner, they could alter the timeline. We can't risk that."

"Yes, sir."

Evans extended his hand. "Good luck."

The private shook it. "Take care of yourself, sir."

Evans and Maria set off for Kammler's tent.

DIETRICH LEANED AGAINST one of the landing struts of the *Haunebu II* and wiped the sweat from his forehead. "This is *scheisse.*"

"We've done guard duty before." Jochen stood fifteen feet away in the shade provided by the ship, his MP40 hanging off his shoulder.

"Yeah, but while everyone else is having a party. Why do we always get—"

A familiar sound caught their attention, but one they did not anticipate hearing in Egypt.

"Is that…?"

Dietrich unslung the *Mauser* from his shoulder. "It's gunfire. And it's coming from camp."

"What's going on?"

"How the fuck should I know?"

Another burst emanated from the compound.

"Go check it out," ordered Dietrich.

"Fuchs ordered us to stay here until our relief arrives."

"We need to know what's going on in case we have to get the weapons out of here." When Jochen didn't budge, Dietrich barked, "Move!"

Jochen ran off toward the compound.

A QUARTER OF a mile to the east, Wilhelm and Erwin watched *Die Glocke* when they heard the battle erupt inside camp. The two men stared at each other, confused.

"That's gunfire," said Erwin.

"I'm not deaf, asshole."

"Do you think the Americans escaped?"

"How should I know?"

Erwin hesitated. "Should we go help them?"

"Kammler would have us executed if we abandon our posts. We'll wait here and see what happens."

HEMIUNU ENJOYED A leisurely dinner with his wife and two children when a loud noise came from outside.

"Is that thunder?" asked his daughter.

"We're not expecting rain, dear." His wife stared at Hemiunu, uncertainty in her eyes.

Hemiunu had no idea what caused the sound. The noise was violent and unfamiliar. All he knew for certain was that it came from the outsider's camp. *What now?* he thought.

Someone knocked on the exterior of his hut. "Come in."

Ankhmare entered and bowed. The man had a concerned expression. "I'm sorry to interrupt your—"

Hemiunu waved off his subordinate. "What's going on?"

"It seems the outsiders are fighting amongst themselves."

"Are our people in danger?"

"I don't think so, vizier."

"Spread the word for everyone to stay indoors, then go find out what is happening."

"Of course, vizier."

Hemiunu noticed the expression on his subordinate's face worsen. "Is there anything else?"

"Yes, vizier. Two of the outsiders invaded the sacred chamber where we prepare the bodies for mummification. One of the original outsiders killed one of the newcomers. He removed his brain with a hook."

Hemiunu slammed his fists on the table with such force that everything shook. Terrified, his two children ran to their mother for comfort.

"This blasphemy cannot be tolerated! Punish the intruder and make certain he suffers."

"Of course, vizier. How do you want me to punish him?"

"I leave that up to you, Ankhmare. Just do not let the outsiders or the Star Travelers know about it. And bury the other corpse deep in the desert."

Ankhmare bowed and exited the residence.

Hemiunu took several deep breaths to calm himself before focusing on his family. "Please forgive my outburst."

"That's okay, father," replied his son, who still hugged his mother.

"I'll be so happy to be rid of the outsiders."

ABOARD THE MOTHER ship, an Anunnaki warrior made his way to the command center. On entering, he noticed the commander seated on his chair overlooking the bridge. The subordinate knew bad news was never received well by the commander, but he needed to be informed about recent developments. The Anunnaki made his way over and snapped to attention.

"Leader?"

"Yes?"

"We detected a discharge of weapons from inside the human's compound. It seems the newcomers are engaged in battle with those who arrived two weeks ago."

The commander stared at his subordinate for a moment and nodded his head.

"What should we do, Leader?"

"Nothing."

"What about the devices, Leader?"

"My orders were to provide the devices to the humans. What they do with them is not our concern. Neither are their internal affairs. We must concentrate on our mission, which is assisting in the building of the pyramid. Keep me informed of what happens to the humans. That is all."

The Anunnaki warrior departed.

KAMMLER SAT AT his table sipping on wine as Gudrun did an exotic strip tease in front of him, or as exotic as one could perform while wearing an *Afrika Korps* uniform. The dance she performed was nowhere near as arousing as the humiliation she put herself through to gain his confidence. He enjoyed women who degraded themselves to be close to those who possessed power and influence. Upon his return to Germany in the morning, he would become the most influential person in the *Reich* second only to Hitler.

Gudrun had removed her brassiere, dangling it enticingly, when gunfire broke out from somewhere in the compound. Kammler jumped up and shoved her out of the way. She stood to one side, her arms clutched across her naked breasts. The hurt expression in her eyes gave way to bewilderment as more gunfire broke out.

Kammler wrapped his belt containing the holster for his *Luger* around his waist.

A moment later, Fuchs burst into the tent. He did not notice Gudrun half-naked. "*Herr Obergruppenführer*. The Americans escaped and attacked my men."

"How many survived?"

"I'm the only one."

"Where are the Americans now?"

"Still at the celebration. I need to get you to the *Haunebu II*."

Gudrun slipped her bra over her shoulders. "Let me get dressed."

"We don't have time," said Fuchs. "The Americans could be here any second."

"Meet us at the ship," said Kammler.

Gudrun started to protest, but the two men had already

exited.

Once outside, Fuchs noticed the commander of the Americans and the traitor Maria approaching the tent one hundred feet away.

He raised his *Mauser* and fired.

Chapter Thirty-Six

KERDOSHIAN AND DAWSON spotted the top of the *Haunebu II* on the other side of a sand dune. Both men fell prone and climbed to the top until they had a better view. One SS soldier stood guard, crouched behind one of the landing struts.

"There's only one," said Dawson. "He should be easy to take out."

"Not with him having a *Mauser*. And we don't know if there are any more inside."

"Shit." Dawson thought for a moment. "I can circle around and sneak up on him from behind. Give me ten minutes and then distract him."

"I can do that."

Dawson patted the sergeant on the shoulder before crawling down the dune and making his way behind the saucer.

CRANE WENT FROM one German to the other, checking their pulses to ensure they were dead. Every few seconds, he would pause and scan the area to make certain no one snuck up on him.

The seventh German he came to was still alive, gasping for air from a chest wound that had punctured a lung. The pale pallor of his skin and the amount of blood loss indicated he would not survive much longer.

The soldier coughed up blood. "*Bitte hilf mir.*"

Crane took the German's hand in his own and squeezed gently. The soldier smiled and closed his eyes.

"*Viele dank.*"

A minute passed before the German coughed again, a vicious spasm. Blood flowed from his mouth and his body went limp. Crane felt for a pulse, but there was none. He released the man's hand and continued checking the bodies.

EVANS SAW KAMMLER and Fuchs emerge from the tent. He went to raise his MP40, but Fuchs had gotten the drop on him. Diving to his right, Evans pushed Maria onto the sand and covered her with his body. The first bullet missed by several feet.

Not wanting to give Fuchs a second chance, Evans rolled off Maria and fired his MP40 where the German stood. Fuchs and Kammler had already made their break toward *Haunebu II.* Fuchs fired a second shot that missed before the two men disappeared behind the *Vril Damen*'s tent. Rather than give chase, Evans crawled over to Maria.

"Are you okay?"

"Just bruised." Maria stood and brushed the sand off her. "Go after Kammler."

"Are you sure?"

"Yes. You have to make sure he doesn't take those devices back to our timeline."

"I'll meet you at *Die Glocke.*" Leaning closer, Evans kissed her on the lips. She did not resist.

Evans raced off after Kammler.

Maria reached behind her. The SS dagger was still wedged between her back and her trousers. She hoped she wouldn't need it.

Taking a deep breath, she entered Kammler's tent.

THE *VRIL DAMEN* approached *Die Glocke.* Wilhelm rushed out into the desert to greet them.

"Are you ladies all right? What the hell is going on?"

"It's terrible." Traute broke down in tears as Wilhelm led them back to the time machine. "The Americans escaped and killed everyone at camp. They're going after Kammler. We were lucky to get out alive."

"What about Gudrun and Maria?"

"We don't know what happened to them." Traute grabbed Wilhelm by the right arm. "You have to help."

Wilhelm shook his head. "We're under orders not to leave *Die Glocke*."

"You have to help. Everyone's in danger."

Erwin eyed Traute suspiciously. "But you said everyone was killed."

She hesitated. "I mean everyone who's still alive."

Erwin's right hand moved to the trigger housing on his MP40. "How exactly did you escape?"

Sigrun stepped to one side and fired ten rounds into Erwin's stomach, practically cutting the soldier in half.

Wilhelm jerked his arm free of Traute's grasp and stepped back, raising his submachine gun. Before he could fire, Sigrun gunned him down.

"Why did you do that?" yelled Heike.

"They were on to us."

"What's done is done." Traute grabbed Erwin by the collar and tried dragging him away, but the body weighed too much. "Help me move them away from the ship."

KERDOSHIAN CHECKED HIS watch. Dawson had been gone for thirteen minutes. Time to cause a distraction.

Standing, he waved toward the guard. "Hey, asshole. Over here."

As expected, the German was not the wait-and-see type. He raised the MP40 and fired.

Kerdoshian dropped behind the dune and scurried several

yards to his left. The bullets chewed up the sand around him, but luckily none found their mark. He popped up and fired three rounds. Two missed. One ricocheted off the strut, causing the German to flinch. He shifted position and let loose another burst toward Kerdoshian, who had hit the sand a moment earlier. The bullets churned up more sand around him.

Kerdoshian stayed low and moved to his right.

Hurry up, Dawson, he thought. *My luck won't last forever.*

DAWSON HAD CREPT to within a hundred feet of the saucer when the distraction began. He rushed forward and took up a position by the strut directly behind the German. Kerdoshian popped up a third time and the German fired, emptying his weapon. Dawson saw his chance.

As the German switched out magazines, Dawson attacked. The German heard Dawson approaching but not in enough time to defend himself. Dawson rammed his knee into the soldier's temple, knocking him onto the sand. Despite the blow to the head, the German fought back. Dawson dropped to one knee, driving it into the German's abdomen and momentarily stunning him. Grabbing the soldier by the back of his head and jaw, Dawson twisted up and to the right, snapping his neck. The German went limp in his hands.

Dawson picked up the submachine gun and aimed it at the ramp leading onto the *Haunebu II.* "All clear."

Kerdoshian cautiously peered over the dune then ran down to join Dawson.

"Now what?" asked Dawson.

"Now we figure out a way to destroy those devices. Come on."

The two men made their way up the ramp.

GUDRUN IGNORED THE gunfire outside the tent, more

concerned with getting dressed and joining Kammler for the trip home. She had slipped on her bra and boots and had started putting on her shirt when the curtains opened.

"I knew you'd come back for... oh, it's you."

Maria stood by the flap leading into the tent.

"What do you want?"

"To come back to our original timeline with us. The rest of the *Vril Damen* are waiting at *Die Glocke*."

"You released the Americans, didn't you?"

Maria ignored the question. "Come with me. You're still one of us."

"Why do you want this expedition to fail?" Gudrun buttoned her shirt. "You saw what happened at the end of the war. The rape of women and children. The mass murders. The destruction of Germany. Do you want that timeline to continue?"

"Of course not." Maria stepped closer to Gudrun. "But Germany got what it deserved. If we're successful, the new timeline will be even worse. Millions will die, and no one will be able to stop it."

"Who told you that? The Americans?"

"Yes."

"And you believed them?" snapped Gudrun. "You've gone soft. You saved the *Reich*. You gave us a chance to undo the horrors of the war and snatch victory from the jaws of defeat, and now you're willing to throw it all away because you fell for the American's propaganda."

"Please come with us." Maria moved closer.

"No." Gudrun backed away and made her way to the table. "I'm in charge of the *Vril Damen*. You can't order me around anymore."

"It's over, Gudrun. There's no more *Vril Damen*. There's no more *Reich*. We lost the war. You have to accept that."

"No, it's not. We still have a chance for victory." Gudrun grabbed her gun belt from the table, withdrew the *Luger*, and aimed it at Maria. "I won't betray my country like you're doing."

Maria ducked to the right as Gudrun pulled the trigger. The bullet whizzed past her. Rushing forward, Maria body checked Gudrun. Both women fell onto the sand. Gudrun tried to raise the pistol. Maria grasped Gudrun's wrist in her left hand and twisted. The brunette cried out and released her grip on the Luger. Maria leaned over and pushed the weapon out of reach.

When she did, Gudrun punched her in the chest, knocking the wind out of Maria. Gudrun rolled over, pinning Maria. Gudrun smashed her right knee into Maria's crotch, momentarily stunning her. In those precious seconds, Gudrun straddled Maria's chest, wrapped both hands around the woman's throat, and pressed her thumbs against Maria's larynx, strangling her.

Maria clawed at Gudrun's arms, her nails ripping into the skin. The brunette would not loosen her grip. Hatred and anger filled her eyes, and the slightest trace of a smile pierced her lips. Maria struggled to inhale but could not. Her mind grew fuzzy and her vision narrowed. She had only a few seconds of life left.

Reaching behind her back, Maria grabbed the SS dagger. She placed the weapon between herself and Gudrun. The latter was so intent on killing her opponent she never noticed. Maria placed the dagger on Gudrun's right arm halfway between the wrist and elbow then sliced. The blade went from one arm to the other, cutting two deep gashes through the skin. Gudrun loosened her hold around Maria's neck.

Bringing up her leg, she kicked Gudrun in the back, knocking her to the side. Gasping for air, Maria rolled onto her hands and knees and scrambled across the sand, hoping to get to the *Luger* before Gudrun did. When she reached it, Maria clutched it between both hands, rolled over, and aimed.

Gudrun stood in the middle of the tent, her arms extended

in front of her. She stared at them in shock. Blood flowed from the twin cuts and the claw marks, running down past the wrists and dripping off her fingers. Nothing spurted from the wounds, so no arteries had been cut. She raised her eyes and focused on Maria.

Maria wrapped her finger around the trigger. "Please don't make me shoot you."

Gudrun pressed her wounded arms tightly against her stomach and ran out of the tent. Maria struggled to her feet and followed, pausing at the tent flap. Gudrun ran off into the desert in the direction of the *Haunebu II*. She had made her choice. Maria wished her friend well.

Still holding the *Luger*, Maria headed for *Die Glocke*.

EVANS STAYED A safe distance behind Kammler and Fuchs, far enough away to keep them in sight but not close enough to be within range of the *Mauser*. The German rifle could throw a bullet a good hundred yards farther than his MP40, making him an easy target. Being the desert, there was not a lot of cover for him to sneak up on the two SS officers. He bided his time and tried to stay out of sight. Once they reached the *Haunebu II*, he would hopefully meet up with Kerdoshian and Dawson. Then the odds would be better.

"DON'T LOOK BEHIND us," Fuchs warned Kammler. "One of the Americans is following us."

"I noticed him shortly after we left camp." The *obergrup-penführer* seemed unfazed by the situation. "He poses no immediate threat."

"He might if we run into the other Americans. I want to take him out."

"Do you think you can?"

Fuchs motioned to the dune ahead of them. "Once we top

the crest, I can use it as cover to ambush him."

"Don't take too long."

When the two topped the dune, Kammler continued ahead. Fuchs waited until he was out of sight of the American, crouched low, and made his way two hundred feet to the right. He laid down and crawled to the crest, pushing the sand aside to create a makeshift foxhole. Exposing only the top of his head, he peered out over the desert. The American remained on the trail, oblivious to him.

Fuchs raised the *Mauser*, moving cautiously so as not to give away his presence, and aimed. He steadied his arms in the sand and waited, centering the sites on the American's chest. When the American closed to within one hundred yards, Fuchs inhaled deep, held his breath, and squeezed the trigger.

The sound of the shot rang out across the desert. A cloud of blood erupted from the American's shoulder, and he fell over backward onto the sand. Fuchs set his sight on the body, but the American did not move. After waiting thirty seconds, he crawled to his feet and raced off after Kammler.

The *obergruppenführer* had paused and stared at Fuchs.

"I assume you were successful."

"Yes. One more problem out of the way."

HERMAN SLOWLY CAME around. He felt sand against his face and a throbbing in his right shoulder. The last thing he remembered before passing out was enjoying the celebration with his comrades and Traute kissing him on the cheek, followed by a cascade of gunfire that cut through the party. A bullet struck him in the shoulder, and he had passed out from the pain. He wondered what happened to the others.

Slowly opening his eyes, he saw his friends lying dead around the tables. It looked as though no one had survived the assault. An American moved along the rows, checking everyone's pulse. When he came to a soldier groaning in pain, he placed a dagger against the soldier's chest and drove it in deep, puncturing the heart. The soldier cried and spasmed before passing on. Typical for the Americans to slaughter the wounded.

Herman thought about reaching for his MP40 but knew, in his condition, he would never be able to get the drop on the American. Instead, he removed his SS dagger and clutched it in his left hand against his chest, then quietly rolled face down onto the sand.

KERDOSHIAN REACHED THE top of the ramp and paused.

Dawson followed behind him. "What is it?"

"I think we found what we're looking for."

The lower deck of the saucer was shiny metal, reminding Kerdoshian of the interiors of the spacecraft from those old *Flash Gordon* serials he watched as a kid at the Saturday matinee, only much more elaborately detailed. On opposite ends of the ship sat two gunner stations directly above each of the twin machine guns. They reminded the sergeant not of the hand-held positions aboard a B-17 but the remote-controlled ones used on modern B-29s. Passenger seating lined the walls between each station, six on each side for a total of twelve. Each contained a seat belt as well as pull-down body restraints like those used on roller coasters. A ladder extended from the center of the lower deck through the upper deck and into the cockpit.

What intrigued Kerdoshian most were the six wooden crates set in the center of the floor on either side of the ladder and bolted to the deck. Kerdoshian stepped over to the closest, undid the latch, and lifted the lid. Inside, held in place by a wooden frame, rested a spherical device a meter in diameter. The exterior surface was smooth. Thirty-six wires protruded from a box on top, connecting to equally spaced locations along the device.

"What the hell are those things?" asked Dawson.

"They're called atomic bombs. There's enough firepower in one of these to destroy a city."

"Can you disarm them?"

"If I do that, the Germans will only figure out a way to repair them. I have to disable them permanently."

"Do you know how to do that?"

"I'll need some time to figure it out."

"Do what you have to. I'll stand watch." Dawson headed for the ramp, pausing in front of one of the gunner stations. "Too bad Crane wasn't here. We could hold off an army with these."

"I assume they're more technical than merely point and shoot."

"You're probably right." Dawson frowned and made his out of the saucer.

Kerdoshian examined the device. He tried to remember the limited intelligence reports he had read about Germany's atomic weapons program. The box on the side with the protruding wires was the arming and fusing system. Setting off one of the devices would be easy enough and would solve the problem of disabling them, along with everything else in the process. However, doing so ran the risk of damaging the pyramid and killing countless Egyptians. They would succeed in preventing the Germans from winning World War II, but with serious alterations to the current timeline that in the long run would create more problems than it solved. He ruled out that option.

Disabling the atomic devices was not enough. The Anunnaki could easily replace them with new ones. They needed to irreparably damage or destroy the *Haunebu II* so it could never return to its original timeline. Only the total failure of Kammler's expedition would ensure Allied victory.

As he considered his alternatives, Kerdoshian recalled one piece of intelligence that not only solved his dilemma but killed two birds with one stone. He rummaged around the lower deck until he found a screwdriver, then removed the cover to the arming and fusing system.

THE GUNFIRE ECHOING from the desert warned Crane the mission was not proceeding as planned. At this distance, he couldn't tell whether the trouble came from the *Haunebu II*, *Die Glocke*, or somewhere else. No matter. His buddies or the *Vril Damen*, or both, needed his help.

Crane sped up the disposal of any surviving German soldiers, foregoing niceties and not bothering to check to see if they were alive or dead. With each one the private came to, he jabbed the SS dagger into their heart and moved on to the next.

Reaching the last row, Crane ignored the first body. A bullet had struck the soldier in the forehead and blown off the back of its skull. No way anyone could survive that. He moved to the next corpse, which lay face down with a bullet wound in its right shoulder. Crane placed a hand on the shoulder and flipped the body over. Only two more after this and then—

"*Verbrecher!*"

The German soldier yelled and jabbed at Crane with an SS dagger clutched in his left hand. His aim was off due to his awkward position, yet he still managed to slice the blade along Crane's face, ripping a deep gash along his right cheek and gouging out a chunk of his ear. Caught off guard, Crane fell back onto the sand, releasing his MP40 in the process. The German kicked the weapon under the table, rolled onto his chest, and reached for his submachine gun a few feet away.

He might have made it if not for the wounded arm.

Crane jumped up and raced over to the German, slamming his boot on the soldier's left ankle. The shattering of bone was accompanied a moment later by a shriek from the German. Crane leaned forward, reaching for the MP40. Despite the excruciating pain radiating up his leg, the German drove the dagger up to the hilt into Crane's gut and twisted. Crane nearly passed out from the agony as he felt the blade cut through his intestines and turn them into chopped meat with the twist of the dagger. When the German withdrew the weapon, the front of Crane's shirt and trousers instantly became soaked, but he could not be sure whether from blood, feces, or both. Crane realized he would die in the next few minutes.

But not before taking out this son of a bitch first.

Positioning his left elbow over the German's face, Crane let his upper body grow limp. As his body fell forward, the extended elbow crashed into the soldier's temple, stunning him. Crane lay down behind the soldier, placing both knees on his lower back and wrapping the palm of his hands under the German's chin. With one swift yet excruciating move, Crane rolled onto his back and raised his legs, lifting the soldier into the air. Crane pulled back on the German's chin. Still holding the dagger in his left hand, the soldier stabbed behind him, but from his angle, could do no more than scrape the blade along Crane's skin. Crane jerked his hands with his remaining strength.

Bones snapped.

The German soldier went limp.

Crane rolled to one side again, allowing the body to slide onto the sand, then rested a minute. His breathing became quick and heavy, and he felt light-headed. Crane forced himself to stand, struggling to climb to his feet. He couldn't afford to rest. He needed to… needed to… what? That's right. Evans waited for him back at *Die Glocke* so they could return to Washington.

Stumbling out into the desert, Crane headed straight, no longer remembering what he was doing. His heart pounded in his chest, critically increasing the loss of blood. He breathed fast and shallow, which only added to the feeling of lethargy overtaking him. Crane barely made it a hundred feet before he dropped to his knees, telling himself he would rest only for a few moments.

A few seconds later, Crane collapsed face-first onto the desert, dead.

ANKHMARE AND HIS two workers topped the dune overlooking the outsiders' encampment in time to witness the final moments of the fight between Crane and Herman. Ankhmare stared aghast at the scene before him. More than a dozen butchered bodies lay strewn about, staining the sand crimson in their blood. And in the middle of it all, two men engaged in a life-or-death battle, one of them from the original group of outsiders and the other from those who joined them a few days ago.

"It's barbaric," whispered Asim.

"The outsiders are barbarians," answered Omari. "They're not civilized like us."

Ankhmare watched the battle unfold until one of the outsiders snapped the neck of the other. He shook his head and mumbled, "If this is our future, then civilization is doomed."

"What was that?" asked Omari.

"Nothing." Ankhmare waved him off.

They watched the remaining outsider stagger off into the desert and collapse not far from the encampment.

Asim headed down the slope.

"What are you doing?" snapped Ankhmare.

"We should check on the others."

"They're not our concern."

"But we can't—"

Ankhmare raised his palm. "We have been forbidden to interact with the outsiders in any manner. I will inform the vizier of what happened and have Ain request the Star Tarvelersi take care of this mess. After all, they're the ones who brought them here."

Asim bowed. "My apologies."

Ankhmare gestured for the two men to follow. "Let's return to the pyramid."

KAMMLER AND FUCHS made their way to *Haunebu II*. Every minute or so, the *standartenführer* would glance over his shoulder or scan the flanks to ensure none of the Americans were sneaking up on them. So far, they had avoided danger.

A lone figure emerged out of the twilight, approaching from the direction of the saucer. Fuchs stepped in front of Kammler to shield him and raised his *Mauser*, centering the site on the individual's heart.

"Stop! Who are you?"

"Don't shoot, *Herr Standartenführer*. It's me. Jochen."

Fuchs lowered the rifle. "What the fuck are you doing out here? You should be guarding the *Haunebu II*."

"Dietrich is doing that. He sent me to find out what's going on and to see if I can help."

"Don't bother." Kammler pushed past Jochen and continued to the *Haunebu II*. "We're returning to our timeline."

"What about the others?" asked Jochen.

"Everyone else is dead. Now keep up unless you want to be left behind."

MARIA TRUDGED THROUGH the desert, grateful she had not run into Kammler or Fuchs. Ahead of her, rising above the top of a dune, sat the top of *Die Glocke*. She had never been so excited to see that infernal machine.

When she crested the dune, she noticed that Traute, Heike, and Sigrun were already there. Good. Once Evans and the others showed up, they could get out of here.

Traute spun around and raised the MP40 at her.

"It's me, Maria."

Traute lowered the weapon. "Don't sneak up on us like

that."

Maria raced down the dune to the capsule, giving each of her ladies an uncharacteristic hug.

"Is everything okay?" asked Sigrun.

"Yeah," Maria lied. They would be once she knew Evans was alive. "I'm glad to see you."

Heike stepped forward. "What about the others?"

Kammler and Fuchs escaped and are heading for the *Haunebu II*. Evans is trying to stop them."

Traute raised an eyebrow. "What about Gudrun?"

"She decided to join Kammler." Maria left out the part about the bitch attempting to kill her.

"Things here are under control." Heike motioned with her head toward the two German soldiers lying on the sand.

"Did you have to kill them?"

Traute's tone grew stern. "We had no other choice."

Maria didn't question her friend. She wished they could have been spared. Too many people had already died because of this idiocy. And there would be more.

"What now?" asked Sigrun.

"We wait until the Americans destroy the *Haunebu II*."

"What if they can't?"

Maria lowered her eyes. There was no chance the *Vril Damen* could stop Kammler and Fuchs on their own. If they failed, the only alternative was to return to their timeline where Maria would have to deal with Kammler and Himmler.

She prayed Evans would be successful.

EVANS CAME AROUND, staring into the night sky and trying to remember what had happened. He rolled onto his right side and cried out when pain shot down his arm and through his body and back. Evans sat up and gazed over at his right shoulder, noticing the wound. It all came back to him. He had been following Kammler. Fuchs must have backtracked and sniped at him. Thank God the German was not a crack shot. Fucking stupid of him not to anticipate that.

Evans rotated his right arm. Another bolt of pain radiated from his shoulder, but at least he had full mobility, and blood didn't spurt from the wound, so the damage probably wouldn't be permanent.

He struggled to his feet and set off after the Germans, hoping he had not been unconscious so long Kammler had time to escape.

PANIC THREATENED TO overwhelm Gudrun. She wasn't concerned about anyone hunting her down. It had become quite clear that no one—the Americans, the *Vril Damen*, not even Kammler—cared about her. Her panic stemmed from being severely wounded and alone in the desert. She did not want to be stranded. She had spent the entire expedition dreaming about her triumphant return to Berlin at the side of one of the most powerful and influential men in all of Germany. Of being the head of the *Vril Damen*. Of basking in the accolades of being instrumental in the *Reich*'s ultimate victory. Now she hoped to make it to the *Haunebu II* before Kammler left her behind in this primitive culture.

Gudrun paused to rest. She could tell by the slight dizziness and loss of breath that she had lost a lot of blood, though thankfully not enough to be fatal. Pulling her arms away from her chest, she examined the wounds. The gashes on her arms were deep and painful. Blood seeped from them, but nowhere near as much as earlier. Crimson drenched the front of her *Afrika Korps* uniform. When Gudrun got back to Berlin, and if Maria made the return trip, she would ask Himmler to send the bitch to Auschwitz to suffer.

Clutching her arms tightly against her chest, Gudrun set off for the *Haunebu II*.

KAMMLER STOPPED AS they approached the dune in front of the saucer.

"What's wrong?" asked Fuchs.

"We don't know if the Americans are waiting for us." The *obergruppenführer* thought for a moment. "Jochen, wait here. Fuchs and I are going to circle to the flank. Wait five minutes and approach the saucer. If the Americans are there, provide cover so we can outflank them."

"Of course, *Herr Obergruppenführer.*"

Kammler motioned for Fuchs to follow. The two men made their way around the dune.

DAWSON CROUCHED BEHIND the landing strut, his eyes scanning the horizon. Concern grew inside of him. By now, someone should have arrived. Evans and Crane. The *Vril Damen*. Hell, even the damn Germans. He didn't like the lack of activity. It made him nervous. What if—

A figure cautiously crested the top of the dune. Dawson hunched closer to the landing strut and raised his MP40, centering the sites on the person. It wasn't one of the women, but he could not tell if the man was one of theirs or a German in the dimming light.

"*Dietrich, bist du da?*"

Definitely German.

Dawson fired. A string of bullets traced their way through the sand. The German dived behind the dune. Dawson couldn't tell if he had hit his target or if the man had jumped out of the way.

JOCHEN HIT THE ground a moment before a string of bullets rang over his head. Fuck, Kammler would have his ass for this.

Jochen rolled twenty feet to his right, stood, and fired at the American. The rounds ricocheted off the saucer's hull. He wondered if he had killed the American when another burst of submachine gun fire tore up the sand around him. Diving behind the dune, he made his way another few yards to his right. This time, rather than expose himself, he raised the MP40 above the rim and fired indiscriminately, only to be met with another volley of return fire.

He hoped Fuchs would be in position before the American got off a lucky shot.

FUCHS LAY IN the sand one hundred feet from the *Haunebu II*, his *Mauser* trained on the landing strut. He could barely make out the figure hiding behind it, knowing his position only by the muzzle blasts from his weapon.

"Why don't you shoot?" asked Kammler, who crouched a few feet behind him.

"He's concealed. I don't want to give us away until I get a clear shot."

"Hurry up."

Fuchs ignored his commanding officer. Kammler may be brilliant at his job but had never seen combat.

Jochen fired a second time from farther down the dune. The American shifted his position, slightly exposing himself. Fuchs' finger wrapped around the trigger and he inhaled. The third time the American fired, he moved around the strut enough that he exposed his back. Fuchs smiled as he pulled the trigger. A single 7.92mm bullet exited the rifle and struck the American between his shoulder blades. He collapsed into the sand, dropping the MP40.

Fuchs jumped up and raced to the saucer, keeping his rifle trained on the American who rolled around, clutching at the wound. Fuchs kicked the MP40 out of the way and leveled the *Mauser* on the American.

Kammler joined them a moment later. He stared down at the American. "It seems you failed in your mission. This time the *Reich* is victorious."

Dawson rolled over and stared at his chest. The bullet had punctured his lung. He would never survive. With nothing to lose, he raised his bloodied right hand and extended his middle finger.

"Fuck the *Reich* and fuck Hitler."

Fuchs pumped three more bullets into his chest.

Jochen ran up to them. "Good. You got him."

"No thanks to you." Kammler removed the *Luger* from his holster, placed the barrel against Jochen's temple, and fired. His body collapsed onto the sand. "Next time, don't abandon your post."

Fuchs checked the *Mauser* to make sure he still had ammunition. "Let me check inside for booby traps, then we can get out of here."

KERDOSHIAN HAD FINISHED making his adjustments to the arming and fusing system when gunshots erupted outside the saucer. He dropped the metal lid to the system inside the crate and lowered the outer cover, not bothering to latch it shut. As he made his way to the ramp, he heard voices. Dawson screamed something about fucking the *Reich* and Hitler, followed by three shots from a *Mauser*. Now it was him versus God knows how many Germans. Moving beside the opening to the ramp, he crouched down and clutched the screwdriver in his right hand, ready to make a last stand.

A few seconds later, Fuchs cautiously emerged through the opening, scanning the interior. Before Fuchs could see him, Kerdoshian lunged forward and drove the screwdriver toward his head. The German caught the movement in his peripheral vision and lurched back. The screwdriver barely missed. In one rapid motion, Fuchs dropped his rifle, grabbed Kerdoshian by the arm, and slammed his wrist on the metal rim to the opening. Kerdoshian's wrist shattered, causing him to drop the screwdriver. Rolling onto his left side, he kicked at Fuchs. The blow struck the German in the chest. Rather than being stunned by the attack, the German grabbed Kerdoshian's leg and slammed it down against the rim. Kerdoshian cried out as the tibia fractured.

"Damn Americans. You're nothing but pains in the ass." Fuchs climbed into the bay. Grabbing Kerdoshian by the collar, he lifted the American off the deck and punched him several times in the face until Kerdoshian was barely conscious. Fuchs released him. Kerdoshian slid to the metal, his face bloody, his nose broken, and several teeth shattered or knocked out.

"All clear, *Herr Obergruppenführer*."

Kammler ascended the ramp. His expression seethed with contempt and smugness. "When will the Allies learn that they can't defeat the Master Race?"

Kerdoshian tried to flip him the middle finger but had no energy.

"Should I throw him out?" asked Fuchs.

Kammler shook his head. "Secure him to one of the seats. That way, he can witness his defeat first-hand."

Kammler handed Fuchs the *Luger* and made his way up into the cockpit. Fuchs dragged Kerdoshian over to the nearest seat, belted him in, lowered the suspension bar, then used rope to tie his hands to the bar. When finished, Fuchs walked halfway down the ramp and checked outside one last time to ensure no other Americans were nearby.

At that moment, Gudrun reached the top of the dune and fell to her knees. He could tell from this distance she was severely injured. Fuchs stepped back inside and called up the ladder.

"*Herr Obergruppenführer, Fraulein* Gudrun is outside. Should I get her?"

Kammler's responded in a cold, emotionless tone. "She's expendable. Buckle up. We're going home."

As Fuchs strapped himself into the seat opposite Kerdoshian, Kammler pressed the green button to return them to their timeline.

GUDRUN FINALLY MADE it to the *Haunebu II* and dropped onto the sand. Relief washed over her. The saucer was still here. She had made it on time. Soon she would be back in Berlin and everything—

The ramp to the saucer raised. An electronic hum emanated from inside the *Haunebu II*, intensifying until Gudrun placed her hands over her ears in a desperate but futile attempt to blot out the noise. A shimmering field of electro-magnetic energy formed around the craft and expanded outward over five hundred feet. The saucer elevated several feet, the landing struts slowly rising into the hull.

"No!"

Gudrun climbed to her feet and rushed the saucer. She had to let them know they were there so they could take her along. Stumbling down the dune, she ran to the saucer.

Directly into the field of electro-magnetic energy.

Gudrun screamed in agony. Her internal organs felt as though they had been set on fire as crystals formed on every tissue. She suffered unbearable torment as the energy turned her skin, muscles, and organs into minerals. Her blood congealed and separated, clogging her veins. Gudrun fell to the ground, thrashing about as the energy ripped her life from her body. Every organ shut down—eyes, lungs, kidneys, heart, and intestines. Her mind ceased to function, momentarily locking her into an insanity that only lasted a few seconds. After a few moments of anguish, Gudrun's body went limp, her skin pale and glistening.

"FUCK!"

Evans ran forward, topping the dune in time to see Gudrun transformed from a human into a lifeless compound of minerals. Behind her, the *Haunebu II* lifted off the desert, slowly climbing into the night sky.

They had failed. Kammler was heading back to his own time with six nuclear devices that would change the course of their original history.

Evans could do nothing but stand there and watch the *Haunebu II* fly off into the altered timeline.

KAMMLER YELLED DOWN from the cockpit. "We're at five thousand feet and rising. Soon we'll be teleported back to Germany."

Kerdoshian laughed.

Fuchs sneered. "What's so funny, Negro?"

"For a Master Race, you're fucking stupid."

"What do you mean?"

"Fifteen thousand feet," Kammler yelled from the bridge.

Kerdoshian spit blood and a broken tooth onto the deck. He motioned toward the six crates. "Those things aren't dropped on a city like a regular bomb. They're detonated by atmospheric pressure."

Fuchs' eyes widened at the realization. Unbuckling himself, he shoved up the bar and ran over to the crates, noticing that one no longer had the latch secured. He lifted the lid and stared at the arming and fusing system. The bomb had armed itself. The display read 35000.

"Twenty-five thousand feet."

"Stop the ascent!" screamed Fuchs.

"You know I can't. The saucer is self-controlled."

Kerdoshian laughed again. "How does it feel to be defeated by someone you assholes consider as sub-human."

"Fuck you." Fuchs aimed the pistol at Kerdoshian.

He never had a chance to pull the trigger.

At thirty-five thousand feet, the barometric switch in the fusing system activated and switched on the firing system. An electric current ran through the thirty-two cables. Beneath the surface, thirty-two symmetrical explosive plates detonated simultaneously. The shock wave pushed inward, condensing the plutonium core into a critical mass and initiating a chain reaction. Within a millisecond, the device exploded with the force of fifty thousand tons of TNT, vaporizing the *Haunebu II* and its occupants.

THE CONCUSSION FROM the blast blew Evans off the dune. He landed hard on his back, the air knocked out of his lungs. It took a moment to regain his breath. Climbing to his feet, Evans stared into the sky.

A massive fireball over six hundred feet in diameter replaced the *Haunebu II*, slowly rising into the night and illuminating the desert like a sun. A rumbling sound reached his ears, like thunder only more ominous. The noise slowly subsided and the fireball dimmed until both vanished.

My God. Kerdoshian had done it. He had succeeded in stopping Kammler from returning to the altered timeline. Evans closed his eyes, saying a silent prayer for his friend. History would never know the sacrifice Kerdoshian had made.

Reality soon invaded Evans' thoughts. He had completed only half the mission. He still needed to save the *Vril Damen* and return to his timeline. Taking a moment to get his bearings, he rushed off in the direction of *Die Glocke*.

A part of Evans wondered what he would return to.

MARIA PACED NERVOUSLY. "What time is it?"

Traute glanced at her watch. "A little before seven."

"Relax." Sigrun tried to sound comforting. "Evans will be here—"

A blinding flash of light illuminated the night, so bright that the women averted their eyes. A few seconds later, the shock wave washed over them, knocking them to the ground. Then the rumbling from the detonation reached them, shaking Maria to her core. She had been in Berlin during several Allied bombing raids but had never experienced anything as frightening. For a moment, she thought the world had come to an end. When things settled down, she got to her feet.

A giant fireball rose into the night, lighting up the sky and slowly consuming itself until it burned out. An eerie silence descended over the area.

Traute stepped up to Maria and placed a comforting hand on her shoulder. "I'm sure Evans is alive."

Maria shrugged her off. "No one could survive that."

"Don't rule it out. You know how resourceful the Americans are."

"Thanks, but we know he's dead."

Sigrun hesitated before speaking. "What now?"

Maria fought back her tears. "We use *Die Glocke* to go back?"

"Get down." Heike raised the MP40 and stepped in front of the others, aiming at a figure approaching from where the *Haunebu II* used to be.

Traute and Sigrun raised their weapons and stood in front of Maria to protect her.

As the figure drew closer, it raised its left hand and waved it above his head. "Don't shoot."

"Evans!"

Maria broke away from the other girls and ran across the desert, jumping into his arms and kissing him passionately. Evans didn't break the kiss for several seconds. When he did, he held Maria close to him and hugged her. Only then did she notice the wound in his right shoulder.

"My God, you've been shot."

"It's only a flesh wound. I'll be fine."

"I'm so glad you're alive." Maria buried her head into his shoulder so he wouldn't see her crying.

"It's all over." Evans held her head against his. "We stopped them."

Traute joined them. "What about your friends?"

Evans merely shook his head.

"I'm sorry."

"Thanks. But none of us ever expected to come back from this mission."

Maria broke the embrace but still held Evans' hands. "What now?"

He motioned toward *Die Glocke*. "We go back."

"But to which timeline?" asked Traute.

"We won't know that until we get there. Come on."

They made their way to the capsule. Heike peered inside. "It only seats two."

"Some of us will have to stand."

"You can stay behind if you want," teased Sigrun.

"No way."

Evans ushered them inside, giving the seats to Maria and Traute. After settling the *Vril Damen*, he climbed in, closed the hatch, and moved over to the console.

"Are you ladies ready?"

Maria smiled and took his hand. "As you Americans say, let her rip."

Evans placed his hand on the green button and pressed.

Beneath their compartment, an electronic whir vibrated through the craft as the gyroscopic rotors switched on. The noise increased, only this time muffled by the sound-proof lining covering the exterior of the compartment. A jolt rocked *Die Glocke*. It rose off the desert until it hovered three hundred feet off the ground. The humming became louder, this time accompanied by a rocking motion. The craft accelerated at an incredible speed. Light passed by the portal so rapidly it could not form into images. Within seconds, everyone inside had passed out.

+   +   +

SEVEN EGYPTIANS ESCORTED Meissner from the pyramid. The one named Ankhmare led the group. Two others held him by the arm while the other four shoved him along every time he resisted.

"Where are you taking me?" Meissner protested.

His captors didn't respond.

They led him into the burial preparation chamber where he had murdered Nigel. Panic set in. Nothing good could come of this.

"Let go of me."

Meissner dug his heels into the sand. The six Egyptians lifted him, two on each leg and one under each shoulder, and carried him into the chamber. Once inside, they placed him on the same table at which he experimented on his friend. Meissner struggled to break free but to no avail. The two Egyptians who held his arms pressed down his shoulders while two more anchored his legs.

Ankhmare spoke in Ancient Egyptian to the other two men. They disappeared and came back a few seconds later with rope.

"I demand you let me go."

Ankhmare leaned over, his face inches from Meissner's. "You must pay for your defilement of the scared burial chamber."

Meissner could not understand the man but, from the with rage and contempt in the Egyptian's voice, he knew there would be no reasoning with him.

Ankhmare nodded to the two Egyptians with the rope who bound the German's legs.

Terror raced through Meissner's mind as he realized his fate. He tried to kick his way out, but his ankles were secured tight, succeeding only in squirming on the table. Within minutes, the Egyptians had wrapped him in rope to his waist, further restricting his movement. Four Egyptians held his arms by his side as the other two began tying his waist and abdomen.

"Help me!" Meissner's cry reverberated through the chamber.

The wrapping now reached up to his elbows. Meissner frantically struggled, succeeding only in slowing the process.

"Someone, help me!"

Ankhmare moved to the head of the table and nodded at one of the workers, who stepped over to a nearby table.

"Ankhmare?"

The Egyptian glared at him.

"Please let me go. I promise I'll be leaving soon and won't come back."

Ankhmare averted his gaze.

The Egyptian returned with a pair of tongs and a knife. Meissner's eyes widened. Dear God, no.

The Egyptian tried to open Meissner's mouth. The German bit down hard, grinding his teeth until they ached. A second Egyptian squeezed together his nostrils. Meissner tried not to breathe but could only hold out for so long. When he parted his lips to breathe, the first Egyptian plunged the tongs inside his mouth, grabbed his tongue, and pulled it out. Ankhmare leaned over Meissner, the knife in his right hand. With a sardonic smile on his face, he sawed through the tissue.

Meissner howled, his screams drowning out when blood flowed down his throat. He gagged and spit. Blood streamed down his cheeks. The cutting stopped but the agony remained. Meissner watched as the Egyptian crossed over to a fire pit and tossed the severed appendage into the flames.

Meissner no longer resisted, too busy trying not to drown in his blood. The Egyptians finally finished their work, tying everything except the Egyptologist's head so he could bear witness to his fate. Once finished, they shrouded Meissner's body in sheepskin, an item the culture considered unclean, signifying for anyone who found the body later that this person had committed some terrible sin. The final indignity.

With the process completed, the Egyptians picked up Meissner and carried him into the desert. They walked for close to thirty minutes until Meissner could no longer see the pyramid or his compound. Eventually, the party dropped him into a hole six feet deep. Meissner tried to beg for mercy, but his words, garbled as they were, fell on deaf ears. Panic overwhelmed him. He attempted to escape but could not stand, thrashing around the bottom of his grave like a crippled rat.

Meissner's last conscious thought was of his captors pushing the sand back in on him, burying him alive.

Chapter Thirty-Seven

?????
?????

AJOLT JARRED Evans awake. Pain rippled from his shoulder, aggravated by nausea. He opened his eyes and stared into the darkness. At first, he could not focus on anything, his vision blurred by dizziness. Evans closed his eyes for a few moments until his senses settled, then opened them again.

The lights inside *Die Glocke* had gone out. The capsule no longer moved. It sat motionless, tilted at a thirty-degree angle.

Evans wondered where they had landed.

And when.

"Is everyone okay?"

A moan came from the other side of the capsule, followed by Heike saying, "My head hurts, and I feel like throwing up. Other than that, I'm fine."

"I think my arm's broken," added Sigrun.

Evans reached out and placed his hand on a soft, warm shoulder. "Maria, how are you?"

"I'm Traute." She giggled. "I feel like I've been in a car wreck."

He removed his hand quickly. "Anything broken? Any internal injuries?"

"No."

"What happened?" Maria asked from the other side of the capsule.

"I think we crash landed."

"Great."

"Stay still," he said. "I'll get us out."

Evans made his way to the hatch and undid it, prepared for a squad of SS soldiers to be circling them. When he pushed it open, he stared out into a forest. Wherever they were, it was dusk. The sun had begun its descent below the horizon and night rapidly closed in from the east.

Once outside, Evans helped the *Vril Damen* onto the grass, being extra careful with Heike. The five of them looked around.

"Are we outside of Hamburg?" asked Traute.

"It doesn't look like the forest near Hamburg." Heike cradled her broken arm against her chest. "For all we know, we could be somewhere in Bavaria."

"Or Russia," joked Sigrun.

Maria grimaced. "Don't even think that."

"We're not going to answer our questions standing here." Evans turned to the ladies. "Let's go before someone comes to investigate."

"Just a minute." Maria reached down to the pocket on her sand-colored pants and removed a reddish-tan leather notebook with an elastic cord wrapped around it. "Kerdoshian told me to give this to you."

Evans thumbed through it. Kerdoshian had kept a detailed account of their entire mission from Valthor's arrival at Roswell up until the time they had escaped. Damn. He'd miss that man.

He handed it back to Maria. "You keep it for now."

"What if something happens to me?"

Evans clasped her hand and squeezed gently. "You'll be safe with me."

He led the way through the forest, hoping they didn't run into anyone until they figured out their location. Four women in *Afrika Korps* uniforms and an American soldier with a gunshot wound wouldn't blend in well in any environment.

Sirens sounded in the distance, drawing closer. Evans urged the women to pick up their pace, worried at first that the local authorities might be searching for them. However, as the commotion centered behind them, he realized they were more interested in the crash site than whoever walked away from it.

After nearly an hour of hiking, they emerged from the tree line. A field opened in front of them. Half a mile ahead sat a small town, if you could describe a handful of buildings scattered over an area of half a square mile a town. Lights shined from the square so, wherever they were, the population did not observe blackout restrictions. The buildings looked more American than European. None of this helped in pinpointing their position. If they had landed back in America, they could be anywhere within the forty-eight states.

Two roads ran along the left and right, converging in the center of town. Evans opted to cross the field, wanting to delay contact with the locals until he knew more about them. Approaching from behind the largest building to provide cover, they passed through an alley between it and a service station. Thomson's Gas was painted in red lettering on the wall. Beneath it and near the corner, a weathered and torn poster of Uncle Sam pointing his finger at the viewer proclaimed I WANT YOU FOR U.S. ARMY.

An old car sat behind the building on four flat tires. Spots of rust dotted the body and undercarriage, clearly visible against the faded red and white paint. Traute walked over and ran her fingers along the right rear fender, which slightly rose off the body like the fin of a fish.

"What's this?" she asked.

Sigrun flashed her a confused look. "It's a car."

"I know that. Who designs cars like this? It's so pretentious."

Stepping into the street, they checked out their surroundings. Hadley's Cinema stood off to the right. The large, black metal letters on the marquee over the entrance read

NOW PLAYING
HARUM SCARUM
WITH
ELVIS PRESLEY

Who the hell is Elvis Presley? thought Evans.

Another building sat directly across the street from the cinema, the lights out and closed for the evening. The sign above the door read Restucci's Grocery. They waited until no one was around before crossing the street, concealing themselves in the shadows. A cardboard sign hanging inside the window read

Kecksburg PA Post Office
Open 11-3 Monday – Friday
Closed weekends

Evans breathed a sigh of relief. At least they were in the States. He could call the Army for help.

"Well, we know where we are," he said.

"Now we need to figure out when," added Maria.

A hundred feet further down the road, another building sat isolated from the others. A sign extended over the sidewalk, the name lit up in yellow lights—Gamboa's Diner. Several cars were parked out front and in the back. Talking and laughing came from inside.

"Come on." Evans headed toward the diner. "We can call for help there."

Maria stopped him. "Do you think we should? Look how we're dressed."

"Trust me. It'll be alright."

Evans wondered if maybe Maria was right the moment they stepped inside the diner. Every patron stopped talking and stared at them aghast. From the kitchen, the cook peered through the serving window to see what caused the disturbance. The lit cigarette fell from his lips onto the grill.

Mustering the most pleasant voice he could, Evans responded. "Hello, everyone."

The patrons went back to eating, though cautious eyes continually glanced in their direction.

Evans and the *Vril Damen* took the five seats at the end of the counter.

The waitress, a middle-aged brunette with an infectious smile, overcame her initial shock and came up to them. She wore a nametag with the name Evelyn printed on it.

"Lordy, what happened to you?"

Evans pointed toward his wounded shoulder. "We've been through a lot today. Can you call an ambulance? And can I use your phone to contact the Army?"

"Sorry, hon. We don't have long-distance service here. But I'll call the hospital in Pittsburgh and have them send someone for you."

"Thanks," Maria replied.

Evans glanced around. Every patron had stopped talking again and stared at them. When he waved, they all went back to eating.

Evelyn came back a few minutes later, clutching five glasses of water. She placed them in front of the time travelers.

"You look as though you could use a drink."

Evans smiled self-consciously. "We don't have any money."

"They're on the house, sweetie. Two ambulances are on the way. The operator is calling the Army and will have someone meet you there."

"Thanks."

A folded newspaper sat on the end of the counter. Evans pulled it over and spread it out. The headline of the *Pittsburgh Tribune-Review* discussed Pope Paul VI signing the Second Vatican Council.

"What's the date?" asked Maria.

Evans checked. It read December 9, 1965.

He passed the newspaper to Maria. "Now we know when we are."

Epilogue

Present Day

THE TWO FBI agents sat on the sofa opposite Evans. Both men had their gaze locked on him, Brady appearing as if he wanted to believe the story, but it sounded too farfetched. At least the younger agent kept an open mind. Carbone glared at Evans as if he was batshit crazy.

After nearly a minute of silence, Carbone asked, "Is that it?"

"Yup." Evans continued to pet Winnie, who curled up asleep on his lap. "We defeated the Germans and came home."

"Fifteen hundred miles and eighteen years later than when you left." Carbone made no effort to conceal his disbelief. "You said the machine would bring you back to the same time and location from which you left. What happened?"

Evans grinned. "*Our* time machine was supposed to return us to Roswell in July 1947."

"So why didn't you go back to Nazi Germany?"

"I don't know. Maybe the Anunnaki technology was flawed and Kammler would have wound up in central Pennsylvania with six atomic weapons. Maybe the nuclear detonation disrupted the instruments. To be honest, I don't care. We made it back safe. I don't look a gift horse in the mouth. I never saw Valthor again to ask him."

Brady leaned forward and rested his forearms on his knees. "What happened after the diner?"

"Didn't my service records contain that?"

The slightest hint of a conspiratorial grin crossed Brady's

lips. "Your service records were destroyed in 1968."

"That doesn't surprise me." Evans laughed, waking up Winnie, who looked up at his master and wagged his tail. "We were taken to a nearby hospital where the doctors set Heike's arm and patched up my shoulder. When the Army rep arrived, I gave him my name, rank, and serial number and told him to check out my story. Maria and the others made up names for themselves."

"Did he believe you?" asked Carbone.

"I didn't tell him anything. He said he'd check with the Pentagon and get back to me. Two days later, an agent from the CIA who called himself Smith arrived. I told him what had happened. Later that week, the five of us were flown to the Farm and went through two weeks of interrogation. My fingerprints checked out but, according to them, I had died at Omaha Beach in June 1944."

"So, how come your still alive?"

"The original me died in 1944. The me from the altered timeline survived and returned to 1965. You'll have to ask Valthor or the Golden Sun about that."

"Do you know what happened to the others?" asked Brady.

"Kammler and the *Vril Damen* disappeared in May 1945 and were never heard from again, at least according to official records. I checked on my team through the Department of the Army. Crane died at Malmedy during the Battle of the Bulge. Nelson went MIA in Korea in 1950. Dawson survived the war and opened a deli in Palm Beach. He died of lung cancer in 1984. Kerdoshian lived and worked at a hospital in St. Louis. I visited him in 1966 and gave him back his diary. Of course, he had no idea who I was. I spent the day with him, telling him what had happened. He looked at me the same way you two are now. He thanked me, and I left. We never talked again. His was killed two years later during the Civil Rights movement."

"What about you?"

"The Army paid me for my missing eighteen years of service, honorably discharged me with a pension, and warned me never to speak about this to anyone. This is the first time I've told my story to anyone other than Kerdoshian."

Carbone frowned and gestured to the house. "You're telling me you bought this on a military pension?"

"The back pay helped. I had been putting away money since 1945 for my retirement. That collected a lot of interest in twenty years."

Brady motioned toward the photograph of the woman with long hair on the mantle. "And you and Maria lived happily ever after?"

"We married the next summer and traveled around the world. We had a great life together." Evans grew sullen. "Until cancer took her from me five years ago."

"And the rest of the *Vril Damen*?"

"They stayed with us for a while. Sigrun eventually returned to Germany and we never heard from her again. Heike moved to Seattle and became a psychic. We got together once a year until she passed away in 1979. Traute lived here with Maria and me until she died in 1973."

Carbone stood. "We have everything we need. We appreciate your time."

Evans placed Winnie on the floor and rose, shaking the agents' hands. "My pleasure. Come back anytime."

He escorted them to the door. Carbone walked out. Brady paused long enough to whisper, "Thank you for what you did."

Evans smiled. "You're welcome. Thank you for believing me."

As the two FBI agents made their way to their car, Evans closed the door. Maybe Brady believed him, or maybe he was being polite. It didn't matter. Evans knew the truth and had no regrets.

He bent down and scratched Winnie behind the ears. "It's late, boy. How about dinner?"

The dog barked and wagged his tail.

✦ ✦ ✦

WHEN THEY REACHED the car, Brady paused by the driver's door. "What do you think?"

"The guy is certifiable."

"He was interesting."

"Listen, kid. If I want science fiction, I'll go to the movies. Let's get out of here. We've wasted too much time on this already."

As they pulled away, Carbone reached into his pocket, pulled out a cell phone, and placed a call. The other end answered on the second ring.

"Hello?"

"Director, it's Agent Carbone. We just left Evans. He still maintains his story about time travel and saving this timeline." He pronounced the last word with contempt. "The guy belongs in an asylum."

"Sorry to hear that. Thanks for verifying his story."

"What now?"

"I'll have the bureau keep tabs on him. You and Brady did well. Come back to Washington."

"Will do, sir." Carbone broke the connection and pocketed the phone. "Take me to the airport. I want to catch the next flight out of here."

✦ ✦ ✦

THE DIRECTOR HAD no intention of keeping tabs on Evans. Let the man live out the rest of his life in peace. He deserved it.

The director was probably one of the few in the government who believed Evan's story. His family had been telling the tale of the time travelers for generations, going back to his great grandfather. Of course, he never put credence in any of it until the archaeologists discovered the *Reichsadler* near the pyramids. He had immediately called his friend Kevin in the CIA, who promised to look into it. Kevin called back the next day and informed him his inquiry caused a stir on the seventh floor, and the deputy director warned Kevin to forget about it. The director thanked him but, not being the type to leave burning questions unanswered, he sent Brady and Carbone to talk to Evans.

As far as he was concerned, the two Agents confirmed what he already knew.

Opening the desk drawer, he removed a reddish-tan leather notebook and opened the pages. Damn. The story had turned out to be true after all.

The director went over to his wall safe, opened it, and placed the diary inside. The investigation would go no further.

A knock sounded on his office door.

"Come in."

Doris, his secretary, stuck her head in. "Sorry to bother you, Director Kerdoshian. Your limo is waiting to take you to the White House."

"Tell them I'll be there in a second."

He closed the safe and privately asked his great grandfather's forgiveness for ever doubting him. America's most outstanding wartime achievement and the heroes who pulled it off would remain a state secret.

A Thank You to My Readers

In addition to working for the CIA and being a stepdad, writing has been one of the most fulfilling things I've done with my life. The best part is having fans who read my books, enjoy them, and crave more. I'm incredibly fortunate and grateful I have such a loyal fanbase. You keep reading, and I'll keep writing.

If you enjoyed *Operation Majestic*, please post a review on Amazon and Goodreads. Reviews are what drive the algorithms that get a writer's books more exposure. It doesn't have to be lengthy—just a rating and a sentence or two about why you liked it. And please tell your friends about the book and post it on your social media. To be successful, I need your support.

A final note. The *Nurse Alissa vs. the Zombies* series will continue as will the Tatyana paranormal stories. I'm currently writing *Nurse Alissa vs. the Zombies VIII* and am in the process of plotting out the next Tatyana novel (which will take place aboard a haunted cruise ship) and the next book in *The Chronicles of Paul* saga.

Thank you all in advance.

Acknowledgments

WARNING: Do not read the acknowledgments before the book, as this section contains spoilers.

The fun part of my job is writing. The difficult part is getting my books published. It's a complicated process involving many people, all of whom deserve to be recognized.

This book has been a labor of love. I've been a student of World War II and Cold War history since high school, getting my Masters' Degree in Modern German and Soviet Studies. I've always wanted to write a novel dealing with Nazi Germany and the occult or supernatural. Originally, I started this book two years ago. However, the *Nurse Alissa* and Tatyana paranormal series temporarily sidetracked me. This past summer, the muses began pushing me to finish this project. I'm so glad they did.

I've tried to keep this book as historically accurate as possible. Hans Kammler, Maria Orsic, and the *Vril Damen* are real, though little is known about them. Except for Gudrun, who drew the unlucky straw of being one of the antagonists, I based their personalities and backgrounds on what few records exist. It's a fact that the *Vril Damen* and Kammler disappeared without a trace in February and 18 April 1945, respectively. An incident involving an unidentified object did take place at Roswell in July 1947; I postulate what might have happened if the claimed UFO successfully landed rather than crashed into the desert. Unverified reports indicate that a craft resembling *Die Glocke* appeared outside of Kecksburg, Pennsylvania, in July 1965. Official documentation suggests that a Majestic Committee did exist within the U.S. government, although the purpose of its creation is still open to debate. And according to ancient astronaut theorists, Valthor is a historical figure (although he went by the name of Valiant Thor and did not appear in the timeline until the late 1950s/early 1960s). Everything beyond that is my overactive imagination.

I have a deep fascination for Egypt and was fortunate enough to visit Cairo and the Pyramids of Giza in the fall of 2002. I did considerable research on Ancient Egypt while writing *Operation Majestic*, especially on the construction of the Pyramid of Khufu. The impressive archaeological discoveries made by John-Pierre Houdin with regards to the construction of Khufu played a significant role in this book. (I highly recommend watching the video *Khufu Revealed* available on YouTube). Houdin's theory has not yet been verified and is still open for debate among archaeologists. Denise Doxby, curator of Ancient Egyptian, Nubian, and Near Eastern Art at the Museum of Fine Arts, Boston, Massachusetts was kind enough to read the manuscript and point out the errors I made in Ancient Egyptian lifestyles and culture. Denise's cooperation was invaluable in making this book a better read and I thank her profoundly for the assistance. Any inaccuracies made in describing Ancient Egyptian society are attributable only to me.

The existence of Nazi UFOs is still a hot topic among historians and ancient astronaut theorists. I purposely excluded any mention of the *Rundflugzeug* privately developed in the 1920s and 1930s by the *Vril* Society and industrialists and entrepreneurs to keep the plot from getting convoluted. The best sources for descriptions of the *Haunebu II* and *Die Glocke* were derived from two sources: *Castle Werfenstein and the Wonder Women of Vril* by William A. Hinson and *SS Brotherhood of the Bell* by Joseph P. Farrell. Hinson's book is poorly annotated. Farrell's book is well documented but contains questionable sources and delves into conspiracy theories irrelevant to this novel. Nick Cook's *The Hunt for Zero-Point* provides a more reliable history of what is known about Kammler and *Die Glocke* experiments but did not provide the details I needed for the novel.

Time travel, the central them of Operation Majestic, is another highly debatable topic. Paul Nahin's *Time Travel: A Writer's Guide to the Real Science of Plausible Time Travel* and *Time Machines: Time Travel in Physics, Metaphysics, and Science Fiction* are the best books on the mechanics of time travel and were used extensively while writing this book. I attempted to portray the methods of time travel, the problems inherent with such a concept, and the conundrums of timelines and multiverses as accurately as possible, but any flaws in the logic are mine alone.

As always, much gratitude is owed to my beta readers, most of whom have been with me from book one. They point out grammatical/spelling errors and inconsistencies and offer their opinion on whether they like the story. I would be lost without them. My friend Jeff Thomson, author of the *Guardians of the Apocalypse* series, read the manuscript with a highly critical eye and pointed out numerous plot flaws, which I fixed.

Uwe Jarling, who created the awesome creature covers for my *Shattered World* series, did the cover art for *Operation Majestic*. He is a good friend as well as a talented and creative artist. Uwe enjoys developing the creatures in my books so they are as gruesome and frightening as possible. He did a marvelous job on the Anunnaki.

Finally, a significant debt of thanks goes to my family, human and furry. Working from home allows me to set my hours, though it's rare if I work less than ten hours a day. The pets are always there as my muses and major distractions. Walther and Bella sit with me on my porch while I write during the day (except in the freezing weather when they abandon me for a warm bed) and, at night, when I'm in my study editing and managing social media, my cats Archer and Michonne stand in front of my desktop computer, Michonne because she wants to be petted and Archer to meow because he ran of treats or because he can see the bottom of his food dish. My family never complains (I think they're glad to get rid of me). I couldn't do this without their love, patience, and support. I love them all.

About the Author

Scott M. Baker was born and raised in Everett, Massachusetts and spent twenty-three years in northern Virginia working for the Central Intelligence Agency and traveling through Europe, Asia, and the Middle East. Scott is now retired and lives outside of Concord, New Hampshire, with his wife and fellow writer Alison Beightol, his stepdaughter, two rambunctious Boxers, and two cats who treat him as their human servant. He is currently writing the *Nurse Alissa vs. the Zombies* and *The Chronicles of Paul* sagas, his latest zombie apocalypse series, as well as his paranormal series. Previous works include *Frozen World,* his first non-zombie post-apocalypse novel; the *Shattered World* series, his five-book young adult post-apocalypse thriller; *The Vampire Hunters* trilogy, about humans fighting the undead in Washington D.C.; *Yeitso*, his homage to the giant monster movies of the 1950s that he loved watching as a kid and still enjoys to this day; as well as several zombie-themed novellas and anthologies.

Please check out Scott's social media accounts for the latest information on future books, upcoming events, and other fun stuff.

Facebook: facebook.com/groups/397749347486177
Twitter: twitter.com/vampire_hunters
Instagram: instagram.com/scottmbakerwriter
Blog: scottmbakerauthor.blogspot.com
TikTok: tiktok.com/@authorscottmbaker

You can also sign up for Scott's newsletter, which will be released on the 1st and 15th of every month. He promises not to share your email with anyone or spam the recipients. The newsletter will contain advance notices of upcoming releases/events and short stories from the Alissa, Paul, and Tatyana universes that will not be available to the public. You can sign up by clicking the link below.

Newsletter: mailchi.mp/0b1401f1ddb2/scott-m-baker-writer